Hammond

Jonathan LaPoma

ALMENDRO
ARTS

This is a work of fiction. The names, characters, places, and
incidents are the products of the author's imagination or are used
fictitiously. Any resemblance to actual persons, living or dead, is
entirely coincidental.

ISBN: 978-0-9988403-5-2

Illustration by Adly Elewa
Interior design by Polgarus Studio
Author photograph by Emilio Azevedo

For more information, contact info@almendroarts.com.
www.almendroarts.com
www.jonlapoma.com

Praise for *Hammond*

"Effectively and evocatively captures James' frail emotional state as he stumbles through boyhood and his early adult years . . . Overall, this is an earnest, hardscrabble story of restless youth, mental illness, and the saving grace of sports-inspired camaraderie . . . A compelling work of fiction that successfully captures the anger, frustration, and freedom of kids on the brink of adulthood."

-Kirkus Reviews, Recommended Review

"Lingers in the mind far after its conclusion . . . replete with interpersonal interactions, personal revelations, and an overlay of mental illness perspective rare in a coming-of-age story. Readers who look for compelling sagas of mental illness struggles will find Hammond a revealing standout in the literature which grabs the reader's attention and swings through a life that too often feels stuck. Few stories can capture this gritty and stark existence, and *Hammond* is reminiscent of the classic *I Never Promised You A Rose Garden*, with its powerful, introspective view of an evolving (and, sometimes, devolving) young man."

-Diane Donovan, *California Bookwatch*

"Succeeds on many levels, LaPoma's use of James, a mentally ill youth troubled by the destructive tendencies of his family, as the central character is laudable. His unique worldview gives the narrative an unforgettable flavor. Fans of Jim Carroll's *Basketball Diaries* will find many similar themes in this book . . . Readers who enjoy a coming-of-age tale with lots of introspection will likely find this book a good match."

-Mark Heisey, *The US Review of Books*

"This is the book that marks Jonathan LaPoma as my favorite underrated author . . . One of the most genuinely emotional novels I have read in a hot minute . . . So emotionally in-depth that at times I felt I was getting overwhelmed by ghosts of my own depression. I don't remember the last book I read that had so much truth and understanding packed into its words (perhaps it was *The Summer of Crud*) . . . *Hammond* is truly a masterpiece of the coming-of-age genre. My biggest hope for this book is that it gets the attention it deserves."

-Audrey L, *Netgalley* Reviewer

"As raw and unfiltered as any coming-of-age book I have ever read . . . lingers in the mind long after finishing it, and I for one am looking forward to reading more from LaPoma in the future."

-Edwin Howard, *Netgalley* Reviewer

To Buffalo, The Little City That Could

Also, to the Skis, the Dellwood All-Stars (especially you, Brownie), and Sister Arthur

How was I to bear up against this? A strange martyrdom indeed, where I must be both martyr and my own executioner!

-Sor Juana Ines de la Cruz

Chapter 1

Keep shoveling. Clear the court of snow. You'll feel better after taking some jump shots—at least, that's always helped before.

When I cleared up to the foul line, I took another sip from my flask, then got back to work. But I slipped on a patch of ice and landed on my back under the rim. God, that rim had once been so red, I could see it in a blizzard. So red, I could hit threes all night. But now it was so gray, fading into the sky above it, I could hardly distinguish it from the clouds. No one was around. Even in winter, you used to be able to catch a game, usually just runnin' twos or threes, but now it was just me—just me and all the gray. Everyone else had been stamped out. Buried under an avalanche. And the ones who weren't buried were moving on. One was heading to Amherst College soon. Another to Yale.

My hands were icicles. Remember how they used to split open? How the blood would freeze on my palms? It'd been months since I'd practiced. I mean, *really* practiced.

Take another sip. Close your eyes. Go to sleep. You'll be warm soon. It'll all be over soon . . .

"C'mon, Ray, lemme out," Gerry said from inside the classroom's back closet.

"Fuck you, you little Nazi," Ray said. "You're my prisoner."

Tony and I both laughed. His seemed genuine, but mine hurt my face.

Julia Costa raised her hand. "Sister Verona."

"What?" Sister clearly didn't like kids—or life all that much—and had no business teaching them.

"So," Julia said, "you mean that missing Sunday Mass, even once, is equal in the eyes of God to blowing up a school full of children?"

"Yes! For the hundredth time, both are mortal sins, and if you die with a mortal sin on your soul, you'll spend all of eternity burning in Hell."

Tony leaned forward and whispered in my ear, "Can't be any worse than this class."

Now my smile was real. For some reason, Sister had let us choose our seats at the beginning of the year, and Ray, Gerry, Tony, and I had all made a mad dash for the far back corner. Ray took the corner seat, which was in front of the closet, and he'd often push Gerry inside at the beginning of class, then barricade the door with his desk. Ray was a big motherfucker and easily passed for a high schooler; no one was shoving him out of the way. He was the first of us to shave. The first to get drunk. The first to smoke, to drive a car. First to kiss a girl. And he was definitely the leader of our group and the toughest kid in school, even though we were only in the sixth grade, and St. Anthony's Elementary went up to grade eight.

"But what if you pray for your—" Julia said.

"It doesn't matter how much you pray!" Sister's eyes seemed to glow red. "If you don't go to confession, your soul will belong to Satan!"

Rachel Crawford raised her hand, but when Sister called on her, Rachel addressed Julia instead. "It's really easy: just don't miss Mass."

"Easy for you, maybe," Julia said. "Some of us got lives to live."

"You just need to have faith, and all your problems will go away," Rachel said.

"Exactly! Why is that so hard?" Sister said.

"Well, Rachel," Julia said, "if you've got so much faith, then why do you have those Clearasil pads in your backpack? Shouldn't God be taking care of that acne? You look like the goalie for the school dart team."

I laughed out loud. Damn, Julia was a badass.

"C'mon, Ray, it's dark in here," Gerry said. As much as he whined about being shoved in that closet, I think Gerry liked the attention.

"Don't make me come in there," Ray said.

Gerry made up a song and sang in an intentionally whiny voice: "If I say I'm sorry, will you say you're sorry . . ."

Tony laughed again and this time couldn't stop.

"Is there something funny about the Word of the Lord, Mr. Da Luca?" Sister gave Tony the Medusa stare.

"Uh . . ."

"I think there's a spider in here," Gerry said.

Ray, Tony, and I burst out laughing.

Sister sighed and mumbled some shit about young boys being forged by Satan himself, then sat down behind her desk to wait out the end-of-day bell. When it rang a moment later, Ray freed Gerry. Ray checked to make sure Sister wasn't looking, then punched Gerry in the arm as he stepped into the classroom.

"That's for what you did to the Jews, you fucking Nazi," Ray said.

It looked as if Gerry was going to scream, but he held it in, and then made a noise that sounded almost like a dolphin. "I already told you I'm only *half* German." Gerry was the runt of the group, the perpetual voice from the closet. His best shot at fighting back was with humor, and he was well equipped. Dude could crack me up at any time, which is why I always made a point not to sit next to him at church. I made that mistake one day, and Monsignor Joseph actually stopped Mass to tell me to step outside "until the Devil passes through you." That was a low point for me, and Mom was none too forgiving.

Rachel came over to our corner. "You should be nicer to him, Ray."

"And you should be less of an ugly bitch, Rachel," Ray said.

"God is watching you," Rachel said.

"Doubt it."

"I'm going to pray for your soul tonight."

"Where would you like it sent?" Ray said.

We all laughed as Rachel walked away pouting.

The four of us said goodbye to Sister, and as soon as we stepped into the hall, a group of seventh graders approached us. Though a year older, they were about the same size as us, except for Ray, who could've stomped any two of 'em together. Normally they wouldn't press us when Ray was around, but they'd been getting ballsier since the start of the new school year. I think because they were only a grade away from being the oldest in the school, they thought they ran the show. They'd been picking on Gerry and Tony for years, so I would always give them shit whenever they passed in the halls, but it seemed they weren't going to let me do that unchecked anymore.

"Hey, Jimmy, what was that you said to me at lunch today?" their leader, Shane Walsh, said. "That you wanted me to beat your ass like your dad does?" Earlier that day, I'd told Shane, a scrawny Irish prick from a Central Park mansion, to "stroke my shillelagh."

"No, I said kiss my ass, you leprechaun fuck," I said, stepping right up in his face.

"Why do you want a guy to kiss your ass? You a fag or something?" he said.

Ray stepped forward. "Fuck off, Shane."

I could see the fear in Shane's eyes, but he got lucky because Sister Carol, the principal, came up the back stairs and approached us.

"We'll deal with this later," Shane said, and he and the other idiots left.

Sister Carol was a large, towering woman whose voice could stop a speeding tank. Gerry liked to joke that she used to play offensive line for the Bills in the sixties but got kicked out of the league when she ripped another player in half—but he'd never say that to her face. Sister Carol didn't mess around, and when she said, "School's over, boys," we walked our asses out of there with a quickness.

We met up with my older brother, Dan, and Tony's older brother, Alonzo, by the bike rack. They were both starting seventh grade. My younger siblings, Diane, Rebecca, and Jeremy, went to St. Anthony's as well, but K–5 started and ended an hour earlier than 6–8, so they were always gone by the time Dan and I got out. Mom would drive them to and from school, but, "Middle schoolers have to walk," so Dan and I were on our own.

Alonzo was small like Tony, but unlike Tony he was arrogant as hell and had a hot temper. Alonzo loved gangster rap and would talk down to anyone who didn't know all the obscure rap facts he did. I once called Dr. Dre "Dr. J" and he never let me live it down. Dan was a little smaller than I was, and, unlike me, he rarely spoke.

"So, how're you guys likin' Sister Ver-gina so far?" Alonzo said.

"That lady scares me," I said.

"Yeah, she's already yelled at me, like, twenty times, and it's only the second week of school," Tony said.

"Get used to it," Alonzo said. "Dan and I had to deal with that bitch for a year, and now it's your turn to hear all about the different ways your soul will roast in Hell if you so much as take your eyes off her for a second while she's speaking."

"I used to see a dark line around her body after staring at her for so long," Dan said.

"She turns every subject into a lecture about religion," I said. "In math today, she went on and on about how God created variables to test our devotion to Him."

"Yeah, it's better in the closet," Gerry said.

Ray slapped Gerry hard on the back. "I didn't tell you to speak."

"Ah, fuck, Ray!" Gerry said.

Ray stuck his finger in Gerry's face, and Gerry shut the hell up.

"Can we come over to play basketball today?" I asked Alonzo.

"I got shit to do. Why don't you just man up and go to Hammond Park?" Alonzo said.

"No way," I said.

"Don't be a pussy," Alonzo said.

"I'm not a pussy!"

Sister Verona exited a back door and started walking toward the convent.

"Tell you what," Alonzo said. "You walk over there and slap Sister Vag on the ass, and you can come play basketball."

The others laughed.

"Fuck that," I said.

Just then, Sister Carol walked out and gave us an evil look.

"Yo, let's get the fuck outta here," Alonzo said.

We unlocked our bikes from the rack, walked them to the edge of the parking lot, hopped on, and took off, Dan and Alonzo leading the way. We all lived a few blocks from one another in a mostly Italian, working-class section of North Buffalo. The neighborhood had its share of problems, but it was relatively safe, and had that All-American small-town feel to it. Most of the homes had been built in the late nineteenth and early twentieth centuries, and had front porches where people grilled hot dogs and drank beers and laughed as American flags waved above the front steps in the cool summer breeze. Summers in Buffalo were green, gorgeous, and well-earned after months of harsh, gray winter, and people were out everywhere, celebrating the sun. They smiled while cutting their lawns and washing their cars and having friends over to eat pizza and wings and play bocce in the backyard. Though we rode our bikes past drunks and crackheads and wife-beaters, most people here would agree that the real problems existed *out there,* not among *us.* The *real threats* were in the Puerto Rican neighborhoods on the West Side and especially in the Black neighborhoods on the East Side, and as long as we stuck to our little slice of Heaven, we'd be all right.

No, nothing bad *here.* Here, if a man beat his kid into a cast, that was just discipline. If he slapped his wife around, she deserved it. But where in small-town America are you gonna get away from that shit? Our little section of North Buffalo was as good as any other, and we were all doing our best. The sunshine and hot dogs helped.

A few blocks south was Central Park, one of the richest neighborhoods in the city. The houses there were gorgeous, and Dan and I would ride our bikes down Nottingham Terrace sometimes to check them out. A lot of St. Anthony's kids lived in that area, but most were from ours.

We all stayed together until we got to my and Dan's street, where the others went their separate ways. Dan and I stopped at the large, blue plastic box with the words *The Buffalo Times* written in white letters on the side, which sat at the curb of our small, two-story house, and we looked inside. Bob had already dropped off the day's delivery.

"Let's get a snack first," I said. I laid my bike on the driveway and headed for the house.

"GOD-FUCKING-DAMN IT! I TOLD THOSE FUCKERS THIS WAS THE WRONG SIZE SCREW!" On a quiet day, you could hear Dad screaming from all the way down the block, even if the windows were closed. They weren't closed that afternoon. Fuck him.

"Eh, forget the snack." I turned around and went back to the box, and we opened it and tossed our bookbags inside. We each filled a delivery bag and got started.

Dan and I had the biggest route in our neighborhood—the entire block, about ninety customers. Before handing it over to us, our boss, Bob, had grilled us to make sure we wouldn't fuck it up, and I think the fact that we already had a successful business cutting lawns and shoveling driveways for elderly neighbors, as well as the fact that we were both dedicated altar servers, convinced him, and after a month he told us we were the best carriers he'd ever had. Maybe he used that positive reinforcement shit with all his carriers, but it worked on me. I wanted to do my best, and not just for him, but for the whole neighborhood. People relied on Dan and me for their news, and I took that seriously. Some of our customers were seniors who never left the house. We were their link to the world.

We each had our own section of the route. I delivered to the section west of our house, then north at the corner, and east at the end of the block. My section was a little easier than Dan's. I had a series of mailboxes at the ends of driveways, so I didn't have to get off my bike and drop the papers inside of screen doors, which was the worst. I also had a few apartment complexes with multiple customers, where I could just drop the papers on welcome mats. In the summer, the apartments were great, but in the winter, going from the cold to the heat and back caused me to sweat pretty badly. Though my route was a little cushier, I did have some of the crazier customers, and I stopped delivering to one guy after he refused to pay up. Some days he'd chase me down, demanding a paper. He never caught me. The one time he almost did, I sped across the street without even looking and got away. Luckily no cars were passing, but even if they were, fuck him.

I also had St. Anthony's rectory, which was my last delivery, and I'd usually wait there for Dan so we could ride home together. The priests were some of my weirdest customers, but they had a mailbox that I could pull my bike up to, so it was all good. While waiting for Dan, I'd often hear Father Mike singing along to Elvis or Neil Diamond tunes blasting from the kitchen window. Father Mike was a great guy, and sometimes he'd tell us dirty jokes before serving Mass. My favorite was, "Why'd the woman slap the midget? Because he said, 'Gee your hair smells nice.'" The rectory was attached to the church, which was also attached to the school, and each of those was surrounded by blacktop. Across the blacktop and behind the school was the convent, and behind the convent was a small garden where students would hang out during recess. The school, church, and rectory had high, steep roofs and beautiful stone walls, and the convent was a large, rectangular building with a flat roof and brick walls. As much as I hated St. Anthony's, I felt safer there than probably any other place in the world. And I don't think I even hated it all that much . . .

That afternoon, instead of hearing Father Mike singing "Don't Be Cruel" off-key, I heard kids shouting. There, in the parking lot behind the rectory, a couple of White kids on bikes were talkin' shit to a big Black kid. One of the White kids got off his bike and said something to the Black kid, and the Black kid bitch-slapped his ass to the ground.

"Don't you ever call Silas Macker a liar, motherfucker," the Black guy said.

A window opened on the second floor of the rectory, and Monsignor Joseph, wearing nothing but a towel, stuck his wet, wrinkled head outside. "Hey, you boys cut the shit or I'm gonna call the cops."

"Sorry, Monsignor," one of the White boys said. He picked his friend up off the ground, and they took off on their bikes. Silas told Monsignor to fuck off, then walked in my direction. I hopped off my bike and hid behind a bush. Monsignor hawked a loogie, spat on the pavement, and stuck his head back inside, muttering, "These god-damned kids . . ."

I didn't know any of the White boys, but I'd definitely heard the name Silas Macker before, and the stories about him always involved broken noses, lost teeth, and shattered egos. He was a sixth grader at Kirkland Middle, a public school about eight blocks from St. Anthony's—just far enough outside of my safe bubble to give me some mild comfort. But worlds had a tendency to collide.

I could feel my whole body tighten as Silas approached, but he didn't even look in my direction and just kept walking down the street. I could see Dan coming from the opposite direction, and Dan passed him without even the slightest hint of fear.

Dan and I rode home, but the screaming hadn't stopped. The screaming wasn't just coming from our dad, though. Our next-door neighbor was an old man named Calvin Rogers, and he'd scream even worse than Dad. He had a garage full of old lawnmower parts that he'd sell to local weirdos, and he'd sit there all day and scream as he tore the mowers apart and haggled over the prices of their components. He had a mentally disabled daughter named Helen who was in her fifties, and she'd sit on the front porch with her cat and say, "Come over" to anyone who passed. Mom forced us to talk to her, and it always made me uncomfortable. I never knew what to say, so I would just ask about her cat. The old man would scream at her all the time for whatever: not washing the dishes, washing the dishes wrong, leaving the dishes on the counter, putting the dishes away. She couldn't win. But she'd always smile, then go inside for more abuse. Nothing seemed to bother her. She had her cat, and she was happy. A part of me was always glad when he'd scream at her while I was over there because then I could walk away—but I could never walk away from the screaming.

Across the street from them was a guy who reminded me of Buffalo Bill from *The Silence of the Lambs*. He always wore a one-piece mechanic outfit unzipped to his bare, hairy beer belly, and he'd walk around eating corn on the cob while staring down anyone who passed, shouting shit like, "Slow down, maniac!" or, "Yeah, that's right. Keep right on walkin'!" He lived with his mother, who he treated like a queen, but he'd scream at her poodle. I felt terrible for that poor dog. I saw him kick it around a few times, but what the fuck can you do about it?

Our other next-door neighbor was a single woman who lived in a huge, three-story house. Her husband and two daughters had been killed in a car accident before we moved in, and she never left the house, except every so often when she'd walk out in full clown gear and get into a small bus filled with other clowns. It was nice to know my family wasn't the weirdest on the block.

My dad was a compulsive do-it-yourselfer. He'd bought the shittiest house on the street and wanted to make it sparkle—and he was succeeding. In the seven years we'd lived there, he'd remodeled almost every room, and each downstairs had new insulation, drywall, electrical outlets, and wallpaper. He'd installed a bay window and oak floors in the dining room, new cupboards in the kitchen, and redid the whole bathroom, plumbing included. Now he was working on one of the three bedrooms, which meant that Dan, our four younger brothers and sisters, and I all shared one room. Being packed in there was torture. Things had improved since the Evil Thoughts had come on years earlier, but I was still haunted by everything that'd happened, and every little noise in that room drove me nuts. I couldn't stand the sound of snoring or heavy breathing or the parties coming from the upstairs apartment Mr. Rogers rented to an endless string of loud tenants. The yelling my dad would do even at night.

I'd found a pair of old earplugs by Dad's workbench in the basement and had been wearing them for months to sleep, but they couldn't kill away all the sound, and they hurt like hell to wear. The skin in my ears was so raw and open that when I put those filthy things back in each night, my ears would sting badly. I couldn't put any pressure on them, so I could only sleep on my back. Sometimes when I'd take the plugs out in the morning, they'd be covered in blood. I'd rinse them off, but they were so filthy, they'd never get clean. Some nights I considered puncturing my ears with nails to stop the noise. Two quick jabs would end all my suffering.

There were so many nights when the stress was so much, I'd feel as if I was drifting off—heading closer to that point I knew I'd arrive at sooner or later.

Insanity.

Complete isolation. I knew what it felt like. I'd already been to Hell. When I was younger and the feeling would come on, I used to cry. But my old man had made extra sure to "toughen" me up, and now I didn't cry about it anymore—even when I did.

Chapter 2

I t started when I was lying in bed late one weekend night, after we'd spent most of the day at my grandmother's house, and it rushed me, fast and without warning. It was as if the truth of the entire universe suddenly flooded my already fragile mind and opened a world of possibilities known only to war heroes and serial killers and genius artists and Alcatraz inmates and Wild West outlaws. It came to me, innocent yet all-knowing. I was already a sad boy. Already so broken down by the yelling and fear that the pieces would never come back together. I wanted to bury my head in a snowbank and numb it all away, but the world had other plans for me. The world wanted me to *know*. Wanted me to feel the pain of all its tortured souls. Feel the punishment of all its criminals. Feel the isolation of all its sick and dying. I could feel the energy burning inside my chest. Could feel my brain teeming with darkness and light. A war had begun inside my head. I was nine. I had no idea I was now both superhero and villain.

While they may have flooded me for the first time that night, I knew the Evil Thoughts had always been with me. As far back as I could remember, I'd thrown fits if my sock was bunched up in my shoe or my belt didn't fit just right. It seemed that even back then I'd known—just not entirely—that the darkness was waiting for an opening. Waiting to catch me off guard. I don't know why it hit me that one specific night. I was tired as hell from playing with my cousins most of the day and night, but the more I tried to sleep, the less I could. The more I tried to calm my thoughts, the harder they raged. I knew then with full clarity that I would never feel peace again. That was a certainty.

I developed rituals to help me sleep. About an hour before bed, I'd drink warm milk, because every shitty sitcom ever made had at least one episode where someone can't sleep until they drink warm milk and all their problems melt away. After, I'd eat a bowl of cereal. When that was done, I'd rub Vicks VapoRub on my chest, because I'd once heard Dad tell my younger sister it'd help her sleep. Then I would rub Vaseline on my hands and cover them with socks. Before walking upstairs, I'd tap the same spot on the wall three times and say, "Good night, night, night, night, night," to both parents, then rub my left hand along the rail as I climbed the steps. I left a huge grease stain on the wall and a trail on the railing that, whenever I saw them, made me feel that life was completely hopeless. When I got to our bedroom, I'd turn on the fan, which I'd rigged to make a ton of noise to block out all the other sounds, and put a huge stuffed animal over my younger brother's head to muffle his snoring. Then I'd head back down to the bathroom and spend about half an hour squeezing out every last drop of that warm milk, only being able to relax enough to pee once I'd taken care of the sound quality in the bedroom.

When I'd get back to the bedroom, after hitting the

same spot on the wall three times and rubbing my left hand on that rail again, I'd climb up to my top bunk bed, put the plugs in my ears, then begin with the prayers. I'd always start with twenty Our Fathers and twenty Hail Marys, then I'd spend the next half hour or so begging God to make me feel okay. To take the insanity out of my brain. It was only getting worse. I'd finish up by repeating, "Our Lady of Lords, pray for us," for about an hour, because I'd heard one of the nuns say that for each time you say, "Our Lady of Lords, pray for us" in your head, three hundred days were slashed from your sentence in Purgatory. Usually by then I was so exhausted that I'd fall asleep. Other nights, though, I wasn't so lucky, and I'd spend pretty much all night praying, sweating, and crying.

God never listened, though. The rituals got longer and longer, and soon I was spending about four hours each night praying and drinking milk and squeezing piss. I got more rigid with the execution and timing, and if even the slightest thing was off, I'd panic. I needed to start the rituals at exactly seven at night so I'd be in bed by nine, which meant that if we were at a birthday party or dinner or whatever, I'd start flipping out as the minutes ticked down to seven. At first, Mom would do her best to calm me, but after a while I wore her out, and she seemed to stop noticing. Dad wasn't so forgiving. If he even sensed my panic, he'd beat the living shit out of me. He didn't want to hear it. Whining was for bitches, and he wasn't raising no bitch. He liked John Wayne and John Wayne didn't put Vaseline on his hands or drink warm milk. John Wayne shot motherfuckers and left them to die in the desert. When you're as sick as I was, you find out right away who really cares. You get right to the deepest, darkest truths about life, and once you've seen them—once you know what's true—you can never unlearn them. I was filled with far too many truths and felt as though they would end me at any moment. The stress was too much. There were several times when I felt as though I'd gone completely over into the world of no return: insanity.

Insanity is torture. I'd take death over insanity a hundred times out of a hundred, and I started obsessing about death. It was the only way out. I knew I'd never make it to eighteen. Adulthood. I'd never make it alone. I'd never make it without Mom there staying up with me in the middle of the night as I cried myself to sleep. I knew I was diseased. That I wasn't one of God's chosen people. Knew that Satan had me. That my parents didn't give a shit about me.

After a few years, though, the intensity and length of the rituals began to subside. But something else rivaled the mental pain. Over the years, my body had taken on so much stress that my muscles had quite literally deformed me. My muscles were so tight they felt like bone, making them impossible to relax. I felt twisted up, one hip inches higher than the other, and my back so crooked I felt as though I might tip over while standing up straight. I'd get intense muscle pulls, especially in my groin. It took five, ten, sometimes twenty minutes to relax enough to piss or shit, and with only one bathroom in a house of eight people, I always felt as though I was going to explode. Everything spiraled inward. My body was strong, so I could take it. And after years of enduring endless screaming and ass-beatings, I felt prepared to deal with the pain. I became at one with the chaos. I took it on. Felt as though I could be its king.

In class, I was always competing with Chris Yangston

to see who'd get the highest grade, but even when I came out on top, I still felt that I was stupid. I couldn't think. Couldn't concentrate. My thoughts jumped all over the place, and trying to hold on to a single one gave me such intense headaches that it wasn't worth the effort. So I learned to read teachers to see what drove them. I watched how teachers would react to other students' responses, and I'd copy what the teachers seemed to like. I became excellent at adapting, and I think that's the only way I was able to survive this period in time. Soon, mostly through sheer bullshit alone, I was able to stay at the top of the class.

My whole life had become one prolonged state of panic, but I was able to find balance with it. Was able to survive with it. My behavior grew stranger, so I started hanging with the weirdos. The assholes. The outcasts. The Kids in the Closet.

But as I adapted, the Darkness evolved too—always staying ten steps ahead of me. It was as if it was trying to find my biggest weakness to rush all at once, to remind me who was in charge. At first, the Darkness hadn't allowed me to sleep, but in time, with the rituals and everything, I was able to cope and sleep through most of the night. So, it shifted to something else. In third grade, Rachel Crawford's mother was killed by a drunk driver while driving home from work one night. She used to volunteer in the library with Sister Rose, and I'd see her almost every day. My mother worked nights at a local diner, waiting tables, and after that, I'd sit in the bay window around midnight and wait for her to get back, even on school nights. If she was even a few minutes late, I'd start to panic. Soon I wouldn't let her go anywhere without me. Whether she went to get groceries or buy tampons or pick up the pizza for the party that night, guess who tagged along? That lasted for a good year and a half and only went away when the disease found a new, and horrific, way to terrorize me: the Evil Thoughts.

In August of '93, the news was alive with stories about a thirteen-year-old boy named Eric Smith, who lured a four-year-old into the woods and murdered him. The story shocked and disturbed the country. It did the same to me, but it disturbed me for other reasons as well. For months after seeing that redheaded kid on TV, I couldn't shake the obsession that if I let down my guard, I'd hurt someone too. It wasn't that I *wanted* to hurt anyone. In fact, that was why it disturbed me so much to think I could. But the darkness was overwhelming, and it felt as though I had Satan inside of my brain, tempting me and calling me to do his will. I knew I couldn't say anything about this to anyone, so I just let it eat away at me. I knew I was an animal. I knew I was evil. I knew the reason God never answered my prayers was because I wasn't under His control.

Most of the time, I didn't think about hurting anyone, but every so often, something would remind me of Eric Smith—maybe I'd see a kid with red hair in church, or some little kid would talk about going camping in the woods—and the thoughts would rush me. It fucking haunted me. That I had no control over any of it. That just by going outside—just by leaving my house—the world could destroy me. I started dreaming that the cops were after me. I felt that all good, moral people knew I was evil, and I felt isolated from them. It all got to be too much.

One afternoon after Sunday Mass, the congregation went to the St. Anthony's cafeteria for a pancake brunch.

Some of the kids ran off somewhere to play, and suddenly I found myself alone in a back room with this five- or six-year-old kid everyone was always gushing over. He always wore this stupid little bow tie and a tiny suit to church, and people wouldn't shut up about how cute he was. Now, here he was, looking up at me with those big, little-kid eyes under a shaggy red haircut, and the feeling overwhelmed me. I punched him in the stomach. Not all that hard, but it was a solid shot. The kid kept smiling. So, I pulled back and socked him in the gut again with everything I had. He started crying and ran off to his mother, and I got seriously spooked and hid in one of the confessionals. I remember thinking that I'd just damned myself to Hell for all eternity and there was no way to ever make up for it. I was shaking and sweating and knew the cops would come soon to haul me away. But the cops never came. Neither did my parents. Eventually, after a few hours, Monsignor Joseph heard me crying, and he whipped open the curtain. I wanted to confess to him what had happened, but he started yelling at me to beat it, so I took off running again. I slept in the garage that night on an old mattress, and when I walked into the house the next morning, no one had even noticed I was gone—except Dan, who asked what was up, but I wasn't telling him shit. I thought maybe I *had* actually gone crazy. No one ever mentioned anything about me hurting that kid, and that terrified me even more than the fact that I'd hit him. Who the fuck out there was going to stop me? It was all up to me—me and my crazy-ass brain—to stop myself from realizing the endless possibilities, both great and evil, I felt were inside of me. There was no hope. If I lived to eighteen, I knew I'd either end up in jail or dead—most likely by my own hand.

In time, the Evil Thoughts began to subside too, and as the news cycle went on to other stories, I tried to forget about Eric Smith. Tried to forget that he was currently in a cell serving his sentence. Tried to forget that I, too, was currently in my own cell, inside my mind. Tried to forget how I hurt that poor kid, all dressed up in his suit. Tried to forget how I wanted to destroy something that everyone loved. Tried to rob that kid of the happiness I'd never be able to feel.

Months later, the news moved on to Kurt Cobain's death, and they made him out to sound like Satan too. It was right around the time I started to get into good music. My brother would play Nirvana and Alice in Chains tunes, and they'd get stuck inside my head, mixing up with the Evil Thoughts and the rituals and the dark and light, and soon music tortured me as well. The songs reminded me of the evil inside of me. Some bands were "good," and those were the ones I was allowed to listen to. The Beatles were "good." The Smashing Pumpkins, my favorite band, were "good." The Cranberries were "good," and so was Pearl Jam. But STP was "evil." Chris Cornell was "evil." Kurt Cobain and Layne Staley were the Devil himself. Listening to the radio was too risky. At any time, Nirvana could come on, and I'd start losing my mind. Katherine Talbot threw our first co-ed party in the summer before sixth grade, and I took the risk and went. For the first hour, everything was okay, until someone popped a Soundgarden cassette in the tape deck. We were playing spin the bottle, and Julia Costa got me, but before she could kiss me, I heard the music starting and ran off to the bathroom. It was on the first floor, so I climbed out the window and took off running home. At school, everybody thought I was scared to kiss her. Ray gave me shit about it, calling me a faggot. One afternoon, I opened Dan's CD player and fucked with some of the wires inside so he wouldn't be able to play music before bed. When he got a new one, I threw it out our second-story window, and I even microwaved some of his CDs. Dad kicked the living shit out of me for it. I knew it was crazy, but I couldn't stop myself. How I didn't go completely insane then still boggles my mind. But I got through it because that's what you do when you're born in Buffalo. Into a world of gray and black and freezing cold. You learn how to survive.

Or you die.

As much as the darkness tortured me, there was something beautiful in it that I could feel but didn't understand. When the thoughts first rushed me when I was nine, it seemed that all the knowledge of the world was suddenly mine. That I just *knew* everything. And in that everything was a world of art I knew I'd never be allowed to touch, for a number of reasons. I felt as if I understood the beauty in the insanity of Van Gogh without even knowing who he was. I knew the source of John Lennon's words when I'd play Dad's Beatles *Anthology 1* CD. My capacity to love and forgive felt endless. I was brimming with desire. But the world I lived in would never allow me to explore any of this. The world I lived in was a stone lid on creativity. Art was for fags. Music, for Satan. And the creative energy inside of me was all mixed up with the Evil, and it was just too dangerous to explore. If I started drawing or making up tunes, I could easily be summoning the Devil. And I needed to go to Heaven, even though I knew I wouldn't. I needed to be good. I needed to make Dad proud so he'd stop hitting me and screaming and making Mom and my sisters sad. I needed to make Mom proud so she'd feel happy and smile for once. I needed to drive the snow and gray away from Buffalo so the city could finally see how beautiful it was. I needed to let Dan know how strong he was, even though I knew he felt so weak. I had my family on my shoulders. My city on my shoulders. Inside of me was the power of the gods, and it was my responsibility to make sure everyone else got to Heaven—even though I knew I was going to Hell and taking everything good inside of me along for the ride.

Chapter 3

The next morning, I woke up in a bit of a panic. Not because of the racing thoughts; it'd been a few years since I'd had the worst of my problems with sleeping, even though they hadn't gone away entirely. No, that morning I panicked because I'd forgotten to do my Religion homework, and Sister Verona would probably condemn my ass to Hell for it. I figured I could try to get most of it done during breakfast—if that was even possible. Mornings in our house were always insane. Eight people getting ready in one bathroom. There was no order to any of it, which stressed me out. I needed my routines. My rituals. But routines were impossible in the mad morning scramble. On days Mom waited tables, she'd usually go in around 6 p.m. and come back at midnight, so she'd just use the bathroom after we all left. She'd get the kids ready first and then drive them to school at seven fifteen, so the house was less crazy after that. I'd hop in the shower whenever I could, and that morning, I got in before Dan. Dad hit me with the, "You got two minutes! No Hollywood luxury showers in this house," line he gave us each morning. If you went over two minutes, he'd stop whatever he was doing to go to the basement and cut the hot water. I mean, he actually fucking timed us. That morning, at the two-minute mark, I was just about to get out when he came in and took an explosive shit. That always grossed me out, but at least it gave me extra time with the hot water. He co-owned a vending machine business, so his schedule was pretty flexible, but he always tried to get on the road before Dan and I left for school. Sometimes his partner, Tim, would pick him up so Mom could use the car, and they'd drive to their warehouse in Cheektowaga where they'd fill up the delivery truck and head out to restock the machines.

When I got out of the shower, I made breakfast. I always ate cereal, and when I reached up for the supermarket's version of Cap'n Crunch, I saw the box of Honey Bunches of Oats behind it. It'd been sitting up there for over a year now. It was my job to clean the cupboards, but I couldn't throw that box away. Mom had bought it with the hope that maybe somebody would like it. We'd never had it before, and she'd wanted to give us all something new to try. But Dad told her it tasted like shit, and it had oats or some other adult-sounding crap, so none of the kids wanted to eat it. So it just sat up there, all alone, nobody ever reaching for it. Nobody ever looking at it. Talking about it. Mom should've known not to make that mistake. You don't try something new in Buffalo. And now, her hope of making us happy was hidden in a cupboard. And seeing it each morning depressed the hell out of me, but I could never, ever throw it away.

I got as much of my homework done as I could, then Dan and I took off on our bikes for school. Even if Mom had offered to drive us, we would have preferred to ride. In Buffalo, you only get so much time to enjoy the good weather, and we savored every moment. At the St. Anthony's parking lot, we had to walk our bikes to the rack, and this time, as we got off, a construction worker standing in a six-foot-deep hole beside the sidewalk stopped working on the water pipe and looked up at us. "Stay in school, kids. Don't be a fool like me." I told him, "Yes, sir," and walked my bike to the rack. Dan and I shared a cable lock, and we locked our bikes together, then went inside. Sister Carol was always there in the school entrance to tell us good morning and make sure we weren't messing around.

The sixth and seventh grade classrooms were next to one another in a separate part of the building from the K–5 rooms, so Dan and I would stick together and split ways when we arrived. As usual, Sister Verona was yelling at someone when I walked in. Karen Blackburn had forgotten her prayer beads or something and Sister made sure to give her hell for it. In the back of the room, Tony and Ray were cracking up. Apparently, Tim Lamonz had brought pornographic playing cards to school, and Tony had stolen them and put a card in each kid's desk. We watched Kristine Manning open her desk, but instead of screaming, she sat down and stared at the card with this strange look in her eye.

"Hey, Timmy," Ray said as Tim was getting his books out for his first class, "check it out." Ray pointed at Kristine, and Tim shot out of his seat, crying, "Oh my God!" He grabbed the card, and Kristine fought him but ultimately gave it over.

Rich Bauer opened his desk too, but Tim snatched up the card before Rich could see it.

"There's one in each desk," Ray said to him.

Tim went nuts and started flipping open desks and

seizing the cards. When he got to us in the back, Ray held up his card, which showed a blond woman rubbing her huge tits.

"That's mine!" Tim said.

"Mine now," Ray said.

The one in my desk had a woman lying on a bed with her legs spread open. Her thing looked like the Predator's mouth. Her titties looked great though.

Rachel opened her desk and screamed. Tim booked it out of the room, and we watched him sprint across the parking lot and disappear down the street. But as it turned out, Rachel was screaming because there was a spider in her desk. Apparently, Tim *had* grabbed her card. He didn't come back to school that day or the next.

First period, Sister turned Reading class into another lecture on Hell. "If a small bird took only one drop of water out of the ocean once every trillion years, by the time there was no water left on Earth, eternity wouldn't have even yet begun. And that's precisely how long your soul will burn if you even think about fornicating."

All these talks about Hell always got to me. I knew that's where I was going. But I'd already been in Hell for so long that I knew I'd be okay there. I was a survivor. But the thought of Mom or Dad going to Hell horrified me. I was pretty sure Mom was going to Heaven, but Dad . . . That was questionable. He always said I was the reason he yelled. I was the reason he had to beat my ass. Maybe it *was* my fault that everyone was always so angry. Maybe it *was* my fault that the city was so depressed. Maybe if I just sucked it up and became a priest, I could absolve his sins and help him get to Heaven. I knew I couldn't make him stop yelling, but I could forgive him. God, I promise I'll become a priest if you'll just make them happy. I'll give you everything I have if it will make them smile. Nobody's ever happy. Please, let them be happy. You can take me. You already have. I may be sitting here, looking normal, but underneath it all my brain is still beyond fucked from the Evil Thoughts. At any time, they'll come back. At any time, Satan will have me. Take me first. Get me before he can. I want to cleanse their sins. I want to help all the tired, sick, and poor people out there. Buffalo is so full of misery. Let me help. I'll anoint the sick. I'll soothe the tormented. I'll stay up all night talking to the lonely. Make me an instrument of your peace.

"You'll burn and burn and burn . . ." Sister went on.

But maybe devoting my life to God would turn me into *her* someday. An angry old woman who hated life. Christ, and think of Monsignor Joseph. That dude was more miserable than anyone. Plus, I wanted to get married someday. I wanted to give my life to a special girl and spend all my time making her happy. God, what's the answer? Tell me what to do. I need something to get through . . . anything . . .

I turned around and whispered to Tony, "Hey, can we play some hoops this afternoon?"

"Naw, this weekend would be better," he said.

Rachel shushed us, and Tony gave her the finger.

"I wanna come too," Gerry said.

"Mr. Kozak," Sister said, "are you paying attention to the Word of the Lord?"

"Uh . . . uh . . ." Gerry savored the moment for all it was worth, then ripped a loud fart, and we all erupted.

"That's it, Mr. Kozak. Tonight I want you to write a one-thousand-word composition on why your bodily functions anger our Lord."

"Yes, Sister," Gerry said.

When Sister turned around, Ray slapped Gerry on the back of the head and said, "Fuckin' Nazi."

Fourth period, we headed for the music room downstairs. In the hall, Shane and Jacob Mancuso, who lived a few blocks from me, pushed me and Gerry into a wall.

"We're gonna get you, tards," Shane said as he continued down the hall.

"Tickle my pickle for a nickel," Gerry said. He started gyrating his hips and grabbing his crotch like an arrhythmic Michael Jackson. Sister Adele gave him a dirty look, and he stopped.

When we got to the music room, Gerry and I sat in the back corner next to Ray and Tony. Miss Amalia was playing the piano and singing "It's Too Late" by Carole King. I knew the song because Mom used to listen to it all the time, and when she did, she always had this look on her face as if she was going to cry. Miss Amalia had that same look. When the song was over, Miss Amalia told us that we were going to be working on two-minute skits that day and performing them in class. Ray, Gerry, Tony, and I started coming up with ideas, but they were all crap. At one point, Gerry raised his arm and I could see a huge welt under his bicep. I got an idea and shared it with the group, and they loved it. Gerry and I wrote a song for it, and it all came together without even having to think all that much. This wasn't the first time we'd created something like this. Gerry and I would get together sometimes and come up with all kinds of crazy ideas for *Saturday Night Live*-style skits. Sometimes they were crap, but a lot of them were hilarious. We'd perform them at Tony's house—usually when Alonzo wasn't there—and Tony even recorded one with his dad's camcorder. That afternoon's skit was called "Life with Uncle Willy," and it was about a hermit named Willy who moves in with his three young nephews who annoy the hell out of him, and he beats the living shit out of them. We couldn't stop laughing as we put it all together.

Miss Amalia came over to see what was so funny, and as she got closer, I could feel my dick shooting up like a rocket. She was half Indonesian and half Spanish, and something about her drove me crazy. One day during class, she leaned over while helping another student, and her butt rubbed against my arm. I had a dream about it that night, and when I woke up, I had sticky white goo in my boxers. I wanted to rub my dick all over her ass, and it didn't make sense to me as to why. She was always smiling, even though it seemed to me she wasn't that happy. Her smiles looked forced. But at least she was trying, which is more than I could say about most of the adults I knew. Most adults were sad and angry and did whatever they could to hurt kids. I didn't want to be an adult, but I also knew I wouldn't live long enough to worry about that anyway. The best I could do was to enjoy each moment. And that afternoon, I was doing just that.

A few of the groups performed their skits. Most were crap. But Julia and Katherine Smith did a dance, and something about the way Julia moved made me see her in a way I never had before. In all the other skits, everyone had just looked embarrassed and nervously grinned their way through it, but when the music started, it took Julia over. Her body, her movements—everything was so deliberate and skillful, yet relaxed and graceful. It was as if she already knew at such a young age that, no matter what stage you were on, and no matter how small the audience, you had to give it everything you had. That a two-minute dance routine in Miss Amalia's Music class was as important as any Broadway show. I watched her absorb all the shame and ugliness in that room and filter it through her and send it back out to us as pure, driven energy, which spread through me with the same force as the dark thoughts spread through me years ago. Most of the other kids were messing around. Ray was drawing dicks on the back of Gerry's neck with a pen as Gerry faked laughter. Rich Bauer was throwing pieces of paper into Katherine's open backpack. Rachel and Jenny Pierce were showing off their new slap bracelets. But Julia was everything to me. I felt connected to her. Felt our spirits align. Felt so close to her, as if she could see the horror and darkness in me, and it didn't scare her. That she knew what to do with it—how to make it go away. Seeing her doing something so beautiful with the ugly hand she'd been played in life made me believe I could do something just as beautiful. And it terrified me.

Julia was a tough girl. She was an only child and lived with her parents in a nice place near the park. Though she came from more money than most, her dad was never around, and when he was, he was worse than Poor Rich. He worked in insurance and was always screaming and talking down to people, and he'd march Julia and her mother down the center aisle at church even if they were ten minutes late, and then sit in the front pew. Her mother didn't work. She sat around the house and chain-smoked and drank and told Julia she was "too fat" even though Julia was rail-thin. Julia had the best of everything—clothes, CDs, jewelry—but she had some shitty-ass parents. Julia always asked great questions in class, which pissed off the nuns, and her taste in music and movies was perfect. Her favorite bands were Mazzy Star and Mother Love Bone, and her favorite movies were *Pulp Fiction* and *Empire Records*. She was way cooler than any of us and knew shit about the world we didn't. Why hadn't I seen her like this before? How could something so incredible be right in front of me for so long without me even knowing it? Like with the dark thoughts years ago, I felt something rushing me that afternoon, watching Julia dance. It was as if some truth had come to me. Some knowledge I'd never again be able to ignore. All those years of talking to her before and after class. All those years of sharing *Simpsons* or *SNL* quotes and laughing. All those years of talking about music and our favorite NBA players. How could I not have seen her before? She was so fucking beautiful, looking just like Sophia Loren in that picture Grandma had on her wall. The picture I loved and had kissed so many times throughout the years when no one was watching. But maybe that was life: one long struggle of being blind until you can see.

Ray slapped me on the shoulder as he, Tony, and Gerry got up and headed for the back closet. We went over our skit one last time, and before Ray walked into the closet, I told him that in order for it to work, he needed to beat the absolute shit out of us for real. No playing. Humor didn't work unless it was real.

When Ray shut the door behind him, Gerry and I started singing our song:

"Life with Uncle Willy, Willy.
Sometimes it can be silly, silly.

He makes me real whiny, whiny,
when he hits me in the heinie, heinie.
He's Willy, Willy, Willy.
He's a suicidal, homicidal, psychopathic, maniac,
do do do wah.
Uncle Willy is his name.
Beating us is his game.
Life with a hermit can be fun
except for the fact that he beats us 'til he's done."

Gerry, Tony, and I started pounding on the door and saying shit like, "Uncle Willy, will you come out and play Parcheesi with us?"

"No, leave me alone!"

"Uncle Willy, will you come out and play baseball?"

"No, piss off!"

"Uncle Willy, would you like to eat some of my birthday cake?"

"That's it—"

Ray whipped open the door. He took a drag from an imaginary cigarette, tossed it on the ground, and crushed it with his shoe, and Tony, Gerry, and I scattered. Tony ran for the room's far corner, I slid under the piano, and Gerry went for the door, but Ray grabbed him right away and slammed him on the ground. Ray ripped off his belt and started whipping the shit out of Gerry, all over his stomach, neck, and face. Miss Amalia tried to stop him, but she couldn't. Ray came for me next. He grabbed me by the ankles and dragged me out from under the piano, then he whipped my back like a motherfucker. I was screaming and laughing so hard I couldn't breathe. When Ray went after Tony, Miss Amalia grabbed the belt away.

"Boys, that's enough!"

Most of the class looked horrified, but I could tell Julia got it. She was laughing just as hard as we were. The rest of the day, we all kept singing the "Life with Uncle Willy" song and cracking up. Gerry had a welt on his cheek that looked pretty nasty, but he'd be all right. My back was too sore to sit against my chair, so I leaned forward and put my elbows on the desk, and soon the day was over.

After school, Dan, Gerry, and I helped Sister Rose work on the garden near the convent. We'd been helping her two or three days a week since the end of the last school year, and it was starting to come together. We'd spent the first few months weeding and getting rid of old plants and bushes, and had finally gotten around to planting new ones. I loved to work with my hands. I spent so much of my time trying to stop my racing thoughts, so it was great to see how my efforts could make something that was actually real. Something I could look at. Something I could touch and smell.

At ninety-two, Sister Rose was by far the oldest nun in the parish, but she was also the kindest. Every afternoon at four, she took a shuttle downtown to help some other nuns work a soup kitchen on the East Side. She also worked in the school's library, and we helped her there in the winter. She was always smiling and telling us all how good and special we were. I loved to spend time in the library with her. It made me feel safe. It made reading feel safe. I loved books and part of that was because of Sister Rose. She loved reading as well, and we'd talk about our favorite books, hers being *Tom's Midnight Garden*, and mine being *Where the Red Fern Grows*. She obviously didn't do much work in her own garden. She mostly just walked around and enjoyed the sunshine and the smell of the flowers and told us how grateful she was for our help. I knew Gerry loved it as well.

At home, Gerry got it the worst of any of us. Gerry's dad was a complete loon and fucked Gerry up all the time. My dad beat my ass, but not like Gerry's dad did to Gerry. I never liked going over to his house. None of us did, really. His dad scared the shit out of us. He was always drunk and screaming about "niggers" and "spics," and I didn't even know what those words meant. Other dads used those words sometimes too. My dad used those words sometimes, along with "liberals." "Those god-damned liberals are ruining this city!" just like the "niggers" and "spics." They were always so angry when they said those words, though, so they must have meant something terrible.

But Sister Rose never said anything like that. Sister Rose didn't think anyone was ruining anything. She loved everyone and treated them all with respect. She wanted to help, and this passion to help people spread to me as well. Sister told us she'd pay us, but she never had any money. Instead, she'd give us prayer cards and say she was praying for us. That was okay with me. God wasn't listening to my prayers, but maybe he'd listen to hers. Besides, a lot of the religious stuff confused the hell outta me. One day Sister Verona would say, "All homosexuals are going to Hell," then the next day she'd say they were going to Purgatory until they could repent for their sins. It seemed as if she was just making up the rules as she went along. Sometimes I'd read the Bible outside of class, and sometimes God would contradict himself from one page to the next. Sometimes He'd say He's the only God, then other times He'd say that He was the best of all gods. Sometimes He'd punish someone for doing something, but then the next person would do that same thing, and they'd be a hero. It seemed to me that nothing I could do would ever please Him. And so many of His rules seemed impossible to follow. Dad had no chance. He'd be in Hell with me. Honestly, I didn't want Dad around me for all eternity, unless he could be happy. He'd been happy when we were younger, when we still lived in Virginia Beach and he was in the Navy, but he'd been so miserable since moving back here. Maybe in Heaven he'd be happy again, though.

I stopped reading the Bible because it confused me. It made me question whether or not God really gave a shit. If God was really up there, or if he was just like all the other gods, like Zeus and Hades, who I knew weren't real. Either way, I had the garden. I had the Earth. The dirt. I had my brother and my friend beside me. I could be happy here. I didn't have to think about those things here. Just me, the plants, and the sunshine. No screaming. No misery.

A car came tearing up near us in the garden and stopped, and Gerry's dad screamed at Gerry for making him wait, then he took off, yelling that Gerry could eat shit for dinner.

"It's all right, you can eat with us," Dan said.

We left around four so we could deliver papers. Sister Rose hopped in the shuttle as we took off on our bikes, but before we parted ways, Sister told us, "God loves you boys very much." That made Gerry smile even though I could tell he wanted to cry.

Chapter 4

Gerry helped us deliver papers that afternoon, and he did the first half of my section of the route. When I passed Jacob Mancuso's house, Shane and a few other shitbags were playing hoops in the driveway.

"Hey, Lombardi," Shane said to me, "you got next."

He and the others crossed the street, heading for me. I got off my bike so I had better balance. Shane and Mancuso got right in my face.

"Real tough guy, aren't you, Jimmy?" Shane said.

"You are too, surrounded by all these jerks," I said.

Mancuso punched me in the stomach, and Shane stomped on the spokes of my bike's front wheel. I was more concerned for the spokes than for myself, but after taking a quick look, there didn't seem to be any damage. Shane motioned as if he was going to hit me, and I stepped to him. Mancuso hit me again, but in the face this time, splitting my lip. I took a step back, then stepped forward, right up on him. Ms. Ricci, one of my customers, came out of her house and started screaming something about calling the cops. The assholes went back across the street. Ms. Ricci offered me some frozen corn to put on my face, but I said no and kept going. When I got to the rectory, Monsignor Joseph opened the upstairs window and yelled down to me, "I called the news and requested you put the paper in the door, but you keep putting it in the mailbox. Why can't you just put it in the door?"

"Sorry, Monsignor." I put the paper in the door, and he shook his head while muttering some crap about "stupid kids," and I rode away. When I got home, Gerry and Dan were already back. Helen gave me the "Come here" deal from her front porch, but I pretended not to see her. Mr. Rogers was on the warpath in the garage, and I could hear him screaming and throwing shit around like a madman. I didn't want to get anywhere near that.

Because Gerry was there, Mom ordered Bocce's. Everyone in Buffalo loved Bocce's pizza, but I hated it because it had so much sauce. Dad calmed his shit down whenever we had guests. In fact, he was a great host. I think a part of him loved entertaining people, and he'd dish one-liners and dad jokes all night, smiling and laughing and patting people on the back, calling them "Champ" and "Slugger" and saying, "Watch out for this one here!" and, "You're a good guy, no matter what they say about ya!"

No one asked about my lip, and the sauce from the pizza burned it when I chewed. The family machine was in gear, and nothing could slow it down. No time to check on cuts or bruises or shattered egos. Always forward! Always, "Suck it up!" Always, "Your brother never complains!" So I did suck it up. But it fucking burned my lip.

After dinner, Gerry left and Dad went back to work on the bedroom. The smiles and laughter were gone, and back was, "None of you fuckers are helping me!" When he was calm, I enjoyed helping him. I liked to see how things worked. Liked to see how to run Romex to the electrical boxes and hook it up to the sockets. How to hang drywall and lay carpet. But I hated to see him go berserk each time he dropped a damned screw. Each time I handed him the wrong size nail. "You should be like a nurse is to a doctor and know *exactly* what I'll need next." So, I'd hand him shit, hoping it was the right thing. Hoping that, just by chance, I'd impress him. But even if I got lucky and handed him the right tool or whatever, the best I'd ever get was to not get screamed at. He rarely ever asked Dan or my younger brother, Jeremy, to help him, and he certainly didn't ask Mom or my sisters. I was always his guy. A part of me felt special about that, but another part felt chained to the job. Felt as if this was just another thing—like the prayers and rituals—that I couldn't get away from. I *had* to do it, and if I didn't no one else would. If I didn't, I was letting the old man down. It was my sacrifice. My burden. Sometimes, he'd call me, "Wayne—I mean, James," and it made me feel as if I wasn't even the one helping him. That I didn't even exist. But still. I had to do it.

Sometimes I'd help him late into the night. But that night, I decided to shoot hoops instead. He'd put a hoop above the garage that summer, after I'd begged him to for years, and I'd spend hours shooting around. Working on my dribbling. Doing layups with both my left and right hands. When I played basketball, it slowed my thoughts. When I got hours of exercise, I could sleep much better. So I started obsessing over basketball, but it felt like a healthy obsession—not like the prayers. This felt good. Positive. I liked doing it. I dedicated a few hours each day just to practicing. And the effort was showing.

I was still doing the rituals before bed, but I'd dropped a few, like the milk and VapoRub. Dan had gotten the hint with the music and didn't play it anymore before bed. I slept in the top bunk, and he was below me. I had the basketball with me that night; I'd been sleeping with it for the last few weeks. I liked to spin it off my fingertips until I fell asleep.

"How's your lip?" Dan whispered.

"What?" I took out my earplugs.

"Your lip," he said.

"What do you mean?"

"I saw you had a split lip. How is it?"

"It's fine."

"What happened?"

"I-I fell off my bike." I accidentally dropped the ball, and it hit my lip. "Crap."

"Hey, why'd the old man put wheels on his rocking chair?" Dan said.

"I dunno, why?"

"Because he wanted to rock *and* roll."

I laughed. "Why did the old man's cat run away?"

"Why?"

I rolled to the wall, slid down into his bunk, and farted in his face. "That's why."

He laughed and pushed me off of him, and I climbed back up to my bunk. Jeremy started snoring, so I hopped down and put the teddy bear over his head, then went to sleep.

The next day after school, Gerry helped us deliver papers again, then we headed to the Da Lucas' to play basketball.

When we got there, Alonzo, Tony, and Ray were inside the house watching a movie where everyone was naked. These two women with huge tits were sucking a guy's thing, which was, like, the size of my arm, and then it exploded this white cream that the ladies started licking up as it dripped down his hard dick. I looked around the room, and all the guys had blankets or pillows covering their laps, and Alonzo's hand was going up and down under his blanket. The movie was terrifying, but I couldn't stop watching, and my dick was hard like the pizza guy's on TV. I didn't know why, but I wished those ladies would suck on mine like that too. Afterward, we watched the first half of *Friday*, which we'd seen like a thousand times, so we knew all the lines, and then we went outside to play.

We wheeled the hoop to the edge of the driveway. One of the Da Lucas' neighbors was always out working on his Camaro and blasting classic rock, and he was out there drinking Labatt Blue and listening to Black Sabbath as we picked teams. He'd come over sometimes and tell us about "real music," and he introduced us to bands like Zeppelin, Pink Floyd, and The Who. I was okay with classic rock, but maybe that had to do with the fact that I didn't start listening to classic rock until after the Evil Thoughts had subsided. Nirvana was enormous when the thoughts first came on, and I still couldn't stand Kurt's voice. But Sabbath, Aerosmith, Lynyrd Skynyrd, Queen. Those were all safe, so I was cool with listening to 97 Rock all day.

We ran threes: me, Dan, and Gerry versus Alonzo, Tony, and Ray. The game was pretty evenly matched at first, but we pulled ahead at the end. Tony put up a wild shot, and Dan grabbed the rebound, kicked it out to me at the top of the key—marked by an oil spot on the street—and I shook Alonzo and put in a layup over Ray.

"Damn, Jimmy, that was nice," Ray said.

"Fuck that," Alonzo said. "You got lucky."

Alonzo checked the ball to me at the oil stain then passed it to Ray in the paint. Ray tried to back toward the hoop, but Dan's defense was too quick, and he stripped the ball as Ray was trying to put in a hook shot. Dan kicked it up to me again at the top of the key, then he set a pick on Alonzo. I burned Alonzo and went straight at Ray, then passed the ball back to Dan. Ray got on him immediately, so Dan hit me with a pass on the baseline, and I sunk a nice fifteen-footer before Alonzo could get there. He shoved me hard before my feet touched the ground, and I fell on the curb.

Basketball was something that came to me as naturally as walking. I rarely had any clue as to what the fuck was going on around me, but when I had a basketball in my hands, it all made sense. I could feel the instincts surging inside of me, guiding me along. Showing me the *real* way to go. My movements were fluid, controlled, and pure. My thoughts were driven and clear.

Alonzo checked the ball to me again. He dribbled between his legs and tried to burn me, but I stripped him, then passed it to Dan on the wing. Dan hesitated, but I yelled "Shoot it!" and he hit a pretty jumper from three-point range. Dan might have been the best out of all of us, but no one seemed to know it. I was a flashier player: spin moves, crossovers, big-point performances—stuff that got people's attention. But Dan was a silent threat. He did all the things nobody else liked to do—set picks, box out players, play solid D—and he did them well. What was more was that the kid had a jump shot unlike any around. He sank almost everything he took. The problem was that, growing up in a world where you always had to put everyone else before yourself, he never shot the damned ball unless someone told him to. A guy like Dan had the ability to strengthen a team in ways you couldn't put on paper. You just needed a special pair of eyes to see it. And I did see it. The rest of the guys played for the fun of it, but for me, and I think Dan too, it was more than a game. We lived and died for it.

Gerry got a steal, then put up a shot that sailed way over the hoop, stopping play.

"Gerry, you stupid fuck," Alonzo said. "Can't you take a break from being a retard for one god-damned second?"

Ray punched Gerry in the arm, and Gerry screamed.

"That's for D-Day, motherfucker!" Ray said.

"I'm fucking half Israeli too!" Gerry said.

Ray hit him again. "That's for insubordination."

Tony grabbed the ball and passed it to Alonzo at the top of the key. He checked it to me, but we stopped play when a car came down the street. When we stepped to the curb, we instantly broke into what probably looked like a choreographed set of stripper moves. We humped the air and licked our lips and pointed at the old woman driving by, who looked mortified as she continued down the street. When she was gone, we tried to get back to the game, but another car came by, and we did the same shit.

"This court sucks," Alonzo said. "Next time let's play at Hammond."

"Isn't that place run by the Kirkland kids?" I said.

"Yeah, the Powells, Luke Harrison, Joey Cartucci, Silas

Macker, and a bunch of others all hang out there," Alonzo said.

"Didn't Joey Cartucci go to juvie for cutting a kid's face with a razor?" Tony said.

"Heard he was just teachin' him how to shave," Ray said.

"I heard it was a teacher at St. Anthony's," I said. "And it was a pencil, not a razor."

"Could we even get on the court?" Dan said.

"*Should* we even get on the court?" I said.

"Don't be bitches," Alonzo said. He pointed at Dan. "We know Joey, and I'm cool with Silas Macker. Let's go up there tomorrow afternoon."

"I'm in," Ray said.

"Oh, shit, here comes Gus," Tony said. He pointed at a man approaching us on a rusted BMX bike and blasting "Strike It Up" by Black Box from a boombox sitting on the handlebars. He kept shouting, "Luke took my jersey!" over and over and looked ready to kill someone. Gus was born a fully functioning kid but suffered a traumatic brain injury after getting hit by a car when he was twelve. For fun, he rode his bike house to house, garbage-picking people's trash. Though in his late thirties, he still lived with his parents at the end of the Da Lucas' street, and inside his bedroom was a mountain of old TVs, broken radios, worn sneakers, and his favorite: basketball jerseys. It was a pile he protected with unwavering vigilance, and if anything went missing, he'd lose his mind searching for it. He had a huge crush on the girl who lived across from the Da Lucas, Bianca Gambino, and he wasn't alone. Though only thirteen, she looked about twenty, and her ass and tits were the cause of more wood growth than the Buffalo-Olmsted Park's Reforestation Project. Bianca came outside when she heard Gus.

"What's he bitchin' about now?" she said.

"He's just upset that Luke Harrison took his Derrick Coleman jersey," Tony said.

"Still? That happened like a year ago," Alonzo said.

"Yeah, and Luke didn't even take it. Remember? Gus found it like a day later under that pile of garbage in his room," Tony said.

"Luke took my jersey!" Gus said.

"Yo, relax, G-Man," Bianca said.

Gus chilled the fuck out whenever she gave him some attention.

"You guys wanna play some hoops?" Alonzo said.

"You wanna play some hoops, Gus?" Bianca said.

"Yeah, I want hoops!" Gus said.

"We'll take Bianca. You guys take Gus," Tony said.

"Fine," I said.

Alonzo stared at Bianca's massive tits. "Let's do shirts versus skins. We'll be skins."

"Fuck that, 'Zo, you ain't getting nowhere near these titties," she said.

Alonzo stuck his face right between them, and Bianca laughed.

"That's twenty bucks," she said. "Ten per titty."

"You take credit?" Alonzo said. He swiped his fingers down the crack of her ass, and she slapped his hand away.

"You guys be skins," Ray said.

Dan and I took off our shirts and tossed them in the grass. Gerry hesitated to remove his, but when he did, we saw that his torso was covered in welts, cuts, and cigarette burns.

"Damn, you get hit by a train?" Tony said.

Gerry tried to put his shirt back on, but Ray ripped it away and punched him hard in the side.

"There's another one for your collection," Ray said.

"Hey—" I said.

Ray looked me dead in the eyes. "What? You got something to say?"

"N-no," I said. I walked over to Gus, instead. "Gus, we're skins, so you gotta take off your jersey."

Gus had some trouble taking it off, but the second I touched it to help him get it over his head, he went apeshit. He started screaming, "Luke took my jersey!" and picked up a fallen tree branch and swung it at my head. I dodged it, hopped on my bike, and peddled as fast as I could out of there. I could hear him still screaming even as I rounded the corner.

As Gus's screaming grew faint, my dad's got louder. Mom stood on our front porch holding my baby sister, Carolynn. I dropped my bike on the driveway and ran to them. "It's okay, sweetie," she said to Carolynn, "just pretend it's the sound of the ocean. Just pretend it's God speaking to you from the heavens. He has to yell to get his voice down to all of us."

"He tried to kill me!" I shouted.

"Where have you been all afternoon? He's been screaming for you," she said to me.

"He tried to kill me! He almost crushed my head with a tree," I said.

"What? Where were you?" she said.

"At the Da Lucas', playing basketball. This guy almost kill—"

"Your father really needs your help in there."

"He always needs help."

"He breaks his back trying to make this house a better place for all of us to live. The least you can do is help him."

"I never asked him to do any of that. Besides, I'm tired of helping. He never asks Dan or Jeremy."

"Get yourself cleaned up, then march right in there."

"But Ma, you don't understand. There's a guy out there named Gus that—"

"I said march!"

I hardly got a step inside the house before he screamed, "SON OF A FUCKING BITCH!" I turned to Mom and gave her a look, and she just covered the baby's ears and said, "Go!" I could hear her trying to calm down Carolynn as I marched alone into Hell.

The old man was in the downstairs bedroom beside the kitchen. He'd gutted the room and removed the studs framing the closet to add some extra space. I think he enjoyed demo, because he never yelled when taking crowbars and sledgehammers to the walls, ripping shit apart, and getting eighty-year-old house dust and filth and crud all over him. His bent, bargain-rack, steel-rimmed glasses would slide down his sweaty nose, and he'd grit his teeth, and put his whole ass into it. He'd pulverize plaster and lath walls filled with asbestos and scrape window frames covered in lead paint, but he'd never wear a mask or goggles. John Wayne would never wear a mask. Masks were for pussies. Real men huffed paint thinner and kerosene as they burned the world to ash.

But once shit was destroyed and needed to be built back up, that was when he'd scream and swear and pout like a toddler. He'd find hundreds of ways to let us know how ungrateful we were. How lazy we were. It didn't matter if I got up at 6 a.m. to deliver Sunday papers so I could finish on time to serve eight-thirty Mass, then spend the day doing homework; if I didn't help him, I was lazy. And I believed him too. He made me believe the worst in myself. I was never good enough. Never strong enough. If he hit his thumb with the hammer, it was because I was standing too close, or breathing too heavily, or I'd given him the wrong nail, or some other bullshit, and the few times I saw those dead, black fingernails fall off his swollen, calloused digits, I felt myself dropping down to Hell with them. Dads have a special way of making their sons feel worthless, and mine was particularly gifted with this.

When I walked in there, he was taking measurements of the studs and marking a panel of drywall. "Here, hold it steady," he said, and I grabbed the top of the panel and held my breath so it wouldn't move a millimeter.

Through the open door, I watched Mom in the kitchen. She'd put the baby down so she could chop carrots for dinner. I tried to hold in a sneeze but couldn't, and the old man screamed, "I said hold it steady!" I grabbed the panel tight with both hands and kept watching Mom as Dad continued to scream. Carolynn started crying, but Mom didn't flinch. She never did. She'd whistle through it or chop carrots or pray the Rosary. I couldn't remember the last time she'd smiled. She had a great smile. The kind you see in the movies when the guy brings the girl flowers then plays her favorite song on the guitar. But no one was giving Mom flowers or songs anymore. She was the lone voice of reason in our household—at least, she was reasonable compared to Dad.

Mom came from a huge family herself—the oldest of nine kids. Her parents were first-generation Italian immigrants who grew up on the West Side while Buffalo was still a flourishing city filled with hope and possibility. They didn't have much, but my grandmother used to say, "Blessed are the meek, for they shall inherit the Earth." I know those words affected my mother because she repeated them all the time.

My mother's father was a cop who'd worked a beat in and around the Fruit Belt, one of Buffalo's roughest neighborhoods. It was tough work, but my grandpa was a charismatic and caring man—so everyone said—and he earned the respect of the community. But in spite of that heart and charisma, the horrors he saw on those streets began to take over his life, and after a few years the smiles and charm were gone. He wouldn't eat, couldn't sleep, and he'd disappear for days at a time. My grandma died when my mom was thirteen, leaving her to care for her brothers and sisters. Mom had to grow up fast. She was a rock. She never complained and always put the needs of her family before her own. She was a brilliant woman; she'd dreamed of becoming a college professor, but was so consumed with the needs of her family that she ended up dropping out of high school and never went back. But no matter how hard she worked at home, she couldn't keep the darkness from spreading, and when she was eighteen, my mother found my grandpa's lifeless body hanging by a rope in the basement. A few years later, she was also the one to discover that her youngest brother, Vincent, had slit his wrists and drained his life away in the darkness of that same basement. My mother prayed the Rosary daily, just as her own mother had, and even though I was just a kid, it still seemed to me that she went to those beads like a drunk went to a drink.

Dan came home while Mom was cooking dinner, and he helped her. He was always helping her while I helped Dad. He'd cook and clean and help with the little kids. Like her, he never complained. When Dad yelled, Dan would whistle through it too. But unlike Mom, Dan still smiled sometimes. Not as much as he used to, though. I still smiled. Sometimes, even after the old man would give me the belt, I'd smile. Sometimes I'd smile even when he was screaming at me. Usually I'd yell back, but sometimes I'd smile to his face. Sometimes I hated that motherfucker so much that I imagined hiding razors in his pillow. Putting nails in his stew. Kerosene in his Pepsi. He wasn't going to beat me. If the Evil Thoughts couldn't beat me, no one would. I was tougher than that motherfucker, and someday I was going to feel all right. Someday I was going to have kids and be good to them. I wanted to believe, I really did. But then again, there was the time I was tagging along with my mother to the drugstore back when I wouldn't let her go anywhere without me, and when I told her that someday I wanted to be happy and not yell like Dad, she told me, "You know what? When I first met your father, he said the same thing about his dad." Even though I wanted to dream that someday I'd feel okay, hearing shit like that, and knowing all I already knew about life and Heaven and Hell, I knew I was a monster that'd just get bigger and bigger until someday it destroyed the whole world and every smiling face in it. Knew that kids deserved every single terrible thing that ever happened to them. Knew that moms had no business waiting for flowers or songs.

The old man and I hung the panel of drywall on the studs quickly and efficiently. I held it up as he drove in a few screws, then when there were enough screws to hold up the panel, we each took a side and a drill and finished the job. Despite the screaming, we worked well together. We could finish hanging drywall in a room like that in an afternoon once we got into our rhythm.

When Mom called us to dinner, we were nearly done with the room. Dad always sat at one end of our dining room table, and I sat at the other, and everyone else filled in the sides. There was rarely a night we'd get through dinner without someone yelling or crying or throwing a glass of milk across the room, and that night was no exception. When my little brother, Jeremy, accidentally coughed on my hand, I spat in his potatoes. I made sure Mom wasn't looking first, of course, but then Jeremy started crying, and Mom made him tell her what happened. I kicked the shit out of him under the table and whispered to him to stop whining like a bitch, but that just made him cry harder. I could see Dad was getting pissed, so I apologized when Mom told me to.

Dan, who sat on my other side, asked how I was doing after the shit that went down with Gus. "He almost killed you," he said, and I responded with, "I know, right?" while giving my mother a disgusted look. She was wiping some green crap off Carolynn's face. I could be bleeding from the eyes, and she'd just sip her milk. I could be coughing up a lung and everyone would just keep eating. But Carolynn farts and Mom sticks her nose right up baby's ass.

Dad asked for the salt but no one could find it, and I could see him starting to lose it. He'd make this sound while clenching his teeth and you knew shit was about to get ugly, and he started making it when Mom went to the kitchen to look for the saltshaker. My father's name was Richard, but ever since he was a kid everyone called him Poor Rich. He was a big, country motherfucker born in some Bumblefuck, New York town southeast of the city that had lost quite a few boys to Vietnam. His parents, like my mother's, were first-generation immigrants—my grandpa from Sicily and my grandma from Poland—who'd struggled their whole lives to make ends meet. My grandfather had been a decorated paratrooper in World War II, and while fighting in Bastogne on a relief mission ordered by Eisenhower, an exploding shell caused him to lose the hearing in his left ear. After the war, he returned to the salt mines where he'd worked for years before being called to fight the Nazis. Sometimes weeks would pass before he saw the sun. When he wasn't working, he hit the bottle hard. And that wasn't all he hit. He gave my grandma, dad, and two uncles regular beatings that, based on my dad's stories, were far worse than anything Poor Rich ever laid on me. Dad reminded me constantly of how lucky I was that he never used a tire iron on me, sometimes while whipping the shit out of me with a belt. My father and his younger brother, Wayne, had both served in the Navy and went to Vietnam on the same ship. My father got through the war without so much as a scratch, but his brother wasn't so lucky. My Uncle Wayne was burned to death in an engine fire while the ship was docked in Singapore and my dad was on a bender with his buddies. My dad's other brother, Tommy, had wanted to go to war with his brothers, but he was in prison for beating a guy nearly to death in a bar fight. He always told Dad that if he'd been there, he wouldn't have let Wayne die like that. That he would have done something. That Dad should have been there. That he should have checked the emergency generators, even though Dad worked in the kitchen. And every time Uncle Tommy starting talking like that, Dad would go off to his old room or the garage or wherever and just stare and not say anything. Sometimes Grandma would jump in and call Dad things like "Bitch," "Drunk," or, "Pussy," while his cousins laughed and threw shit at him.

While Dad and Uncle Wayne were on the ship and Uncle Tommy was in jail, my Aunt Rhonda ran away one night and never spoke to any of them again. No one ever talked about her, and the only reason I knew she existed was because I'd found a picture of her in a box in the attic and asked Mom who she was. Apparently she was Dad's baby sister, and after she left, it was almost as if she'd disappeared from Earth. No one went looking for her. Nobody seemed to care. It was probably best she got away.

When the war ended, Dad was in and out of prison too, mostly for shit related to the benders he'd go on. According to Grandma, it was as if Dad had a bottle of Canadian whisky surgically attached to his hand, and whisky combined with PTSD and uncontrollable rage ain't pretty. He was a big, angry, drunk lunatic, who came from a long line of big, angry, drunk lunatics, and I'm surprised he survived that period in time. Uncle Tommy told us stories sometimes about the crazy shit he and Dad did together, but he never gave me any details. He'd just say, "You don't wanna know, Jimmy. Trust me." They were both enormous. People in town still talked about the time Uncle Tommy won a bet by ripping a car door off its hinges. And when he was fixing our roof, Poor Rich would toss three eighty-pound bundles of shingles over his shoulder and climb the ladder no problem. Grandpa died when I was four, but I remember watching him bend horseshoes with his bare hands while Dan and I cheered him on. He was a big, Luca Brasi-looking motherfucker, and I was glad to have gotten my looks from

Mom's side of the family.

When my father met my mother, he was a hardcore alcoholic, but he quit cold turkey once they became serious. He never touched a sip since. My mother prided herself in knowing she'd helped him kick his addiction.

"WHERE'S THE FUCKING SALT?"

Dad smashed the table with both fists before Mom could find the saltshaker, then stormed into the unfinished bedroom, screaming, "I NEED SOME FUCKING HELP! NO ONE EVER FUCKING HELPS ME! YOU UNGRATEFUL SONS OF BITCHES!" He started up the drill, and Carolynn started to cry.

Mom picked her up and said, "Look what you did, James. Now help me clean all this up." Her words weren't like Dad's. Her words weren't filled with anger and aggression. When she said things like that, it was always with sadness and disappointment. Dad screamed so much, his words meant little to me. But when *she* said things like that, it made me feel really low. I cleaned the food off the floor as Dan cleared the table. While under the table, I rubbed some mashed potatoes on Jeremy's bare foot, and he started crying again.

"James, you get in there right now and help your father," Mom said. I didn't argue—I just marched into the bedroom and helped Dad finish hanging drywall as Dan helped Mom clean the table and do the dishes.

I helped Dad until late that night, and when I got to the upstairs bedroom, all of my brothers and sisters were asleep, except for Dan, who was writing in a black-and-white marble journal under a book light. He did that sometimes, especially after nights when the screaming had been the worst. My rituals had eased considerably by that time, so I no longer panicked when I wasn't in bed by nine; I no longer said goodnight to my parents, but I did still tap the section of wall three times before walking upstairs. I also still put stuffed animals over Jeremy's and my sisters' heads, and I'd pray for about an hour before going to sleep. While praying, I'd spin the basketball on my fingers and it would usually be on the floor in the morning.

Chapter 5

That morning, Dan and I were up at six thirty to deliver Saturday morning papers. When I got to the rectory, I got off my bike and watched the nuns walk across the parking lot on their way to church: Sister Rose, Sister Verona, Sister Adele, and all the rest, walking so quietly and confidently toward the Lord.

Dan and I finished by eight thirty, ate breakfast, and headed outside to shoot hoops. Alonzo called Dan around ten, and Dan came back outside to ask me if I wanted to go with them to Hammond.

"Let's just play here," I said.

"They want to go to Hammond," he said.

"We'll get murdered there," I said.

"GOD-FUCKING-DAMN IT!" Dad had already started working on the bedroom. "I NEED SOME FUCKING HELP IN HERE!"

"Fuck it, I'll go," I said.

We hopped on our bikes and headed to the Da Lucas' house. When we got to the corner of their street, I saw Gus rummaging through someone's trash, and I got off my bike.

"Don't worry about him," Dan said. "Alonzo says all

you have to do is say, 'Friend, Gus, friend,' while holding out your hand, and he'll shake it and forgive you."

Gus found a hockey stick and started hitting it against a tree.

"Can you just go get them?" I said.

Dan shrugged and rode ahead while I hid in a bush. When he and the Da Lucas got to the corner, I rode with them to Hammond Park. Though it was only a few blocks from my house, it was like another world. The park was rundown, and at the west entrance there was a small playground with rusted swings and slides. Behind that was a series of baseball diamonds where girls' softball teams played. In the far corner was a basketball court, which was nothing more than an uneven spread of blacktop with a heavy-duty hoop at each end. The rims were bright red and had chains for nets. For years, the court had been all but abandoned. During the day, the park was filled with kids playing at the playground and girls playing softball, with parents scattered all over, but no one ever used the court other than to jump rope or play hopscotch or whatever. At night, the park was filled with drunks and crackheads who'd stab your ass and steal your shoes and wallet. But for some reason—even though there were better courts nearby—a group of local kids had started playing hoops at Hammond a few months back, and it quickly became one of the city's top spots for streetball. Kids would come from all over to play there: Black Rock, Allentown, the East Side. They'd even come from the suburbs like Kenmore, Tonawanda, and Amherst.

My neighborhood was mostly White, but a lot of the kids playing there were Black, Puerto Rican, Indian, Pakistani, Korean—all the people I'd been warned not to interact with because "they just don't behave civilized like we do." I'd heard stories about what happened on that court and was terrified to go there. If you said the wrong thing, you'd get your ass beat with a quickness. I didn't know why Alonzo and Tony and the others even wanted to go there. I was happy at home. Well, happy enough at least.

We rode our bikes past the playground and up to the court. Two teams were running fives, and the court was surrounded by about thirty guys and a few girls all shouting and cheering and messing around. They mostly looked older, but not too old. They were probably all in the upper grades of middle school or in high school. Bianca was there, rubbing her ass on some older dude's crotch as he drank from a bottle wrapped in a brown paper bag. When Dan saw this, he looked sad.

A softball rolled toward the older dude, and a dopey dad wearing knee-high white socks and jean shorts walked over. "A little help?" he said, but the guy with Bianca just spat in the dad's direction and turned around again. When the dad bent over to pick up the ball, Bianca slapped him on the ass, and he jumped. She licked her lips and said, "Call me," and he walked away with a tentpole in his pants like we'd all had when watching that naked movie at the Da Lucas'.

Though the court was filled with kids from all over the city, a group of locals ran the show, and they were currently whoopin a team from Manigault High School. The locals were some of the youngest kids out there, but from what I'd heard, they kicked some serious ass. Silas Macker was a regular. He wasn't the tallest, but he played power forward bigger than anyone. He was quick and strong as hell and had great instincts around the hoop. He could hit jumpers from fifteen feet and played some of the best D on the court.

Tom and Dorian Powell, or T. Pow and D. Pow, as everyone called them, were brothers notorious for attacking anything that moved. They were bull sharks and sometimes when they ran out of other people to fight, they would turn on each other. D. Pow was older than T. Pow, but he'd failed fourth grade, so they were in the same class. D. Pow was a big, mean dude, while T. Pow was a little more relaxed and charismatic. D. Pow usually played center and could out-rebound most other players. He was quick, too, and scored easily in the paint. T. Pow was also quick and hit mid-range jumpers. He also had handle and could push point if needed. They played rough and dirty and weren't afraid to put elbows in noses and knees in thighs.

Joey Cartucci was supposedly the son of a mafia boss. I didn't know if this was true, but there was no way I was ever asking him to confirm it. It didn't take long to realize that here Joey was the boss. He was a wiseass and bullshitted with other guys, but if they crossed the line, he'd give them this look and they'd shut right up. Joey wasn't the most skilled player, but he was all energy. He'd run up and down the court, always moving, and guys would have to switch up covering him because no one could keep up. He had a nice jumper and played solid D, but his best quality was his hustle. He'd dive for loose balls and grab rebounds and keep his team moving.

Then there was Luke Harrison. By age thirteen, Luke was already widely considered to be one of the top streetballers in Buffalo, and it took only a minute to see why. He owned the court and could do just about anything he wanted. He had a rare combination of power, skill, and grace only possessed by the finest of athletes. He had the best handle, the best vision, the best defense. He could burn any defender, drive to the hoop, and put in layups over guys a head taller. He'd guard the opposing point guard and press him the length of the court, and some of these point guards couldn't even get past half court without Luke stripping them and putting in easy layups. Luke played point but had the size of a power forward. Though he wasn't as big as D. Pow, D. Pow would often cool his shit if Luke stepped to him. Unlike Joey, whose power came from his reputation, Luke's power came from his fists, and if it came down to it, he'd probably knock out every motherfucker who stepped to him. A lot of other guys had size and talent, but what separated them from Luke was that Luke wasn't getting outworked by anyone. He played hard. He played dirty. And he was the King of Hammond.

The Hammond Crew won the game quickly. D. Pow missed an easy layup that would have been the game winner, but Silas got the rebound and put it in. D. Pow picked a trash can up over his head and smashed it against a tree. The dopey dad looked over from the softball diamond, but he didn't say shit.

"Yo, that was a nice pass, Lukie," Silas said as he stepped off the court and walked to the water fountain.

"No shit," Luke said. Like my brother, he didn't say much.

Alonzo approached Silas. "Hey, who's got next?"

Another player on the sidelines said, "You're gonna get next ass-whoopin unless you step away from my court."

Across the court, Joey and T. Pow walked up to a big and tall but timid-looking country boy named Steven, who'd recently moved up from North Carolina. He lived behind my family in a small house with his dad, and sometimes I'd see Steven working on his dad's Buick when I delivered papers.

"You think this is a hoedown or something?" Joey said to him.

"I-I called next earlier," Steven said.

"Shouldn't you be off fucking your sister?" Joey said.

"I don't h-have a sister," Steven said.

"Maybe you wanna fuck *my* sister, that right?" Joey said.

"You tryin' to fuck his sister, Steven?" T. Pow said.

"Fuck that shit," Joey said. He and T. Pow picked up some small branches that had fallen near the court and started breaking them on Steven's back as he ran away. They chased him to the playground, then backed off. Steven sprinted across the street and kept going.

"Let's get outta here," I said to Dan. I could feel the rivers of chemicals racing up my back, locking my muscles and twisting my spine.

"Alonzo, ask him again if we can play next," Dan said.

Alonzo tried to gather some confidence, but I could see it was shot. Either way, he walked up to Silas again, who was now back on the court.

"H-hey, uh, you think me and my friends could get next?" Alonzo said.

"Get the fuck outta here, man," Silas said.

Alonzo came back over. "Fuck this place. I don't wanna play here anyway. Let's go."

We rode back to the Da Lucas' and played tackle football in the field behind their house. Ray came over, along with a few other guys from the neighborhood, and we had a good game. I loved that field. It was in the middle of a block and didn't belong to anyone's yard—at least, not that we knew of. All the houses had high wooden fences in back, so it was like this hidden spot just for us. You had to go through a dense section of trees to get to it from the Da Lucas' yard, but after that it was just this open field, surrounded by wooden fences and trees.

After the game, Dan and I went home and shot hoops in the driveway. Dan mentioned something about me always sticking my left foot behind my right when shooting and twisting to the left in midair, and after shooting a few jumpers, I understood what he was saying. I tried to shoot with my feet square, but it threw me off balance. While we were playing PIG, Mom came outside looking really sad.

"James," she said. "That was Monsignor Joseph on the phone. Gerry's mother died last night, and Monsignor wants you to serve her Mass Monday night."

"What?" I said. "What happened?"

"Monsignor wouldn't say how it happened, just that it did and that he thinks it would be good for one of Gerry's friends to serve Mass."

She went back inside, and I didn't know how to respond. Part of me was sad for Gerry, but the other part of me—the Evil part—started kicking into motion again. It'd been a while since I'd needed to follow my mother everywhere, and I didn't have the energy to do it again. I started feeling dizzy and had to sit against the garage.

"Let's go collect," Dan said to me.

We hopped on our bikes and rode house to house to collect payment for our paper deliveries. We worked seven days a week in the rain, sleet, and snow. Neither Dan nor I had slept in on a weekend since we'd started delivering two years earlier. But collecting was the worst part of the job. It was always a struggle to get the bums to fork over the loot, and even when they did, they rarely included a tip, which was the only way we'd earn anything. And even when they did tip, it was usually only a few dimes or quarters. We split the earnings down the middle and averaged about five dollars a week each. Some people might have complained and quit, but I—and I think Dan too—needed those handfuls of change to keep moving along.

When we finished collecting, we rode to the Burger King across the street from St. Anthony's. I started toward the entrance, but Dan had a better idea. "C'mon," he said, as he rode to the drive-thru line and over the tube that lets the person inside know to start speaking. We ordered and pulled up to the window. A middle-aged man poked his head outside. He had long hairs sticking out of his nose. "Hey, you punks shouldn't play around in the drive-thru line." He handed us our food, and Dan dumped a handful of change on the counter without counting it.

"Hey, don'tcha kids have any paper money?"

We sped out of there laughing and ate in the garden behind the convent. I felt bad about what happened to Gerry, and I got really quiet thinking about him. At one point I almost felt as if I was going to cry, and I think Dan could sense this.

"Why'd the jalapeño wear a coat?" Dan said.

"I dunno, why?" I said.

"Because it was a little chili."

I smiled.

While riding home, we passed the deadbeat's house, and

he chased us down. "Where's my paper? You little shitheads haven't delivered in weeks!"

"We'll deliver when you pay," Dan said.

"Yeah, fucknuts," I said.

The deadbeat almost caught up to me, but I peddled as fast as I could and pulled ahead. Out of nowhere, I saw Gus rummaging through a pile of garbage, and when he saw me, he hurled a lawn mower blade at my head as if it was a Frisbee. I ducked just in time to keep my melon in one piece while shouting, "Friend, Gus, friend!" I peddled my ass home and didn't stop until I was back at the garage.

Mom was on the back deck with the baby. I walked up to her and gave her a long hug, which she returned with her free arm. "Thank you, James. This is very nice."

Chapter 6

After Sunday Mass, we hurried back to the station wagon. The parking lot was always chaos after ten o'clock Mass, and that morning we had places to be. Dad started backing up, but so did the car behind him. Poor Rich muttered a few swear words while pulling forward to let the other guy through. When the other guy was gone, Dad stepped on the gas but had forgotten he was still in drive, and he slammed into the car in front of us. Dad looked around; no one seemed to have seen, so he backed out and sped out the exit as we all cheered him on.

We laughed all the way to Mom's diner, where I ate a huge stack of pancakes with scrambled eggs. I loved pancakes and could eat them all day. Mom said breakfast food made her sick, so she only drank coffee. When we were little, Mom used to bring Dan and me to work with her. The diner was connected to a mall in Amherst, and she'd let us wander around for the duration of her shift. We'd go to the arcade and mini-golf course and movie theater and food court. We loved it, but after Mom found out Jeffrey Dahmer had picked up some of his victims at malls, she never let us come with her again.

After breakfast, we drove to Bumblefuck to visit Grandma. She was a bitter, angry woman, but she always made these Polish cookies covered with powdered sugar, so I didn't mind so much. Dad got the brunt of her anger, anyway, and she was kind of nice to us. She always asked us how we were doing in school, and I'd brag about how I was at the top of my class and complain about how dumb all the other kids were, and Dan would try to avoid having to tell her he was a C-student. All of my younger siblings would tell her about what they drew in school and who was being mean to them and all that, and she'd ask them how Dad was treating us. If we were eating well. If the house had heat in the winter. When Dad would hear these questions, sometimes he'd yell at her, but mostly he'd just go out to the garage and stare at the wall for a while. I'd try to tune out all the yelling and watch basketball games on TV. Sometimes Uncle Tommy would be there too, and he'd complain about how, "The NBA is so Black now I can't even watch it." I would always tell him that the Black players were just better than the White players, except for Larry Bird, but he wouldn't hear it. Sometimes I'd wander around the house to get away from everyone. Over the years, I'd found Grandpa's handgun in Uncle Tommy's old room, Grandpa's stash of full-bush *Playboy* magazines in the basement, and Uncle Wayne's guitar in the attic. Of everything I found, that guitar was the best. I always wanted to play it but didn't dare. I felt as if Uncle Wayne was watching me with a disapproving look, just waiting to beat my ass if I strummed those strings. Just waiting to say, "Don't try, Jimmy. It's only gonna hurt." I could hold it but couldn't play it.

When we got home, Dan and I shot hoops in the

driveway. Jeremy wanted to play too, but I told him to fuck off, and he ran off crying inside the house. Dan suggested we go back to Hammond, and even though a part of me never wanted to set foot there again, there was something about it that called to me. I might have said no, but Poor Rich was on a rampage again, screaming for me to help him, so I grabbed my bike and we took off.

But while riding down the driveway, I saw Gus going through our trash, so I stopped and hid behind the station wagon.

"WHERE THE FUCK IS JAMES!" I could hear my old man screaming. God, Gus, move!

The back screen door opened. "WAYNE—I MEAN, JAMES!"

Gus grabbed an old bike chain and took off, and I peddled so fast in the opposite direction that I didn't even realize I was in the street until a car almost hit me. I could hear my old man screaming my name from half a block down.

"Why do you even want to go to Hammond?" I asked Dan.

"Because that's where the best people play, and that's the only place you're ever going to get better."

When we got to Hammond, the court was far less crowded than the day before. They must have been between games, because Silas, Joey, the Powells, and Luke were sitting on the blacktop, fucking around, while Steven shot jumpers on the far side of the court.

"Whatchu mean you're never gonna toss salad?" Silas said to D. Pow. "How're you supposed to know if you never tried it?"

"It sounds nasty," D. Pow said.

"Why don't you toss my salad to see if you like it?" Joey said. He started pulling down his shorts.

"C'mon, man, nobody wants to see your shiny White ass," Silas said.

"Hey, Stevie," Joey said. "You wanna toss my salad?"

"I-I don't really like salad." Steven gave him a confused look. "I prefer steak . . . and hamburgers."

They all laughed at him.

Dan walked right up to the court, no fear. "Hey, guys, you wanna play a game?"

"Yo, look at these two," Joey said. "We got Horace and Harvey Grant."

"You two twins?" Silas said.

"No," Dan said. "This is James, and I'm his older brother, Dan. You remember me, right, Joey?"

Joey gave Dan a confused look.

"We went to kindergarten at St. Anthony's together," Dan said.

"Whatever," Joey said. "Fuck that place."

"Naw, you're Harvey, and this is Horace," Silas said.

"How are you older? He's bigger than you," T. Pow said.

"You wanna play or not?" Dan said.

"I'll tell you what, Harvey," Joey said. "You tell me what tossin' salad means, and we'll play a game."

"Doesn't it mean licking someone's fanny?" Dan said.

They all burst out laughing.

"Yo, he called it a fanny," Silas said. He walked over and clapped Dan on the back. "This guy's all right."

My brother was one of my heroes, but I never told him. When I saw it was safe, I walked onto the court. It felt as if the eyes of the world were now on me. It felt as if my life finally had purpose. As if God was finally listening.

"We got fours with these two and Steven," Luke said.

"Fuck Steven," Joey said.

"He makes fours," Luke said.

Joey walked up to Steven and stared deeply into his eyes. Steven didn't flinch.

"Okay, we got fours," Joey said.

T. Pow dribbled to the foul line. "First four to make it." He shot and missed. Luke also missed, but me, Silas, Dan, and D. Pow all made it. Luke shot for ball and made it. Joey tossed it in to Luke, and Luke pushed it up court. When he got to the half, I slapped the blacktop and got right on him. He shoved me to get some space, but I stayed on him. From watching him play the day before, I knew he liked to fake left then go hard to the right, so when he tried this, I pretended like he'd faked me out, then quickly shot to my left to stop him from driving. He cut back left, but I was on him, so he kicked it to Joey on the wing. Dan got on him, and Joey passed it back to Luke at the top of the key. Luke gave me a pump fake and tried to drive again, but Silas stepped up to him and blocked his ten-footer. Dan grabbed the ball and passed it to me, and I quickly pushed it past half court to prevent Luke from pressing me the length of the court and waited for everyone else to catch up. When we set up on offense, Dan picked Luke at the top of the key, and I drove the lane. I faked a shot, getting T. Pow to jump and dumped a no-look, backdoor pass to Silas as he cut to the hoop. Silas put in a pretty reverse layup as a smile burst across his face.

"God-damn, Horace! Now that's some vision!"

He gave me a high five as we got back on D. Luke

pushed the ball up court again and crossed me just past the half, but I caught up, preventing him from taking a fifteen-footer. Luke passed it to T. Pow in the post. T. Pow gave Silas a fake, then tried putting in a hook shot, and Silas swatted the hell out of it. Dan dove to stop it from going out of bounds and passed it to me with one hand before he fell onto the grass surrounding the court. I caught it in stride and took it the length of the court for an easy layup.

Joey passed the ball in to Luke. I pretended to be running back on D to catch Luke off guard, then quickly turned, stole it from him, and put in another easy layup.

"Horace is trimmin' your ass, Lukie!" Silas said.

I knew that comment would hurt me too, but I was still glad to hear it. Joey passed the ball in to Luke again, and Luke came at me with a head of steam. I stuck with him as he drove to the top of the key where he elbowed the shit out of my chin so hard, I bit through my tongue. He sank a ten-footer, and I walked to the grass to spit a mouthful of blood. We stopped the game for a second as Silas and Dan walked over.

"You okay, Horace?" Silas said.

I spat another mouthful of blood, then said, "Yeah, I'm good," and we kept going. When I pushed it to half court, I could see a change in the way Luke was playing me. It went from *I need to hurt this dude* to *All right, now it's time to play some D*, which actually made it harder to get around him. Now, he was playing the game rather than defending his kingdom.

As the game continued, Luke's team caught up and tied it at twenty–twenty. Games usually went to twenty-one, and it was no different that afternoon. There was no win-by-two bullshit here, so I knew how important this possession was as I pushed it up court again. I dribbled at the top of the key and watched Dan set a back pick on Steven, allowing Silas to pull another backdoor cut. When Silas cut, I drove left, then cut back to the center of the lane and hit Silas with a behind-the-back pass just as he reached the hoop. He put in another reverse layup and our team exploded in celebration.

"Horace! Harvey! Where the hell you two boys been?" Silas said as he grabbed Dan by the shoulders and shook him with joy. "Man, you fools better be comin' to Kirkland High. We're gonna win us a state championship."

"You think so?" I said.

"Shit, I *know* so. That's some of the best hoopin' I've seen on these streets. You just wait. It's gonna be our time soon."

"Yo, you guys are for real," D. Pow said, and he didn't seem like the type to dish out unearned compliments.

"Where you go to school?" Silas said.

"St. Anthony's," I said.

"Well, St. Anthony done had enough of you two. You're transferrin' to our shit. Man, with me an' the Powells in the paint, Luke pushin' point, and one of you two at shooting guard, we're gonna be tight."

I smiled wider than I had in a long time. This was it. This was my shot at Heaven.

As we walked off the court, I asked Dan, "How'd you know what tossing salad meant?" and he grinned and said, "Alonzo told me."

When I went to bed that night, I realized I hadn't thought about Gerry's mom once that afternoon, nor had I thought about my own mother. I had no idea where she might've gone or at what time she'd returned. I hadn't jumped every time I heard the door open or the car start and rushed to the driveway crying and screaming her name. No, I'd rushed to the hoop, and I'd screamed in victory. Wherever I went with her, I always felt so weak and out of control. Even if she was with me, I felt sick and dizzy. But on that court I'd felt great—even though my tongue still hurt like hell. I'd felt in control and powerful. I spun a basketball on my fingers as I prayed that night for a state championship. I thanked God for finally bringing me something good. For finally giving me something that worked.

Chapter 7

I spaced out but didn't dare take my eyes off Sister Verona as she went on and on about how "Satan *wants* you to eat meat during Lent. Even if you eat a cheeseburger accidentally, forgetting it was Friday, Satan now has complete control of your soul." After staring at her for so many consecutive periods, I was starting to see the black outline around her that Dan had mentioned. I was trying hard to think about Hammond, but it was impossible with Gerry's empty seat beside me, sucking at my attention like a black hole. I wished he was in the closet, but that was all behind us now. I hadn't spoken with him since I'd found out about his mom, and I had no idea how he was doing. I felt guilty spending my weekend playing hoops while he was suffering. Class had gone on as normal that day. No one even mentioned Gerry until Julia raised her hand, cutting Sister Verona off from her lecture on how Lent was prime season for Satan to hunt weak souls, and asked, "Sister, can we say a prayer for Gerry's mom?"

Sister gave her an irritated look and said, "There'll be plenty of time for prayers at her Mass this evening. Now, can we please get back to the Lord's sacrifice, or is that too much to ask?"

If I hadn't already loved Julia, I would have loved her when I saw the look of contempt she gave Sister Verona after that bullshit answer to Julia's sincere question. Somehow, seeing her concern for Gerry made me feel closer to her. She didn't seem like this far-off goddess living on top of a mountain somewhere. She was right here in the trenches with us. But I guess she always had been.

I met Dan in the parking lot after school. He wanted to help Sister Rose in the garden, but I had to go home and deliver my section of the paper route before serving Gerry's mom's Mass that evening. I walked my bike across the parking lot and was about to get on, but I stopped when I saw Shane and the rest of the dipshits waiting for me. I walked my bike over to them and dropped it on the blacktop. They said some shit to me and acted tough, and they gave me a few shots to the stomach and face before a man came out of his house with a baseball bat, and they all scattered. The man asked me if I was okay, and I told him I was. My eye was sore and so was my stomach, but at least they hadn't hit me in the mouth. My tongue was still killing me from Luke's elbow the day before, and I didn't want to have to leave the altar to spit blood during Mass.

When I got home, Mom was in the kitchen feeding the baby. She called me over, but I didn't want to go in there, so I spoke to her from the dining room.

"Your report card came in the mail today. You made first honors again, but you got an unsatisfactory for conduct. Sister wrote that you never seem to be paying attention in class and that you mess around too much with the other boys."

"Sister Verona is really mean," I said.

"Sister Verona has given her life to the Lord. You need to show her some respect," Mom said.

"She never shows us any respect," I said.

"I don't care what she shows you. If she says, 'Pray,' you say, 'How hard?' Got it?"

"Yeah, fine."

"I think you'd benefit a lot from praying the Rosary with me before bed each night."

"Please, don't even say that. You have no idea—"

"'Don't even say that?' That's a terrible way to talk about the Virgin Mother! You ask Her for forgiveness right now."

"Fine. Forgive me, Mary."

"You're lucky she's so compassionate."

"I know."

"Your brother made honorable mention for the first time, so we're going to celebrate after Gerry's mom's Mass."

"Can we get pancakes?"

"We'll see what your brother wants." She came into the dining room, and I spun around quickly. "Face me, Mister."

I turned around.

"Oh my God! What happened to you?" she said.

"I fell off my bike."

"You know how I feel about fighting. What would Jesus say if He saw you?"

"Doesn't He see me?"

"Don't get fresh with me. You know what I mean." She went to the kitchen, grabbed a pack of frozen peas from the freezer with her free hand, and gave it to me. I put it against my eye.

"But what if someone attacks me? Can't I defend myself?"

"Violence never solves anything. You just turn the other cheek."

"What if they already hit that one first?"

"You just keep turning, then."

"I feel dizzy."

"You better not let your father see you like this."

I hung my head and tears gathered in the sides of my eyes.

"C'mere." She hugged me with her free arm, and I wrapped around her and squeezed as tightly as I could, but had to let go when Carolynn started crying. Mom went back into the kitchen, and I went to get ready for Mass.

Mom dropped me off at church, but before she drove away, I stuck my head through the window and said, "Will you come too?" Carolynn started crying again, and Mom drove off.

When I got to the sacristy, I pulled a white smock over my black robe, then went to light the incense. Lighting incense was my favorite part of serving funerals. I'd light the wick, then flip it upside down so the flame would get huge, and I'd heat the incense puck double-time. Afterward, I went to sit on the wooden bench and waited for Monsignor Joseph. Father Mike walked by and, when he saw my eye, asked me how the other guy looked. That made me smile, but when Monsignor took a look at me, he shook his head. "Now what in the hell did you go and do? You have a Mass to serve. Don't you have any respect for God?" My head already felt so heavy I could barely keep it up, and his words felt like more concrete being poured inside.

Monsignor rang the bells, and we walked to the front of the altar, where we stood as the casket was rolled down the aisle. Gerry and his two younger brothers hung their heads as they walked behind their mother. I thought I'd be able to make it through that Mass, but seeing that casket moving toward me sent my thoughts into overdrive. I started obsessing over whether or not my mom had made it home safely. I started thinking about the song the organist was playing getting stuck in my head and never leaving. I started thinking I was never going to sleep again, and that I'd get so exhausted I wouldn't be able to control my anger, and I'd start hurting people for real this time. I started thinking about the kid I'd punched and how I'd run off to the church to hide, but when God found me, he threw me back out on the streets. I started thinking about how, no matter how hard I prayed, or how many Masses I served, there was no way I'd ever get to Heaven. My only shot might be if I became a priest. You need to become a priest, James. Mom is going to Heaven, and you won't be able to spend an eternity without her. Worrying about whether she's okay. Whether she got into a car accident. Whether she slipped on some icy steps and hit her head and was now unconscious and freezing to death. I couldn't spend an eternity in Hell with Dad, always screaming at me. We all needed to go to Heaven and be happy. I could do that as a priest. I could forgive all our sins—maybe even my own.

The casket stopped, and Gerry and his family sat in the first pew. I could tell Gerry was trying to look tough, though he didn't meet my eye. His dad sat next to him, looking dazed. Maybe drunk. They both remained like that—distant, unemotional—until the end of Mass when the casket started to be wheeled away. At that moment, Gerry looked up at his dad and then burst into tears. I started crying too, but I wiped my tears on my smock so Monsignor wouldn't yell at me again.

After church, I waited on the street corner for my parents to pick me up. They came a half hour later than Mom had said they would, and each passing moment they didn't arrive was more agonizing than the last. When they pulled up, I tried to stop sobbing, and I got into the station wagon, squeezing in next to Jeremy. Dan sat at the other window seat in the back and asked, "So, you hit a tree?" I nodded and didn't say anything. I felt that if I opened my mouth, I'd scream at Dad for being late. At Mom for lying about when they'd be there. For making me think they were all dead too. After a few minutes, I calmed down.

"You know, the brakes are going on this thing, and soon we're gonna be screwed," Dad said as he drove.

"It's okay," Mom said. "We'll deal with the problems as they come."

"Yeah, well, these kinds of problems come at about three hundred bucks a pop. You got that kinda money? 'Cause I certainly don't."

"We've always been fine before, and we'll be fine again."

"Shows how much you know."

We made a right onto Main Street, and soon the sound of the engine was the only noise in the car.

"Don't you think it'd be nice if we all died in a car crash together right now?" I said.

"Of all the dumb things I've ever heard in my life, that has got to be the dumbest," Dad said. "What the hell is wrong with you, James?"

"Rich, don't take your anger about the car out on your son," Mom said.

"Well, I'm sick of wasting money on this damned thing," Dad said. "We shouldn't even be going out to eat anyways. We got no fucking money."

"But I'm hungry!" Jeremy said.

"Oh, yer hungry, huh?" Dad said. "So, I'm supposed to just bend over for you? That's it, we're going home. You fuckers can eat shit tonight."

The old man took a wild U-turn at an intersection without even looking, and I watched with wide eyes as a truck came straight at us—lights getting closer and closer, filling my entire field of vision in pure, blinding white . . .

But the truck driver slammed on the brakes, preventing a collision, and we all kept going down the highway to Hell.

Chapter 8

While inserting ads into papers one afternoon, I saw a woman in her underwear, and it gave me the same feeling I had when Miss Amalia accidentally rubbed her butt against my arm in Music class. After delivering papers, I took the ad into the attic and locked the door and stared at the woman. I remembered Alonzo always making this motion with his hand when telling people how gay they were, so I tried it on my dick and it felt really good. But the woman just wasn't doing it for me, so I grabbed one of Mom's Victoria's Secret catalogs from a box near the window and flipped through the pages until I got to Tyra Banks. I remembered seeing her on episodes of *The Fresh Prince of Bel-Air*, and she was all the woman I needed to feel that explosion work through my body for the first time—while I was awake, at least. After that, I didn't feel like a little kid anymore. All the other guys were always talking about jerking off, and now I could do it too. Even though it felt great, I knew God and Grandpa and Grandma and my other grandpa and Uncle Wayne were all watching me, so it also made me feel evil. Anything that felt good had to be the work of Satan, so I couldn't ever do that again.

I felt ashamed of my dick and started getting rushed with Dark Thoughts, so I left the attic and asked Dan to go to Hammond with me.

When we got there, we played twos with two other brothers and almost shut them out. When I hit a twenty-footer to win it, the smaller brother came at me. "You're a fucking cheater!" The bigger one walked toward me as well, and I froze. The thing was, I was used to getting my ass beat. I could take shots to the head and stomach and shake 'em off and keep going. I could take Luke's elbows to the chin or D. Pow's forearms to my nose and keep playing. But something about fighting made me freeze up inside. I think it was some combination of poor confidence and feeling like God and the saints were watching me and judging me and then having to go home and see the look in Mom's eye when she heard I'd fought someone. It was worse for her to find out her son had sinned than it was for him to get his ass beat. I could get slapped around all day, but if I hit someone back, I was a terrible person. Also, I felt that by fighting, I was inviting the Evil Thoughts back. That if I hit someone at Hammond, maybe I'd hit someone while eating dinner at Denny's. While walking through the mall. Maybe I'd start putting cats in microwaves and feeding seagulls antacid tablets. Maybe I'd start luring kids off into the woods and crushing their heads with rocks. No, no fighting back. No hitting. You can beat your younger brother's ass. Dad never hits him, and he needs to know how shitty life is. Jeremy deserved for me to give him the occasional bitch slap or karate kick here and there. But you start hitting people outside of the family, and you might be summoning Satan. He's everywhere, and he wants your soul. Don't ever fool yourself into believing

God's running this game. There's nothing good out there for you or for anyone else. Just keep taking your beatdowns, and shut up about it. Just keep hanging your head. You won't make it past eighteen anyway, so why worry? At least you don't get it as bad as some people do. At least you ain't Gerry.

The brothers started pushing me as I backed away.

"Air ball, double dribble, flagrant foul, traveling," Dan said to them. "Brick, bad defense, offensive odor . . ."

They stopped coming at me and went after Dan, and Dan kept telling them the reasons why they sucked at basketball. The big guy took a swing at Dan's head, and Dan dodged it while I just stood there frozen. The little guy pushed Dan just as Luke, Silas, Joey, and the Powells came around the corner. The brothers stopped immediately.

"Yo, Ricky," Joey said, "I thought I told your fat, dumb ass to stay off my court."

"Uh, sorry, we just wanted to play," the bigger guy said.

"Take your sack-of-shit brother and go on home. Nobody wants you here," Joey said.

The brothers grabbed their ball and started walking away, but they dropped it when Joey said, "Leave it." Joey picked up the ball and said, "Shoot for threes?" just as Steven rounded the corner.

"Fours with Steven," D. Pow said.

A junker stopped on the street and a scary-looking guy got out. "Tommy, I told you to cut the lawn ta-day!"

"Fuck," T. Pow said as he headed for the car.

Everyone started laughing at him, even though they knew his stepdad was a raging alcoholic monster.

"Down to threes again," Luke said.

A group of boys rounded the corner on their bikes.

There were seven of them, and among them was Doug Warsaw, a sixth grader at St. Matthew's, an all-boys school that had some of the best athletes in the city. And Doug was probably the best of them. I'd played with Doug a few times, and we always covered each other. He was good, but I usually burned him on offense and shut him down on D. Everyone else—Alonzo, Tony, and Ray included—thought he was the best sixth grader around, but I knew I was better. Doug, and most of the others, lived in Central Park, but they came up to play at Hammond from time to time. We decided to run fives: the Central Park Crew vs. the Hammond Crew. There were six of us, and Dan offered to sit first, as he usually did.

"Yo, Dougie, we're gonna shoot for ball," Silas said. He walked over, and they slapped hands.

"Man, you know everybody, Mack," Joey said.

"Hell yeah," Silas said. "I got more friends than Santa Claus."

We laughed.

"Let Horace shoot it," Luke said.

Silas tossed me the ball. "Sink it, Ho-dingies."

I dribbled to the top of the key, took a deep breath, and put it right through. More guys showed up, and they stood around the court. Joey tossed the ball in to Luke, and he pushed it as the rest of us ran up court. The guy defending Luke played tight D, and Luke was having trouble getting by him. He passed it to Joey on the wing. I gave Doug a fake and ran to the top of the key. Joey hit me with a pass, and in one fluid motion I grabbed it and sank a twenty-footer. The crowd erupted.

Doug pushed point, and I covered him when he got past half court. Usually Luke covered the other point guard, but I wanted Doug—wanted everyone to see me shut him down. Doug was definitely quick, and he burned me, then tried hitting the same shot I'd just made from the top of the opposite key, but Silas stepped up and swatted the ball down the court. Joey grabbed it and pushed it up, then bounced a pass to Luke, who took it in for an easy layup. One of the other players landed on Joey's ankle, so Dan came in for him as he walked it off.

When Doug crossed the half again, one of the other players set a pick on me, and Doug got by. But Luke picked him up and stripped him with no problem. Dan ran up the court, and Luke hit him with a wild pass that Dan tipped to D. Pow with one hand. D. Pow shook the guy on him, then put in an easy layup. The crowd was definitely on our side.

Luke and D. Pow both slapped Dan's hand as they dropped back on D. We kept grinding them down and out-hustling them, and you could see their spirit breaking apart. But that's what we did to teams. Though we'd only been playing together for a short time, we came together instantly. We weren't the biggest or quickest guys out there, but we made up for it by playing together and wearing our opponents down. We'd find their weakness and hit it as hard as we could. Even if the other guys were more talented, we'd break their hearts and bring 'em under our control. It was an instinct. And our instincts switched on automatically in those fractions of a second when they were needed most: grabbing loose balls, fighting for rebounds, waiting to cut to the hoop until the perfect moment. Games were won and lost in those fractions of a second. Lives were won and lost in those fractions of a second. None of us knew fuck all about shit in this crazy-ass world. But we did know that when we were on that court, nobody was gonna get the best of us. Nobody was ever going to dull those instincts. Not Mom. Not Dad. Not the Evil Thoughts. Certainly not God. And I felt that, with the right team, I could do anything.

We beat the hell out of the Central Park Crew. By the end, Luke, Dan, and I had put on a full court press that they couldn't break, and we ended their misery quickly. They were some of the best players our age in Buffalo, and they couldn't last twenty minutes on our court. They took off soon after the game, and we went to the water fountain. I was happy about just about everything from that game, except for one thing: about halfway through, Doug had crossed me at the top of the key, and when I shuffled to keep up with him, I felt a pulling in my groin that I hadn't felt in years, and I couldn't stay with him. It went away after that, but it scared me. Hammond was my sanctuary. I couldn't have any of that ancient evil bullshit coming back to haunt me there.

The next team stepped on the court to face us, but before the game could start, another junker stopped on the road near the court. This time, two twenty-something-looking hotheads got out, and one was carrying a baseball bat. The driver stormed up to Luke, but Luke didn't flinch.

"Where the fuck is my stash, shithead?" he said to Luke.

Luke just kept staring.

"I'll smash your fucking face in. Where is it?"

Luke shrugged and gave a casual "I dunno" face.

Joey walked over. "What're you bitching about, Moretti?"

"This little shithole stole half a pound of weed outta my house last night, and he's gonna give it all back to me, plus some," Moretti said.

"How you know it was him?" Joey said.

"Pete here saw him snoopin' around last night. My back window was open this morning. He musta crawled in there like a little worm and stole my shit. And now I'm gonna break his face."

"Naw," Joey said, "what you're gonna do is get back in your piece-of-shit car and drive away, after apologizing to my man. And if you ever press him about this or anything else, you're gonna be blowin' dicks on shattered knees, capisce?"

"This doesn't concern you, Joey," Moretti said.

"Everything concerns me," Joey said. "You fondle Pete's balls here as you drive away, that concerns me—and greatly, might I add. You suck a gallon of horse cum out of an elephant's ass, that concerns me."

"Yeah, whatever," Moretti said.

"Not 'whatever,'" Joey said. "What'd I tell you?" Joey pointed to Luke.

"S-sorry, Luke," Moretti said.

"Now get the fuck outta my face," Joey said. "We got more teams to stomp."

Pete and Moretti went back to their car and drove off.

"You go through his window last night?" Joey said.

"Naw, he left his side door unlocked," Luke said. "So, fuck him."

They both smirked.

We stayed on the court all day, beating every challenger. Dan and Steven had some good games. Steven was a tough dude, but he also had a nice jumper that I never knew about until he started raining twenty-footers. Dan hit some big shots as well. Anyplace else, he never shot the ball, but at Hammond I think he felt comfortable enough to shine, and he'd shoot most of the time if he was open. We kept playing well into the night, and when we couldn't see the hoop anymore, we hung out in a gazebo by the court instead. Steven stayed on the court, trying to grab rim.

"Man, you're six-foot-forever and still can't get it," Silas said from the gazebo. "Give it a rest, Stevie."

"I'll get it," Steven said.

"I'm tellin' you boys, we're gonna get that state championship," Silas said. "Coach Sterling runs Kirkland's varsity team, and he's one of the best in the city. He cultivates talent like Phil Jackson."

"Aren't there some sick teams in the city?" I said. "You really think we can even get past them to win a state championship?"

"Hell yeah, man!" Silas said. "I mean, Rucker High is sweet, and Archibald's always a contender—especially this year with J. Peg pushin' point. That right there's the biggest beast in Buffalo. Dunkin' on fools from the circle and shit. But we'll be just as good by then too."

"Who's J. Peg?" I said.

Steven gave up trying to get rim and came over to join us.

"Jerome Pegos. Sophomore at Archibald. Dude averages like forty a game. I was chillin' with him last weekend. He's friends with my cousin. I used to live on the East Side before my daddy moved us on up to North Buffalo."

"The East Side's a dump," Steven said.

"Thank you, Steven," Silas said. "Harvey, those were some sick passes you dished today."

"Guess so." Dan shrugged his shoulders.

"So, you really think we can win a championship?" I said.

"Man, we keep playin' like we did today, and we'll be winnin' an NBA championship."

A cool breeze blew, and I didn't realize how cold I was until I shivered. The temperature was starting to drop again at night, and soon we'd be covered in long gray winter.

"I saw you fighting a kid in the St. Anthony's parking lot. Why'd you hit him?" I said.

"Terry Stanford," Silas said.

"Who?" I said.

"That's his name. Terry Stanford," Silas said. "The guy I hit."

"Why'd you hit him?" I said.

"Don't worry about it," Silas said.

I could see a lighter spark on the far side of the court, followed by someone saying, "Yo, don't Bogart that shit."

Silas sniffed the air, then took a deep breath and walked over to the other guys, who were giggling like idiots. "Ahh, Hammond Afterhours," Silas said.

"What's that smell?" I said.

"You're an idiot, Horace," Steven said.

Dan smirked as if he also knew what Steven did.

Chapter 9

Tony and I stood at the end of my driveway, gyrating our hips and humping air each time a car passed by. Alonzo tossed a shovelful of snow at us.

"Will you two pervs help us?" Alonzo said.

In the winter, Mom agreed to drive us to school, and the Da Lucas were coming with us that morning. Dan, Alonzo, Tony, and I were clearing the driveway from the snowstorm that had hit in the night. December had just begun, but in Buffalo you can get hit with a blizzard even in October. From September on, the weather slowly gets colder and grayer until winter dominates the Northeast for the next four to five months.

We cleared the driveway and car, but halfway to school, the station wagon stalled. Mom tried starting it up again, but it wasn't working.

"I'm sorry, guys, but we're going to have to push it the rest of the way," she said. "I can call a tow truck from the school."

We got out and started pushing, but Mom told me to steer because I was the lightest. I felt guilty about leaving her out there to push, but I didn't put up much of a fight. While sitting in the driver's seat, my thoughts started going crazy. What kind of son does that to his mother? You're supposed to insist that she steer, not you. What kind of pussy are you? But I liked the warmth. I liked not getting my feet soaked with melted snow. I liked steering, even though that wheel was so hard to turn I had to practically jerk it with my whole body. Did liking all that make me bad? Did letting Mom struggle, and not me for once, make me Evil?

The streets were in horrible condition, but they always were after a snowstorm, and the trip was up a pretty steep hill, so I imagined they were all miserable back there. Why did I get to sit up front? Was I the smartest? The strongest? The fastest? Did I have the best vision? I belonged in the driver's seat. I belonged in the place where I could show the others the way.

Or maybe they thought I was the weakest and should be the first to get whatever was coming for us.

I pulled a wide right into the parking lot, and we left the car in the far corner by a huge snow pile the plow driver had made. Mom went to call a tow truck, as the rest of us trudged through the snow toward the church. When we walked in, Mass was almost over, so Dan, Alonzo, and Tony sat in the last pew. I walked past them and continued down the center aisle to the front row. Father Mike held up the Eucharist and everyone kneeled. I bowed my head and could feel the tears streaming down my cheeks. When I looked up at the cross, for the first time I felt that maybe Jesus actually was dead.

Dad took us to Gino the Barber's that afternoon. He'd take the boys there every month or so, and I'd always get a buzz cut, even in winter. Dad said Gino used to work for the mob. I didn't know if that was true, but a lot of people said the same thing. Gino had a small place near Kenmore that was always packed, and he was always telling jokes and stories that made everyone burst out laughing. He had a bar in a back room, and he'd tell guys to go back there and take a drink. He was a big guy with tattoos all over his arms, but despite his looks and what everyone said about his past, he was one of the nicest people I knew. Whenever I got in the chair, I felt as if I was the most important guy in the world. He'd tell me how handsome I was and how all the girls would be lucky to have me and how smart I was and how Dad was always bragging about me. When he asked me how I was doing, I felt as if he actually listened to my answer. As if he actually wanted to know—not like when Grandma or my aunts or uncles would ask. Sometimes I hoped he wouldn't ask me because I felt as if maybe I'd start crying in front of all the other guys and never be able to come back again. Gino loved basketball and would always go to local games to support his customers, and we'd talk about our favorite players and teams. He was a huge Celtics fan, even after Larry Bird retired, and I always reminded him that Jordan dropped sixty-three against them in the '86 playoffs, and he always said, "Yeah, and who won the Finals?" Almost all the guys I knew got their hair cut at Gino's. Our cuts were always uneven and looked like crap, but he charged six bucks a head no matter what style you asked him for, and his jokes were the best, so we all kept going back. I'd been getting a buzz cut ever since we moved back from Virginia Beach, even though all the guys in my favorite bands had long hair and so did all the famous guys Julia was always saying were so hot. But I was born in Buffalo, so a buzz cut from Gino the Barber was the best I could hope for.

On the drive back, Dad would always listen to this one guy's talk show on the radio, and the guy was so angry. Like my dad, he hated liberals and would blame them for everything while Dad pumped his fist and shouted shit like, "You're god-damned right!" and, "They're ruining this country!" I knew I was supposed to listen to the angry guy too, and even though I tried, it always made me feel bad, so I did my best to ignore him. The guy was always going on and on about how *he* was the real victim, so it made me feel guilty that I didn't feel as angry about that stuff as he did, and it all confused the hell out of me. I knew not listening to him made me a bad person, but I already knew I was a bad person anyway, so what did it even matter? I had my haircut and my lollipop and fuck the rest of the world.

After dinner, Dad took a break from working on the bedroom to watch the Bulls play the Pistons, and we all joined him. We took up two couches, while Poor Rich took the recliner. Our TV was a thirteen-inch RCA, and even with foil on the antennas, the display was blurry and discolored. Even so, it was good enough for us. My family may have been the definition of dysfunctional, but one thing brought us together: our love of basketball—especially the Chicago Bulls. Even though Michael Jordan had retired the season before, we still watched every Bulls game and lived and died on overtime battles and buzzer-beating shots. Even if Buffalo still had a team, we would have rooted for the Bulls. They were the perfect combination of raw talent and proper coaching. Phil Jackson got the most out of his players, even without Jordan there, and that made him the best coach in the NBA. It sucked not getting to watch MJ dominate the league anymore. For years, he not only carried his team, but also all of us. I wanted to be Air Jordan—I think my whole family did—and after watching him drop fifty-four against the Knicks in game four of the playoffs the year before, I started begging Dad to put up a hoop on our garage. My mother used to walk around the house singing the song from the Gatorade commercial. Even she wanted to "Be Like Mike." But there were a whole lot of us and only one Mike. Watching NBA games was pretty much the only time we'd all cheer together as a family. We loved football too—obviously the Bills were our favorite team—but basketball was our sport. But after the game, Poor Rich went right back to it: "I TOLD YOU WE DON'T HAVE ANY FUCKING MONEY . . ."

In the winter, Dan and I had to get up extra early to deliver papers because we couldn't ride our bikes, and so that Sunday we got up at six. When I got to the rectory, I saw the nuns crossing the snowy parking lot on their way to church. It was still dark and the wind was blowing, but nothing could keep them from the Lord. Were they stronger than I was? Or were they more foolish? I was haunted by the potential answers to those questions.

When we got back to the house, Dan and I ate breakfast. The box of Honey Bunches of Oats was still up there, but I went with Trix. I grabbed my basketball and shovel and went off to clear a few of my neighbors' driveways, and afterward I headed to Hammond. I cleared the court up to the top of the key and shot jumpers until my hands couldn't take it anymore. I had huge cracks between each finger, and they stung and bled. I'd usually try to sink five straight jumpers before leaving, but I kept going that day. Ten. Fifteen. If I hit one more, Julia will love me. Sixteen. If I hit one more, Dan will be my friend again. Seventeen. If I hit one more, I'll get into Heaven. Eighteen. I stopped there. If I missed nineteen, I'd have to start all over again, and my hands and heart couldn't take it.

When I got home, we spent the rest of the day setting up Christmas decorations. I helped Dad staple the lights to the porch and around the windows, while the rest of the family made cookies, listened to Christmas tunes, and set up the tree. Dad and I joined them when we finished with the lights, and we all spent the night watching *The Bells of St. Mary's*, which was one of Mom's favorite movies. I actually liked it too, and I'd often tear up at the end—not so much because the movie was sad but because I'd cry whenever Mom did during movies, and she usually lost it at the end of *The Bells of St. Mary's*. After, Dad covered my sisters in plastic holly as he sang "Holly Jolly Christmas" and danced around like an idiot. We'd finally finished remodeling the downstairs bedroom, so now the girls had their own space. Dad had even bought them all new beds, so they seemed pretty happy.

I still believed in Santa and was the last of my friends to do so. Ray and Tony both told me I was being stupid, but I swear I woke up one Christmas Eve and saw bright lights flashing across the sky, and when I went downstairs, the presents were there. Whether he existed or not, I needed to believe. I already felt I was losing God, and I couldn't lose Santa as well. Neither listened, but there was always the chance they'd bring me what I needed. If the guys wanted to call me an idiot for it, I didn't care. I had faith. Faith was about all I had.

But I also needed Santa to be real because I couldn't handle any more lies. If Santa wasn't real, then what else were adults lying about?

In school, we'd hear stories about Jesus's birth. We'd sing "O Holy Night" in Music class while Miss Amalia played piano. We'd gather into the hall, and Sister Carol would light the Advent candles, and then we'd sing Christmas songs. I always got really excited when she'd light the pink one, because that meant Christmas was almost here but not too close, so we still had time to savor the season. The closer we were to Christmas meant the closer we were to Christmas being over, and that third week of Advent was always my favorite time of the season. Although I felt I was losing connection with God, participating in those beautiful rituals made me feel closer to Him. Sister Carol would turn off the lights, and the candlelight would be enough for us to see. During the lighting of the pink candle, I remember looking at Julia, the firelight dancing across her face, and thinking how truly beautiful she was. All I wanted to do was walk over to her. To hold her hand. To rest my cheek beside hers. Maybe with her beside me, I'd still be able to believe. Maybe with her beside me I could feel happy. I'd endure even more Evil Thoughts if she would just be mine. I wanted to kiss her so badly. She looked up and our eyes met, and I wanted to scream, "JULIA! I LOVE YOU, AND I DON'T CARE WHO KNOWS IT! I LOVE YOU, AND I'M NOT AFRAID OF ANYTHING!"

The days were short and dark and freezing cold. The snow was always coming down, and icicles hung from the classroom windows. But I always felt safe and warm in that school. As nasty as some of the nuns were, the others were so nice, and they made me feel special to be there.

In December, each grade from six to eight would put on a Christmas play, and I played the lead in ours: a cranky old man who hated Christmas but learned to love it after the toys in his shop came to life and taught him the true meaning of the season. Miss Amalia put the whole thing together, but she made a nasty comment about my singing the day before the main performance, and I spent the night screaming so that I'd lose my voice. Unfortunately, it didn't work, and I sang my song in front of hundreds of people. Miss Amalia apologized after the show and told me I did a great job, even though I was pretty sure she was lying.

On Christmas Eve, we'd go to my Aunt Sadie's house on the West Side. She'd been a model when she was younger, but even though that all ended years ago, she still wore tons of makeup and fancy clothes and acted as if she was a big star. All of Mom's brothers and sisters would be there with their husbands and wives, crammed into that small, two-story house. My uncles would watch college football and get drunk off beer while my aunts would sing songs and pound back boxes of wine. Even though they were all grown up, everyone still came to my mom with their problems. She'd clean up the house and tell her sisters to go easy on the wine and make sure the turkey wasn't burning in the oven. Like my dad, Mom didn't drink at all. Not a sip of champagne on New Year's Eve, not a mouthful of wine on Thanksgiving, and Christmas was no different. One of her brothers was the same way. As far back as I can remember, they were like that. Everyone would get shitfaced while Mom and Uncle Johnny stayed sober.

Uncle Johnny was my favorite uncle. He was the youngest in the family after Uncle Vinny had slit his wrists, and he was a really cool guy. He was handsome enough to be a movie star and had longer hair and played drums and would always tell me, "You got it in you, kid." When I'd ask him what that meant, he'd just say, "You'll know soon enough." He was always dating a different gorgeous woman, even though Mom would tell him to "just pick one, already." Mom said that growing up, he'd been the wild one in the family, but that he overcame his drinking and drug problems, and now he didn't drink at all, like Mom. But the rest of them went hard—Uncle Jake going the hardest. His hands would shake really bad if he didn't drink, and he looked as if he was already in his fifties even though he was one of Mom's youngest siblings. Mom and Aunt Sadie were always going back and forth about whether or not to invite him each year. Even if they didn't, he'd still show up, and would yell if they didn't let him in, so they'd open the door and say, "Okay, okay, but you need to go *easy* this year, all right?" Then he'd get piss drunk and stumble around as they bad-mouthed him in the kitchen.

I think Dad was uncomfortable whenever he was over there because he was one of the only sober ones. Also, he was kind of an awkward dude. When people would talk about the latest Bills draft pick or the latest serial killer murdering homeless people by the bus station downtown, Dad would wander over and start talking about the cracks he'd noticed in the basement walls and the water damage on the ceiling. Or he'd turn every conversation into a story about his time in the Navy. Sometimes he'd say things that didn't even make sense, and I started worrying that he was losing his mind. Worrying that this was how I sounded when I spoke to people too. Alonzo was always telling me I was halfway retarded, and maybe he was right. Like Dad, I never knew what to say to my aunts, uncles, or cousins, so I'd usually find an empty room and hide until it was time to open presents. People in my family never stopped talking, but it didn't seem as if they ever said anything. I could be sitting in a dark room all alone, and no one would come by and ask me how I was doing. I could be coughing up blood on the carpet, and they'd just keep pounding wine and dancing around and singing. I loved my family, but maybe I didn't. I mean, what the fuck was love anyway? It was less a feeling and more a duty, and I was tired of working so hard for them to give me some of it. I was better off alone. I never spoke with any of them longer than to answer their questions about school. Like Dad, I didn't want to talk about draft picks or murders or whatever. I wanted to talk about how to make Julia love me. I wanted to talk about how to make the Evil Thoughts go away. I wanted to talk about how I schooled Doug Warsaw on the basketball court, even though everyone always said he was so great. I wanted to ask them what was going on with my body: where was this hair coming from and why couldn't I stop thinking about boobs? But that never happened, so this time I fucked off to the attic and read a book that Sister Rose had recommended, *The Diary of Anne Frank.* I'd never had to hide from Nazis, but still, I felt as if I knew exactly what she was going through. As if she was telling *my* story as well. And even though it made me cry, I couldn't stop turning the pages.

I went downstairs when it was time to open presents. At first I only got clothes until I unwrapped *Super Mario*

Bros. 3 from Uncle Salvatore, who kept pinching my cheeks and saying, "I don't even know what these games are," while I tried to open the packaging. *Super Mario Bros. 3* was my second favorite game of all time, behind *The Legend of Zelda*, which I could easily play for twelve hours straight.

That Christmas Eve, there was a blizzard, and before we left, all the guys went outside to clear the driveway. Although it was late, I always stared at the city as we drove through. A fresh snow could hide a lot of the ugliness. Deaden a lot of the screaming and chaos. But it couldn't hide it all. Though it was brimming with heart, Buffalo was a depressed city, and it showed. Abandoned houses and shops, trash everywhere, graffiti, drunks walking the streets. And even though it was Christmas Eve, I still couldn't shake the thought of all the wives and kids currently getting their asses kicked, all the kids smoking crack for the first time, all the dads drinking themselves into a depression so deep they'd never climb out. Every time we drove through that city, I felt as though I was absorbing all of its problems, intending to solve them someday when I was better and stronger. Felt I was absorbing all its broken pieces and marking them, trying to remember where to return them when I had the strength to clean them and put them back together again. Felt someday I'd turn all the crying and screaming into singing and dancing. I was a sponge for sadness, and growing up in Buffalo, I was always oversaturated. God. Santa. Please make us all happy. I'll become a priest. I'll do your bidding. Tell me how I can make it all right. Tell me how I can make it as beautiful as I know it can be.

On Christmas Day, we'd visit Grandma in the sticks. Uncle Tommy would be there with whatever woman he was currently seeing, and some of his kids would be there too, depending on who was in prison or rehab. We'd eat tons of ham and pie and ice cream, and I'd always leave with a huge stomachache. Sometimes Dad and Uncle Tommy had a good time, talking and laughing late into the night. But other times Uncle Tommy would say things that would make Dad go off to the garage and stare at the walls. When he'd come back in, Uncle Tommy would say things like, "Oh don't be such a woman," and, "You a fag or something?" and soon after Dad would tell us it was time to leave.

I spent the rest of my Christmas break delivering papers, shoveling neighbors' driveways, playing *Super Mario Bros. 3*, finishing *The Diary of Anne Frank*, and shooting hoops at Hammond. There was only one way to become a state champion and that was through unwavering discipline. My hands could split and bleed all they wanted, but someday they'd hold that trophy, and I'd raise it up high for everyone in the city to see what winners we all were.

Chapter 10

In eighth grade, we got Sister Adele, the toughest nun I'd ever met and hands down the best teacher in the school.

"There my brother Adam stood on the top of Mount Suribachi, dodging bullets from the Japs as he leaned tough into the wind." Sister walked past our desks, crouching down, and jumping up, always acting out every action from her stories. "He and his fellow Marines were storming that hill, when suddenly, a K-ninety-eight bullet ripped into his chest. His buddy turned and asked him if he was okay. Then Adam pulled a small Bible from his front shirt pocket. It had stopped the bullet from tearing through his heart . . ." Sister kept walking around, taking aim and pretending to shoot Japanese soldiers. "Adam fought in the Pacific, but I had three other brothers in that war who were after Hitler and the Nazi scum in Europe. Sadly, Teddy never made it back." Sister dropped character, then walked back to her desk and grabbed a stack of papers. "Okay, now clear your desks for your catechism test."

Sister Adele lived to tell stories. But the best part was that she told the same stories over and over, only the details were always different. Her brother Adam had fought at Iwo

Jima, once losing an arm and another time losing a leg. He'd tripped over Hitler's body in the bunker in Berlin and, another time, watched Hitler take the cyanide pill, "But he just smiled and nodded his head. He didn't dare stop him." He stormed the beaches of Normandy, losing every man to his left and right, but he was also a paratrooper who flew behind enemy lines, helping the Allied powers win D-Day. He drove tanks, steered aircraft carriers, and shot down more Nazi planes than any other pilot in history. I loved Sister Adele and her stories. You could get her on a rant about almost anything, which got us out of a hell of a lot of school.

Sister walked to the front corner desk with the tests in hand. She started counting off a stack to hand to Rachel Crawford, but Ray knew what to do.

"Sister," Ray said, "did you read that article in the paper last week about the teenage girl who let her friend abort her baby with a rusty coat hanger behind the Kmart on Main Street?"

Sister stopped counting and walked back to center stage. "Of course I read it, and it's the tragedy of your generation . . ."

Sister had let us pick our seats, and Ray, Tony, Gerry, and I sat in the back corner, just as we had in sixth grade. But things no longer felt the same. After Gerry's mother died, he got pretty serious. He wouldn't even respond when Ray hit him. If Ray pushed him into the closet, he'd shut up and go to sleep. None of the adults ever gave me a straight answer when I asked how Gerry's mom died, and neither did Gerry. But Ray told me she'd overdosed on heroin. In seventh grade, a police officer had spoken with our class and told us that "heroin is about the worst drug you could ever put in your body. It'll completely ruin you." I knew drugs were bad, but something about those words made me think that heroin was made by Satan himself for the sole purpose of finally destroying me. I had to stay away. I had to not think about it. If I started thinking about it, maybe I'd fall wrist first into a pile of trash while walking through a Hertel Avenue alley, and a used needle filled with China white would pierce through the plastic bag and my skin, and the Devil would finally have me. If I started thinking about it, I'd have to avoid alleys, and walking down Hertel, and I'd just plain never be able to leave my house again. I'd never touch garbage bags. I wouldn't go near the trash. I'd toss all my garbage on a rotting pile in my room, and I'd barricade myself in and never dare to leave. Pissing in mason jars and eating bugs crawling on the walls. Don't think about heroin. Don't think about Hell. Don't think about insanity or insomnia. Fuck, just don't think, period.

Julia sat in the other back corner with her friends, Sarah, Emily, and Stacy. The year before, they'd gotten Sister Agnes to quit teaching. Any time Sister would say something about religion, they'd ask her: what does this have to do with science? Or math? Or reading? Or life? When Stacy McMurphy told Sister that "God isn't real," Sister walked to her own desk, grabbed a few things, left the room, and never came back. She didn't look angry or frustrated, but rather, completely defeated, as if maybe she too didn't believe that God was real and had finally admitted it to herself after a fifty-plus-year marriage to the guy.

Also, the year before, Emily Browning had told me that Julia liked me. When I heard those words, I could have floated up to Heaven and hugged the Lord, real or not. Emily and I walked home together some days, and one day Emily smiled and said, "Yeah, she won't stop talking about you. It's kind of annoying actually." I went to the basement that day after delivering papers and called Julia on the rotary phone by Dad's workbench, and she actually answered and didn't hang up when she heard it was me. I didn't know what to say, so I invited her over to play basketball that Saturday at noon. It was late spring, just before summer, and the weather was getting great again. I spent that Saturday morning trying on different T-shirt and mesh shorts combos and finally settled on a bright yellow tank top and neon pink shorts. Some of the other girls had mentioned liking my arms, so I wanted to show them off to Julia. In the bathroom mirror, I saw that if I put my hands on my head, it made my biceps look big, so I figured I'd pull that move while talking to her. I went outside and shot hoops while I waited for her, but noon came and went, and she didn't come. I went to the basement and called her but no one answered. Then by about twelve forty-five, Julia came out the back door with Poor Rich trailing behind.

"Everyone kisses Clinton's ass, talking about how he stimulated the economy, but they all forget it began with Reagan," Poor Rich cornered her on the deck.

"Yeah, yeah, Reagan was the best," she said, trying to get around him.

"He's just what this country needs right now," Dad went on. "A real American hero."

"Hey, Julia." I walked over. "Dad, we're going to play some basketball now."

"Oh, okay, but hurry up. I need some help in the bathroom upstairs." Dude just finished making a bedroom in the basement, and now he was turning an upstairs closet into a bathroom.

The lunatic walked back into the house, and we went to the driveway. Julia told me she'd gotten there at eleven fifty, and when she'd knocked on the door, Dad had come out and started going on and on about "these god-damned liberals," and she couldn't get away. The girl I'd been praying for the entire year. Dreaming of her. Waiting for the day she'd be mine, and the old man held her up for almost an hour just ranting about Clinton as I'd sweated bullets out back and cursed myself for being so stupid, thinking she could actually like me. Even though she was there to play basketball, she was in her Doc Martens boots and a short dress with a flannel shirt wrapped around her waist. She had the best style, and somehow even managed to make her St. Anthony's uniform look cool. She had the shortest skirt and wore tight necklaces and peace sign earrings and her boots. I felt embarrassed to be in all-neon gear and resolved to start thinking a little more about my style. We shot hoops and talked for about an hour before the old man started screaming inside.

Julia invited me to her place. "Nobody's home, so we can just hang." But as we were walking down the driveway, Poor Rich stormed outside and screamed at me to come help him. I told him no, and he lost his shit, throwing a plumbing wrench at me from across the yard and saying I was grounded, which was the first time he'd ever said that to me. The wrench didn't come close to hitting me, but when Julia saw that shit, she said, "You'd better go help him," and gave me a look as if she knew the true repercussions of upsetting Daddy. As she walked away, I knew she was never coming back. I wanted to kill him. I wanted to cave his skull in with that wrench. I'd never hated him more. Julia started liking Tim Lamonz after that, and they went out for all of seventh grade until she broke up with him over the summer. Rumor was that she was seeing one of the hockey players from Fillmore State and that this grown-ass man had fingered her in the back seat of his Mustang after scoring a hat trick against Albany U.

Sometime over that last year, Ray, Tony, Gerry, and I had started hanging out a lot with Julia, Emily, Stacy, and Sarah. We'd go to the coffee shop across the street from school, and the girls would drink cappuccino as the guys drank Snapple. I loved kiwi strawberry and would drink, like, three each time we went. The girls always wanted to sit on the couch because it was just like their favorite show *Friends*, which none of the guys watched. They'd talk about their favorite cigarette brands and which guys in high school threw the best parties, and we would talk about music and basketball. Even after a year, *Mellon Collie and the Infinite Sadness* was still my favorite album. I remembered seeing the video for "Tonight, Tonight" for the first time at Emily's birthday party the previous year, and every time I heard the song, I'd think about how Julia kept looking at me that night. God, what she made me feel . . . and that song made me understand the urgency of that moment. Made me feel that tonight was the only one I'd ever have. My only chance to touch her. To win her heart. That anything was possible. And it made me understand the power and beauty of music. It also reminded me that Emily's party was the first I'd ever been able to attend without losing my mind, worrying that someone might play Nirvana or STP. I figured I could just go outside until the songs were over, or go upstairs and put pillows over my head, and knowing I could do this and then come back and hang made me feel more powerful than I ever had before. It made me feel more powerful than any of my prayers ever did. It made me feel as though I could maybe survive past eighteen. Billy Corgan's voice was like the voice of God, and it saved me so many, many times. I was even able to sleep over at Ray's one night—something I'd never been able to do. I always blamed it on my parents, saying they wouldn't let me, but really, I could spend the night sleeping on train tracks, and they wouldn't care. Sleeping in the lion pit at the zoo. Sleeping with my legs dangling in the Niagara River, just before the falls. I wanted to try it. We stayed up most of the night watching *The Simpsons* and making prank phone calls, and at one point Gerry popped in his Smashing Pumpkins CD and played "1979," and I felt as though anything on this Earth was possible. I felt the power I'd pushed way down when the Evil Thoughts came on. The power of creativity. Inspiration. I felt that I could make music like this as well. Someday, when all the fear and Evil had gone away, I'd save the world with music. When I woke up the next morning on Ray's living room floor, sunlight shining in through the windows and sliding glass doors, I felt that I could go toe-to-toe with the Devil.

We all had different tastes in music. Tony was big into Bone Thugs-N-Harmony and Tupac and wouldn't stop playing *All Eyez on Me* whenever we got together. Ray loved Metallica and White Zombie and said heavy metal was the only real music. Gerry's favorite album was *Sublime*, but like me, he loved almost anything. He'd listen to Coolio, Radiohead, Pearl Jam, Prince, whatever.

Sometimes we'd talk about music with the girls too. They had similar tastes, but it seemed their favorite band was

Dave Matthews. Julia was also into singer-songwriters like Ani DiFranco and Tori Amos, but she still liked corny shit like the Spice Girls and *Friends*. The girls even did a little dance routine whenever "Wannabe" came on the radio, and as much as I'd say that song was stupid, every time I heard it, I thought about how incredibly Julia moved. God, she could dance. The others were just messing around, but she looked as if she could be in a music video. She was so cool. So graceful and smooth.

We'd all go to movies together, too, our first being *Happy Gilmore*. Ray and I argued over who got to sit next to Julia, and I won. I didn't care how big he was, I'd stand up to Evander Holyfield for her. Even though Julia had pretty much rejected me, she'd still look at me sometimes the way she had at Emily's party. She'd still sit close to me and joke with me, and it made me feel as if I were a superhero. During *Happy Gilmore* she touched the top of my hand, and I started to turn my hand over to try to hold hers, but Ray looked to be watching, so I stopped.

One day as we walked to the coffee shop, Sarah gave our group a name: the Freaky Deaks. I had no idea what it meant, but I did know that being called a Freaky Deak meant I was on the inside. I realized then that I was one of the cool kids. I'd never really cared about being cool until it was right there in my hands. But once I realized how much I liked being cool, I slowly started doing everything I could to be a loser again. The obsessions started coming back when we'd be listening to music at someone's house. I'd start panicking when I got songs stuck in my head and couldn't get them out, and even if I'd go outside for a bit, the panic wouldn't subside. The trees would start dancing around, and the air would get black and heavy, and planes seemed to fall from the sky. I started having trouble sleeping again. I'd replay scenes from movies I saw with the Freaky Deaks until they drove me nuts. I mean, it fucking tortured me. The Evil let me taste just enough of something good before taking it all away again, reminding me just who was in charge. After we watched *Congo*, I couldn't get away from the image of those gorillas smashing people's heads open, and it terrified me. Just before the end, I practically ran out of the theater, sweating and crazy, and called Mom on a payphone to come pick me up.

It all but came to an end in August, a few weeks before school started. I went to join them at Ray's one afternoon, while his mom was at a casino in Canada. The others were always joking around about drinking and smoking cigarettes, and I'd figured they were just talking tough until I walked into the living room that afternoon. Gerry was puking in the corner, and Sarah was so fucked up she could hardly walk. Julia and Emily were laughing at Sarah as she slapped her own face and said, "Get it together!" Ray popped the lid off a bottle of beer with a lighter and handed it to me. "Be a man," he said.

Julia did a shot and then took a drag of her cigarette, and I kept getting visions of that hockey player's hands all over her. Until then, I'd thought maybe it was all a lie. But now . . .

"Oh, uh, no thanks," I said. The room was a cloud of smoke. I coughed and backed toward the door.

"You gotta be kidding me," Ray said.

"No, you can have it," I said, trying to be quiet so Julia wouldn't hear.

But she did.

"Don't be a bitch, James," she said. She always called me James, even though the others called me Jimmy. Something about her formality always reminded me about how high above us she was. Not that she thought she was better than us—I just knew she was. And I feared that someday she'd know it too.

But her words didn't sway me. Ray tried to hand me the beer again, and I again refused. Maybe I should have grabbed it and pretended to take a sip, then dumped half of it down the sink when no one was looking.

But I didn't, and they punished me for it. We went outside, and Ray pushed me in the pool with my clothes still on, and then they started throwing lawn chairs and grill brushes and shit at me. Tony did a cannonball, trying to land on me, but I moved out of the way.

Julia, stop them. Julia, I know you're better than all of this.

But Julia shook up a beer and dumped it on my head as I tried to pull myself out of the water.

I got out of the pool and rode my bike home, crying the whole way. Drinking was Evil. Didn't they know that? Didn't they know they'd go to Hell for it? How could Julia do that to herself? She was an angel on Earth. She was one of the only good things in the Hell in which we lived. She was pure. More godly than God. I couldn't put that shit in my mouth. Not after seeing what it did to Uncle Jake. Seeing how his hands shook so wildly whenever he wasn't holding a drink. Not after hearing all Dad's stories about when he was drunk off whiskey. Not after hearing the nuns go on and on about how drinking alcohol and smoking cigarettes was a surefire way to end up in Hell. Not after thinking about what those gorillas from *Congo* did to my brain. Not after thinking of what it would do to the Evil Thoughts in my head. The nuns said alcohol made you feel less in control, and I couldn't let down my guard. The moment I did, maybe the Evil would take over again. Maybe I'd start dragging kids off to the woods and crushing their heads with rocks. Maybe I'd find that kid with the bowtie and strangle him with it. And that's without even considering what it'd do to my body. The nuns all said alcohol would kill you. Turn you into a raisin. A vegetable. Make you weak and stupid. I needed my body to be strong. I needed to keep it in perfect shape so I could beat Dougie and J. Peg and anyone else who stepped on the court. I needed to stay disciplined so I could win a state championship my junior year. So I could hold the trophy up high and make everything and everyone clean and happy and nice. No, I couldn't drink. I couldn't smoke. I certainly couldn't do drugs. My body was a sacrifice to God. A sacrifice to my family. My city.

My own crazy-ass brain.

I just wished Julia could see that. I just wished she could see that it wasn't due to weakness, but strength, that I chose not to drink. That it wasn't due to weakness that I told her that God still existed even though I had my doubts. That it wasn't due to weakness that I told her she was better off staying in Buffalo and not moving to New York after she graduated from high school. It was due to strength that I wished she'd stay in my arms, where I could help her, save her, show off her talent to the world. Julia, please don't laugh at me! Not you. You have no idea how badly it hurts. I don't care about the others. Fuck Ray. Tony can eat a turd. Emily,

Sarah. They're cool, but I don't give a shit what they think. You, Julia, you're everything. You're better than all of them. Come with me. Marry me. We'll build a house together and have kids and be nice to them and be happy. We'll never waste our time working on the house. Adding extra rooms. Changing the wallpaper. We'll be happy with what we have. We'll spend our time together. We can be happy without alcohol or cigarettes or sex before marriage. We can be happy just doing what the nuns and priests say. We can be happy obeying the Evil Thoughts inside our brains. We'll be good. We'll listen. And the world will let us be.

But I know you won't listen, Julia. I see the wildness in your eyes. I see your need to explore and experience and indulge. I know now, Julia, you'll never be mine. I know now *I'll* never be mine either. We can never be happy together— even though I feel the same wildness inside of myself.

God, I'll never listen to you. I hate you as much as I hate Dad. As much as I hate Buffalo. As much as I want to burn all this shit to the ground.

Though I still sat with Tony, Ray, and Gerry in the back of that room, I felt that I was starting to hate them as well. They could burn in Hell too for all I cared.

Chapter 11

I told Ray no when he asked me to go with him to the coffee shop after school that day, and I rode my bike home alone. It was weird riding without Dan. He'd started at Kirkland High, and while he did pass St. Anthony's on his way home, he got out much earlier than we did, so he was always home by the time I got out. It had been a few months since the last time Shane and the other assholes had chased me down after school, but I think I would have taken those beatings again if it meant I could ride home with Dan. Since we were little, he'd never really spoken all that much, but now that he'd started at Kirkland, he pretty much stopped speaking entirely. When I asked him about school, he'd just stare at the wall or walk away or something and never answer me.

We delivered papers and then headed for Hammond. Though everything seemed to be changing, Hammond was there for us, without fail. Dan, Luke, Steven, Silas, and I played fives against some older guys who'd graduated from Kirkland High a few years back, and they were good. One guy was dunking on everybody, even though he was shorter than I was. The older guys beat us by a few points, but it was a close game that could have gone either way. After the game, I saw Bianca rubbing her ass on one of them, and she grabbed him by the junk and led him away. All the other guys kept shouting shit like, "You better titty-fuck her!" and "Get your money's worth!"

Silas and I walked to the water fountain.

"Damn, it's hot as slavery out here," Silas said. "First thing I do when the Bulls sign me is get some AC. This shit's brutal." Silas took a drink. The water pressure was weak, so he had to get his mouth close, almost touching the fountain.

"Hey, Silas," I said. "What's the best way to get a girl to like you?"

"Well, you've come to the right place for advice, man," Silas said. "The ladies love the Mack. What you need to do is approach her with some confidence. Even if you're scared as shit, just walk up like Coolio. There's nothing chicks dig more than a guy who can control the swayin' of his nuts, ya feel me?"

"What the hell does that mean?"

"It means you need to dig deep and find that guy inside you that you're most comfortable with—that guy you truly are—and just let him out. Once you do that, the words and confidence will just flow."

But inside is where the Evil lives, Silas. So does that mean there's no hope for me . . .?

"Man, it's hot as Africa out here," he said as he headed back to the court. "Imma catch Ebola or some shit . . ."

Silas came over for dinner that night. He'd been coming over a lot that year, and my parents loved him. He always told my mom she was the best cook, which was something none of us ever said, since we were all too busy arguing and complaining our way through dinner each night. Even Dad loved him—Dad who, my whole life, had done all he could to avoid driving through the East Side. Who would never shop at the Tops on Main Street because, "Those people are just waiting to steal your wallet or tires. Better to go to the one in Amherst instead." Who would say things like, "It's not racist if it's true." He rarely used the N-word, unlike Uncle Tommy, who said it all the time, but he did often say they were "all rotten to the core." But he loved Silas, and the two of them would toss one-liners back and forth while laughing all night. It confused the hell out of me. Dad would pump his fist at the TV, shouting, "God-damned thug!" whenever the news would show a Black man being taken away in cuffs, and Dad would talk about how we needed to move further east to protect ourselves because, "They're starting to invade our neighborhood," but if a Black man came to the door asking to call a tow truck, Dad would be on his back fixing that car until it started up again. If a Black woman shivered in the seat next to him at the movies, he'd offer her his jacket without a second thought. In person, he'd go above and beyond to be a good neighbor, but when reading the paper or watching the news or listening to that angry man on the radio, he was terrified of those same neighbors he'd just helped. I didn't know whether I was supposed to be neighborly or afraid, but Silas was my friend and I knew he wouldn't hurt me, so I tried not to let any more fear inside of me. Besides, the White people I knew argued and fought and stole just as much as any of the Black people I knew.

In the mornings, Dan was usually at school by the time I got up. I'd get ready and ride my bike in without him. It sucked not seeing him in the halls. Even though we'd rarely spoken while he was still at St. Anthony's, it had been nice to know he was there. Nice to know he was looking out for me. Now, I had to look out for Diane, Rebecca, and Jeremy, but I did a worse job of that than Dan did. If I saw them, I'd say hi, but not much else. One day, when I saw Jeremy crying outside of his classroom, I just kept walking. It didn't even hit me until like an hour later. I felt like a shitty brother, and I was. I was always doing things to make him cry. Hiding the soap when it was his turn to take a shower. Changing the channel when he was watching *Barney* or *Power Rangers*. I'd call him a fag for listening to Hootie and the Blowfish and the Spin Doctors. I'd hit him and push him around, and when he'd tell Dad or Mom, I'd wait until they stopped yelling at me, and then I'd hit him even harder.

I was terrible to my sisters as well, but I never hit them. Instead, I'd find their insecurities and rub them in their faces. They were fat and stupid and ugly and had no friends. I'd go at them with as much energy as the Evil Thoughts had come at me, and I'd try to wear them both down. Carolynn was little, so I left her alone. But the other two . . . Sometimes they still smiled, but that wasn't okay. It wasn't okay to smile. Not in that house. Not in that city. No, smiling was for other people, in far-off places like Los Angeles or Florida or Europe. You smiled in that house, and boy, I'd punish you for it. You tried laughing, and I'd come at you like Poor Rich with his sledgehammer. Oh, you got a new toy? Oops, it slipped out of my hand and fell into the toilet. Oh, you were on the phone with a friend? Sorry, I unplugged the cord. The box of Honey Bunches of Oats was still in the cabinet. Nobody was allowed to smile in that house.

I didn't like being a prick, but I couldn't stop. It was

almost as if the nastier I was, the less I could stop myself from being nasty again in the future. I was worried I'd go too far one day. I think I did a few times, but with Dan, not the younger ones. Dan pissed me off one afternoon, and I threw a baseball bat at his head. I didn't even realize what I'd done until he'd already dodged it. I was in a blind rage and in that split second of insanity, I realized that I wanted to hurt him—bad. There's something intoxicating about rage. It's almost as if you get sucked deeper and deeper into this world where all consequences and feeling temporarily cease to exist. In that moment when you explode, you can do anything. You'll smash the guitar you'd spent all year saving up to buy. You'll drive your car over a cliff just because you spilled a drink on your lap. Toss a TV through a window because your team lost. Slit your wrists or shoot yourself in the head because fuck it all. In those brief moments, everyone fears you. Everyone's paying attention. For once, *you* don't have to fear *them*. You don't have to worry about controlling your every word and movement. You can do anything. You're free. I saw what Poor Rich was hooked on. What Grandpa and Uncle Tommy were drunk on. None of my brothers or sisters had the rage. But I did. Like Poor Rich, I felt I could smash anything apart at any time, and look what *you* made me do, huh? This is what happens when *you* piss me off. See what *you* did?

But, after the rage subsided, I'd feel horrible. Terrified of what I was capable of. And the worse I felt, the more likely I was to hurt someone again. It was a cycle I couldn't escape. A cycle I was born into. I had generations of rage coursing through my veins, and who was I to stop it? How dare I be ungrateful to Grandpa? To Great-Grandpa? Don't you know what he sacrificed to provide for you? Don't you know Grandpa saved this world from the Nazis? Have some god-damned respect, and smash this fucking lamp!

What was the purpose of building and growing and developing when at any moment you might burn it all to the ground anyways? What was the point in hoping when hope was just kindling for all your fires? I was born to smash. Born to destroy. Born to take a sledgehammer to the backbone of the world. And you're a fool for trusting me. A fool for dating me. A fool for being my friend. Serves you right for being my kid. It's not *my* fault. I *am* anger. And I do whatever I damn well please.

Whatever I'm told.

But I know I'll always do it alone. Whatever I do. Better alone. Better to push everyone away. You can't hurt them if they won't come near you. You can't hate them for making you lose it if they're never around.

Why do I feel this way? God, please let me feel peace. Make me more like Mom or Dan, who try to work through their problems without yelling. I'm sorry for hurting my brothers and sisters. But I can never tell them that. If I let them get too close, I'll only hurt them worse. If I let them get too close, they'll only hurt me too. Plus, *he's* never said sorry. Nobody says sorry in this house. Why do *they* deserve it? What makes *them* so special? I'll make them sorry. I'll show them what sorry feels like.

It wasn't that I was trying to toughen them up. There was no silver lining to what I was doing. I was trying to crush them the same way everything in this world, both inside and out, was trying to crush me. And I was damned good at it. Far better than Dad, Grandpa, and all the others.

Chapter 12

They were working on the street near St. Anthony's again, and a guy marking the blacktop stopped to say, "Don't do drugs, kid," as I passed. When I got to the parking lot, I hopped off my bike and walked it to the rack. Each passing day brought me closer to Kirkland High School—the place I feared most in Buffalo. What new tortures awaited me there? At St. Anthony's, I was the smartest. The best athlete. I always got the lead roles in school plays. But Kirkland was huge, filled with smart and talented kids. It was also filled with bullies and drug dealers and atheists. Kids who didn't believe in God. Kids who would hurt me if I prayed or thanked God. If they knew I still prayed for about an hour before going to sleep each night, begging Him to take the pain away. But at least Dan was there. Each day brought me closer to him. Maybe when I got there, we'd be friends again. Maybe he'd start smiling again.

Each passing day also brought me further away from St. Anthony's. I started appreciating the school much more that year. Started being grateful that Sister Carol would be there at the door every morning to welcome kids and wish them a nice day. Started smiling when I saw Sister Rose reading to the younger kids in the library. Started looking forward to all the Masses I'd get to serve and finals I'd get to ace and gardens I'd get to weed. As much as I talked shit about that school, I felt safe there and didn't want to leave. But time and circumstance can change everything. The tension between me and the Freaky Deaks was getting worse. I started hating them. Hating their rebellions. Hating how they'd talk back to the teachers. Hating how they challenged Sister Adele when she canceled our field trip to the zoo because they were treating her like crap. Couldn't they just shut up and leave her alone? She told them three times that if they said one more thing, she'd cancel the trip, and they said plenty more things. Didn't they know their actions had consequences?

As I pulled away from them, I tried to get closer to God, but even He felt like a stranger to me. I tried my hardest to love Him and serve Him, but it was no use. It was like with the Evil Thoughts: the more I tried to ignore them, the stronger they got. Well, the more I tried to love God, the more difficult it got. I was losing my friends and faith slowly, watching them pull away from me like a receding tide. But I was done crying about it. I felt numb. I sided with the teachers. The parents. Fuck those ungrateful brats who drank and smoked and talked back. Why did they want to grow up so fast anyway? Didn't they know what was waiting for us? Didn't they ever take a walk through the neighborhood and see what the adults looked like? Fat. Angry. Loud. Lonely. Miserable. Why were we pushing so hard to leave St. Anthony's? Why did the girls want to date high school and college guys? Why did the guys want to drink whiskey and drive their parents' cars when Mommy and Daddy weren't around?

I was finally starting to understand why Sister Carol was always so angry at me whenever I did something stupid. I got called to the office more than any other student in seventh grade, and she'd always have me sit beside her on the couch and tell me why what I'd done had hurt the Lord and what I could do to make it right. She'd go on and on about how it was wrong to call Rachel Crawford's mother a plastic piece of crap. To throw Kevin Jenkins's hat in the toilet. To slap Brian Kramer's fat stomach so hard after gym class that it left a welt. To sneak into the art closet and destroy the girls' paintings. To sing, "*Jump* from the highest mountain," during Mass instead of *shout*. To make fun of the way the cafeteria lady spoke. To hide the janitor's mop. And bucket. And car keys. To drive Miss Davis so crazy in Spanish class that she left school crying. To write *House of Satan* in chalk on the school door.

I'd always nod and say sorry even though Poor Rich never said sorry when he smashed crap and went crazy, and Sister would call Dan into the office and tell him to tell Mom what I'd done. But Sister must have been stupider than she looked, because Dan never told Mom crap. I was afraid of Sister at first, but once I realized she couldn't do anything to me, I stopped worrying when I'd hear, "Will James Lombardi please report to my office" over the loudspeaker. Ray, Tony, and Gerry would say, "OHHHH, JIMMY'S IN TROUBLE AGAIN!" and I'd smile, take a bow, and head down for a couch session. Once, Sister called Tim Lamonz to come to the office and he started crying like a little bitch. We gave him hell for it when he came back. Timmy, they can't do shit to you. Don't you know that? Don't you know that no one really gives a shit anyway?

But now, I was starting to see why Sister was so upset with me. She'd tell me that she expected more from me. That God was watching and I shouldn't let Him down. That I was wasting my talents doing such stupid things. She had to have known Dan was, and would always be, on my side. Maybe she never told Mom because she wanted me to accept responsibility for my own actions. I could see that now, and I resolved that I wouldn't get called back to her office for that whole last year. I wanted to make her proud of me. Even when she was angry at me, she always made me feel special. She never called me stupid or ungrateful or nasty. She never hit me like Dad did. Even when she was mad, she made me feel as if I could maybe become a better person. Made me feel good and strong and capable. Not like Ray and Tony and Julia and the others had made me feel that day at Ray's house. Sister would never dump a beer on my head. Throw a grill brush at me. No, I was going to use my eighth-grade year to help build St. Anthony's up, not break it down. Poor Rich was good at demo, and so was I. I needed to work on construction.

Sister Carol greeted me when I walked into school that morning, and I said hi back to her. But, observant as she was, she never called Gerry into her office when he'd come in with black eyes and bruised lips, and that morning he came in with a huge shiner. He told Sister Adele he got it playing baseball, but in reality he threw like a bitch and was really self-conscious about it, so he avoided playing baseball at all costs. Sister Adele just said, "That's too bad, slugger," then told him to take a seat "over there in the dugout." We'd all stopped going over to Gerry's house because his dad was even worse now. He was drunk all the time and once even slapped

Ray when Ray turned Gerry's CD player up too loud. After that, none of us went back. Ray's mom was always drunk as hell, too, and probably wouldn't have done shit about it anyways, so Ray never told her.

The next day Gerry didn't come into school. Out of the blue, his family up and moved to West Virginia. Gerry didn't tell any of us goodbye, and after that, Ray was the only one who ever spoke to him again. A few years later, I heard Gerry OD'd on heroin just like his mother. He and I were supposed to write skits for *SNL*. He might have had a shot. But he didn't make it to seventeen.

How is it that when one kid dies anywhere, the whole god-damned world doesn't just completely fall apart?

Losing Gerry didn't slow us down, though.

"Rooster! Rooster!" I said, when I saw the back room door opening at the Merry Mart down the street from Tony's house.

Ray and Tony hopped over the counter, pockets and arms filled with as many packs of cigarettes as possible. We ran to the Da Lucas', pushed through the loose board in the back fence, walked through the trees, and arrived at the field, where Alonzo had set up some coolers, lawn chairs, and folding card tables earlier that day. Tony and Ray opened a briefcase on one of the tables and dumped the cigarettes inside.

"I can't believe that idiot fell for it," Tony said.

"What'd you ask him to search the back for? Dick shits?" Ray said.

"A dick for," I said.

"Yeah, that's it," Ray said. "When he asked you, 'What's

a dick for?' I almost died. I can't believe he actually waddled back there to look for one."

"Never underestimate people's idiocy," I said.

Ray grabbed a few beers out of one of the coolers and passed them around. He handed me one, but I declined.

"Don't be a pussy," Ray said. "You earned it."

"You guys lifted the stuff, I just watched," I said.

"This is just as much yours as it is ours," Ray said.

Alonzo and several other guys pushed through the trees, cheering and carrying armfuls of cigarettes, beer, condoms, liquor bottles.

"Gentlemen, we are going to make a killing," Alonzo said. He dumped the beers in a cooler, then lit a cigarette.

"You really just grabbed a case and walked out?" a chubby kid asked.

"The fucker didn't know whether to shit or go blind," Alonzo said. "That's how you gotta roll. Just let it all hang out."

While Dan and I'd been spending our afternoons and weekends at Hammond, these guys had been using their free time to rip off convenience and drug stores. They sold their takings to local kids. It had become a pretty lucrative business once word spread, which it usually does quickly at that age.

Dan emerged from the tree cover, but his arms were empty.

"How'd it go?" Alonzo said.

Dan lifted his shirt, showing the cigarette packs he'd slid inside his waistband.

"Yo, we got the Sun*dan*ce kid here," Alonzo said.

Dan dumped the cigarettes in a briefcase, then grabbed a beer from a cooler. I walked over to him and whispered, "I didn't know you drank." Dan shrugged, and I started feeling dizzy. We'd made more money in that one afternoon than we ever had from a month of delivering papers and cutting neighbors' lawns. Even so, I knew I couldn't keep it up. Pretty soon, the other guys would ask me to do more than just act as a lookout.

Everyone else was laughing and smiling and chugging beer. Dan sipped his beer alone, staring into space. It seemed as if I could just push him over and he wouldn't do shit about it. Seeing him drinking and smoking was far worse than seeing Julia drinking and smoking. As much as I knew about her, Julia was still a stranger. I had no idea what went on in her house. Her bedroom. In the back seats of hockey players' Mustangs. But I'd shared a room with Dan since we were babies. We used to piss together, trying to cross streams from start to finish. We'd taken baths together as babies and showered together when Dad screamed about saving water. We served Mass together and delivered papers together and dominated kids at Hammond together.

This year was the first time we'd ever been apart. What's happening to you at Kirkland? What are you doing there? Why won't you talk to me anymore? Why do you just stare at the walls and floor?

Dan lit a cigarette and kept sipping his beer.

"Yo, Jimmy," Ray said. "Let's go hit the Stop & Shop while that four-eyed fucker is still working his shift." Ray and Tony started for the trees.

"I don't want to fuck with that guy. He's old," I said.

Ray stopped, turned around, and looked me dead in the eye. "Fuck. Him."

"I-I've gotta cut Mrs. Prendergast's lawn," I said.

Ray stared into my eyes, studying me. He saw something and gave me a look as if to say, "I see you, Jimmy, and I want nothing to do with you." I knew right then that we were no longer friends. He and Tony walked away, and I stood there alone watching Dan drink and stare into the void that seemed to be growing around us.

When I pushed through the fence and started riding my bike down the street, a brick fell from a tree, almost hitting me. I looked up and saw Gus climbing down. He chased after me, but I was long gone.

When I got back, Mom was in the kitchen making dinner. I wanted to hug her, but she was mixing ground beef with her hands, so I didn't.

"Hey, Jimmy-Boy, what's up?" she said. She popped a chunk of raw beef into her mouth, then handed me some, and I ate it.

"I-I feel like everything I do is always wrong," I said.

"What do you mean?" She wiped her hands with a towel and gave me her full attention.

"I feel like the world could just eat me up at any minute, and I don't even know how or why."

"I think I understand what you're feeling. Growing up can be tough sometimes."

"It's not growing up. It's something else—I just don't know what. My head feels so heavy and dark . . ."

"You've got to have faith in Jesus. Someday it'll all make sense."

"But that's the thing. I don't think Jesus can help me."

"Jesus can always help you. He's the only one who'll always be there for you."

"Won't *you* be here for me?"

"You know what I mean."

"I don't think I do."

"Look, whenever I feel life's weight on my shoulders, I try to help somebody else out. It's a blessing to give yourself away to the world."

"Yeah, but if you're always giving, what's left for you?"

"There's no need to be selfish. I know life can be tough, but you're a very brave guy, and you'll figure it all out."

"I don't want to be brave, and I don't want to wait for *someday*, I just want to feel okay. I want to feel normal. Everybody else seems to be having so much fun, and they're not even worried about the consequences. I feel like anytime I take a step in any direction, it's the wrong direction, even if it seems like the direction everyone else is moving. Does that make any sense?"

"It does. Jimmy, you're not like a lot of the other kids. You're not like your brothers and sisters. Some people are happy with what they have. Some people are content to just sit on their butts and smile all day long. But you want more. Ever since you were a baby, you've wanted more than we could ever give you. You want to know how everything works. You want to know how you can break it all apart and put it back together in a way that's better. You want to know everything there is to know. And that can be very difficult for someone so young."

"I just want to help people, but sometimes I feel like I'd rather hurt them. People say so many different things. I don't even know what to believe."

"Put your trust in the Lord. He's always helped me through everything. Just have faith."

"I hate that word. Everybody's always telling me I need

to have faith in God or the Bible or all this other crap that can't be proven—that isn't real. All these things, and people that say one thing and do another. Nobody seems to know what the hell they're talking about, but they're all so damned confident. And they're all so damned miserable. The Bible says one thing on one page, then a completely different thing on the next. Sister says God will condemn you to Hell for missing one Sunday Mass, but the next day she says it's just a venial sin. I feel like I'm going crazy."

"I won't have you talking all that filth in this house. We respect the Lord in this house."

"GOD-FUCKING-DAMN IT!" Dad probably smashed another finger while working on the bathroom upstairs.

"Sounds like it . . ." I grabbed an apple and went to the front porch. The house next door was empty. A few weeks back, they'd found Mr. Rogers's body, days after he'd had a heart attack while working in the garage. A neighbor finally called the cops after Helen spent nearly two days straight on the porch with her cat. She'd even been sleeping out there. The cops took her away. A part of me was sad for her and her entire life. But another part of me was relieved I'd never have to go back over there and talk to her. Relieved that there was one less thing around me now that reminded me of how hopeless it all was.

Chapter 13

Dad had bought the wrong size pipe for the sink in the upstairs bathroom, and before I could stop him, he took a sledgehammer to the cabinets, toilet, and sink. I grabbed Dan, and we headed for Hammond. I wasn't cleaning up another one of the old man's messes.

A game had just finished.

"But that's only if you wanna drive 'em wild," Silas said to D. Pow. "And you gotta do it like this." Silas brought his index and middle fingers to his mouth and slid his tongue between them.

Joey snuck up behind Steven, who was shooting jumpers at the far side of the court, and as Steven jumped up, Joey pulled down his shorts, revealing Steven's stained and torn tighty-whities.

"Yo, that's wrong for so many reasons," Silas said about Steven's underwear. "Anyway, you gotta work the outside of the snatch before you hit the money spot. I'm tellin' you, they go wild . . ."

Joey snuck up behind Silas and pulled down his shorts too, but Silas wasn't wearing any underwear, or a shirt for that matter, and he just stood there naked, talking to D.

Pow as if nothing had happened. "They'll just start creamin' in your mouth."

"So, it's true about Black dudes," T. Pow said.

"Hell yeah it is," Silas said. "You wanna get some of this?" With his shorts around his ankles, Silas started chasing T. Pow. T. Pow took off running and didn't stop.

When we stepped on the court, Joey said to Dan, "I like Bianca so much. Someday I'm gonna marry her."

"Maybe if you got the loot she'll pretend to be your wife," D. Pow said.

"Cut the shit, fellas," Silas said. "Acting like you've never liked a girl before. Yo, Harvey, you know that dude Gus that claws through everyone's trash?"

"Yeah," Dan said.

"Well, he garbage-picked your journal out of a bag in front of your house, and when Bianca got her hands on it, she started spreading it all over town."

"Just like her legs," Joey said.

I hadn't seen Dan smile in months, and the look on his face made me think he wouldn't ever smile again. Silas walked over and patted him on the back. "Fuck it, man, let's hoop."

It was probably for the best Bianca stayed away from Dan. A few weeks later, they found her body in a dumpster in Black Rock with twenty-seven stab wounds in her torso. I heard some rumors about what happened; it seemed a client wasn't too happy with her services. Sometimes, early development can be a terrible thing, and Bianca paid the ultimate price. The news shook up the Hammond Crew for a few weeks, but we hooped our way through it.

We stayed for Afterhours that night and hung out in the gazebo near the court.

"I just feel like I try so hard, but nothing ever works out for me," I said to Silas.

"Some things aren't meant to be no matter how hard you try for 'em," Silas said. "You gotta learn to work with what the good Lord's given you."

"You have no idea how much I like Julia. My heart feels like it's going to explode," I said. "I mean, I feel like she's just right there, but I'll never be able to get close enough, you know? I can't imagine life without her."

"I do know, Ho-dingies," Silas said. "You got a lotta heart, and it shows. But sometimes having a lotta heart can hurt you. And sometimes it can be dangerous if you don't know what to do with it. Look around. A lot of the people you see drinking and yelling their lives away, those are people who don't know what to do with their hearts, so it starts killin' them. Learn to control that shit, and you'll be unstoppable."

"I guess. . . . I think as long as we can win a state championship, it'll make all this other shit worth it."

"Well, us winning a championship is a certainty, so all this shit will definitely be worth it."

Steven came over and sat down beside me. "Your dad can really work some magic with a hammer, Horace."

"You should see what he can do with a sledgehammer." I gave Dan a knowing look, but Dan just kept staring into the dark.

"He should be running some big-time construction crew, not stocking vending machines," Steven said.

"That man missed his calling," Silas said.

"He's really good at that stuff," Steven said.

"He'd better be," I said. "It's all he cares about."

"Poor Rich is awesome. I see him out there all the time workin' on your house," Steven said.

"Yeah, and screaming like a maniac," I said.

"Don't be ungrateful, Horace," Steven said. "At least he's around. My dad's been on the road for the past few years. I only get to see him once or twice a month, and then he's back on the highway truckin'." Steven sang the word *truckin'* like the Dead, his favorite band.

"You're a crazy cat, Steven," Silas said. "Well, my dad's got all yours beat. Maniac Marty's a beast, you don't even know. Dude whooped my ass the other day because I ate the last cherry popsicle in the freezer. And my mom's drunk ass just sat there cheerin' him on like she was watchin' *Jerry Springer* or some shit."

"When I grow up, I'm gonna be nice to my kids," I said.

"I don't know what I wanna be when I grow up," Steven said.

"Man, you should be a linebacker for the Bills," Silas said.

"Or a bouncer," I said.

"You're a beast and a half," Silas said.

"Yeah, you could kill Joey or the Powells, and all those other guys who make fun of you," I said, keeping my voice down. Those dudes were getting high at the other end of the park.

"Shut up, Horace," Steven said.

"I'm just saying that you shouldn't let them push you around. You're so much bigger than they are. Don't be a pussy," I said.

"I told you to shut up!" Steven got up and chased me out of the gazebo. I sprinted straight for one of the softball diamonds and ran circles around the chain-link backstop until Steven gave up and went back to the gazebo. I went back over too after he promised not to kick my ass.

In the distance, we could hear Luke, Joey, and the Powells laughing. Joey read more of the journal, loud enough for us to hear. "I wish James would be happier and stop making Dad yell. It bothers everybody and makes Mom sad."

They laughed even louder.

"Hey, Horace," Joey said, "you better start smiling more or your dad's gonna make your mom sleep in the garage from now on."

Dan's head already looked so heavy he could barely hold it up, and Joey just dumped more weight on.

Silas got up and headed over to the other guys. He said a few words then came back with the journal. He handed it to Dan and said, "Forget those guys. They're just goofs. They don't mean nothin' by it."

As far back as I could recall, Dad had always blamed me for making him yell, but even when I was little, I'd known he was full of shit. But hearing Dan blame me for it hurt me so much worse than the old man ever could. That was the first time in my life I thought that maybe Dan wasn't on my side. Maybe he never had been.

"What do you think is the worst thing that can happen to a person?" Sister Adele walked through the rows, asking that question over and over. One kid said cancer, another said death, another mentioned losing their parents. When she got to me, I said loneliness, and the class erupted with laughter.

"You think that's worse than poverty, hunger, and murder?" Julia said.

"I think it's worse to be sitting all alone on a mountain of gold in a castle than it is to be living in a shack in the woods surrounded by people who love you. Who understand you," I said.

"So, even worse than getting robbed or being burned alive, you still pick loneliness?" Ray said.

"What's the worst part about being robbed or cheated or beaten up? Worse than the physical pain is the feeling of being alone. Being scared to go back out into the world. Of trusting people. The loneliness is the worst part of being hurt. I mean, what's the point of life if you're all alone? Alone even from yourself?" I said. "When you're alone, you might as well be starving or in prison or being beaten or tortured. Loneliness is torture. It's starvation. And what's worse is that you suffer right in front of other people and nobody even knows because that's the point of loneliness. Nobody knows. Nobody cares. Nobody's watching. At least if you're starving, people might offer you some food. When you're alone, you stay alone, and people blame you for it, even as they're turning away from you."

"You're never alone with God above you," Sister Adele said.

"You're always alone with Satan below you," I said.

"Dark, dude," Tony said.

I knew I'd already crossed a line with all of them and that I'd never be able to come back to their side. But now it was war. They didn't know I could take all seven of them on at once. Even Julia. Love can turn to hatred so quickly, and I could feel that change taking over me. I didn't want to lose her from my life, but I was starting to see who she really was. Maybe she wasn't as perfect and compassionate as

I'd thought. And I didn't know what to do with the feelings I still had. Did I really hate her? Would this all just pass? I hoped it would, but the hatred and anger could also serve as a wall to protect me from her and all the others.

From seeing my good friends turn on me, I realized that all along my allegiance had never been with them. Nor was it with my parents, or Dan, or the nuns, or even God. There was only one God I'd ever truly serve, and that was the Evil God inside my head. These fuckers didn't realize that, for years, I'd been destroying all the good inside my mind—sacrificing it to the Evil that controlled every aspect of my life. As long as I did its bidding, it would allow me some comfort. I'd never be lonely as long as I served it and respected it. I'd only been friends with them because it had allowed me. I needed to learn how to lose everything and be okay with it, because, serving this God, you could lose anything at any minute. They didn't know that turning on me couldn't hurt me all that much. It would only make me stronger. It would only feed the Evil.

When the final bell rang, Sister Adele called me to her desk. Ray walked past me and said, "You better not narc on us," and those words hurt worse than him laughing at me. It was one thing to give someone shit. It was another to assume they'd rat you out. I wasn't telling on him or anyone else. If God really was up there, He could see it all anyway, and He'd dole out punishment. I didn't need to rat out anyone.

"Hey, kiddo," Sister said. "I've been meaning to tell you that your creative writing story was incredible. You really got some talent there, sport."

"I was just messin' around," I said.

"Nothin' messy about it. When I was reading it, I didn't

even hear the phone ring. I missed a call from Monsignor Joseph, but between you and me, sometimes I prefer not to pick up when he calls, if you know what I mean."

"Yeah, I think I do. And thanks, I guess."

"You know, I'm one for stories myself."

"I know. I love your stories."

"I think the art of storytelling is creating characters people care about. To find the life in them and draw it out."

"What if you don't see life in anyone?"

"Oh c'mon. It's very clear to me that you do. You pick up on things that go over most people's heads. I think you got a talent for seeing the beauty in this world."

"Would it be all right if I changed desks? I can't see so well from the back."

"Can't see so well, huh? That's the only reason?"

"Yeah."

"Sure, I'll switch you with Terry."

"Thanks."

"Don't let the others bring you down. As a nun, I come across a lot of people who are lonely, and I have to say, I think loneliness is about one of the worst things in this world too. But you know what? Reading stories like yours makes people feel less alone."

"Really?"

"Oh yeah, sport! I talk about this with Sister Rose all the time. We're both huge readers. I think reading a book is the closest you can ever come to being inside someone else's heart and head. When you've got a book, you're never lonely. You just keep telling your stories, kiddo. Let's put an end to the loneliness out there."

"Sister, can I ask you another question?"

"Absolutely."

"Do you ever regret being a nun?"

"Whoa, now that is some question. I took my final vows when I was twenty, just like my Aunt Barbara did. I didn't have a choice back then. It was just expected of me. But even after all these years, I'd do it again. I'm absolutely certain that my purpose on this Earth is to love and serve the Lord. I have no regrets."

"How can you be so sure? I don't feel like I'm sure of anything."

"God has a plan for every person. You just have to trust Him to show you what that plan is. He's talking to you right now. If you learn how to truly listen, you'll never go wrong."

"Then why are there so many miserable people out there?"

"I think most people don't know how to listen. And I think a lot of people don't *want* to listen."

"Do you ever wish you could have gotten married?"

"I am married. I'm married to God."

"I mean, like, actually married."

"Love can be different for every person. You can love someone in so many ways. God may not be a person here on this earth in physical form, but I can feel Him. I can touch Him with my thoughts and feel Him in my heart."

"When I was younger, I wanted to be a priest. But I think I'd like to marry a woman someday."

"You don't have to become a priest to serve God."

"I'm sorry for asking so many questions. I've just been feeling pretty bad lately, and I don't know what to do."

"Follow your heart. Learn to hear what it's truly telling you. It will always be your best guide."

"Thanks, Sister." I grabbed my backpack off a desk and started for the door.

"Wait, I have something for you." She went to her desk and grabbed a black-and-white marble notebook—the same as the one Dan used to write in. "Take this. Write in it whenever you're feeling lonely. The characters in your stories will always keep you company."

I smiled and took the journal, then walked out the door. I thought about Dan's journal being passed around Hammond. Writing was such a risk. Putting any part of yourself out into this world was dangerous. But so was keeping the best of yourself bottled up inside.

God, I'm listening. I'm truly listening. Please, tell me where to go. I'm falling down. I need to be strong. I need to save Dan. Tell me what to do. I'm listening. Please, speak louder than the Evil. Show me what's right and what's wrong. I want to be good. I want to be nice to Jeremy and my sisters. I want to make Dad stop yelling so Dan will be friends with me again. I want to be able to have fun with my friends without feeling as if I'm going to go to Hell for it. I want to listen to music and watch movies and sleep over at people's houses without feeling as if the world is going to swallow me whole. God, it's all falling apart. Show me how to put it back together again. I'll build it up right this time. I'll make everyone happy. I can do it. I'm so powerful. I feel so powerful. I can save us all.

But, God, how can I trust my heart when it's telling me you don't exist?

Chapter 14

After school, I headed to the garden behind the convent and found weeds everywhere. Sister Rose had been in and out of the hospital, and Dan and I were busy with other things, so no one was taking care of it. It was almost as bad as when we'd first started working on it years ago. The thought of starting over was too much for me. If Sister asked me to help again, I'd have to lie. Tell her my paper route had doubled in size, and I didn't have the extra time. It made me sad to look at. It didn't seem to matter how much effort you put into anything—it would all fall apart the second you walked away. After so much weeding and planting, you just lose the energy to ever do it again. Maybe that was why Mom didn't smile anymore. Maybe she was tired of weeding her family.

After Dan and I got back from delivering papers, Dad came home bitching about the car. He'd gotten a new mass air flow sensor or something because the station wagon had been stalling, but it had stalled again on the way home.

"THOSE CROOKS SCREWED ME!"

"So take it back and have them fix it again. It's their fault. Tell 'em you're not paying another cent," I said.

"YOU DON'T FUCKING GET IT!"

"Yeah, I do. They charged you to fix something, but they didn't fix it. Go make them do the job right. Don't be a pussy."

"YOU SON OF A BITCH!"

He chased me around the dining room table.

"Haha, you called Mom a bitch," I said as I threw the old man a fake, then ran upstairs to my room. I locked the door behind me and sat against it so Poor Rich couldn't get in. When I flipped on the light, I saw Dan sitting on his bed, staring at the floor.

"You okay?" I said.

He nodded. I could hear Poor Rich stomping up the steps.

"Help me hold back this maniac, will ya?" I said.

Dan sat beside me against the door.

"YOU SON OF A BITCH! I'LL KICK THE DOOR DOWN!" He pounded the hell out of it.

"You can try, Poor Rich," I said.

"I'LL SHOW YOU SOME RESPECT!"

"And I'll show you my dick, old man," I said.

I thought Dan would like that one, but he just kept staring at the carpet.

"Hey," I said to him, "you wanna head to BK as soon as this shithead punches himself out?"

The maniac pounded on the door a few more times and then left, grumbling some shit about his back. Too bad he didn't fall down the steps.

"You should stop being such a jerk to him," Dan said. "He does a lot for us, you know. Show him some respect."

"I think you mean show him some blind faith, right?"

"Stop being so selfish."

"Well, if sticking up for myself is selfish, then I guess I'll be eating your burger too. Fuck you both."

I stormed out of there and took off on my bike to Burger King. I got my order to go, but when I reached the garden behind the convent, I decided to eat in the parking lot instead. That was the first time Dan had spoken to me in days. Fucking asshole.

Sister Rose died that November just before her ninety-fifth birthday. I served her funeral and watched her casket get wheeled toward the altar where Monsignor Joseph and I were standing. Apart from the nuns, some students, and a few other people, the church was empty. Sister Rose had humbly served the Lord for seventy-six years and had just about everything she'd ever owned inside that box with her. She'd helped feed tens of thousands of people in her life— maybe even hundreds of thousands—but hardly anyone showed up to her funeral. What was the point? Why even get out of bed in the morning?

As they wheeled her away, I ran back to the sacristy, grabbed a copy of *Tom's Midnight Garden*, and put it on her casket just before they carried her outside. Monsignor Joseph yelled at me for running in church and "disrespecting the dead," but Sister Adele told me later that what I did was "really nice, kiddo," even though she had tears in her eyes when she said it.

I sat beside Dad's workbench in the basement and called Julia. Her mom picked up and said Julia wasn't home but that she'd be back soon and would call me then. The basement was dark and cold, and I was just wearing shorts and a T-shirt, but I didn't want to go get socks and warmer clothes because Julia could call back at any minute. I sat there for about an hour waiting and shivering before Mom said we had to go to Dan's game at the Kirkland High gym.

Dan had made the junior varsity basketball team, and my parents were both really proud. They wouldn't stop talking about how Dan was going to lead the team in scoring and help win a championship. But when we got to the game—the first of the season—Dan sat at the far end of the bench, where he remained the whole time, with the same heavy head and despondent eyes. He hardly watched the game, which was probably a good thing, because even with Luke out there they were getting crushed.

Over sixty kids had tried out for the team, but only twelve made it.

"PUT ME IN, COACH!" T. Pow said, sitting a few rows behind us.

Coach Flemming, a dopey forty-year-old with a porn mustache, pretended not to hear, but he gave T. Pow a quick, nasty glance.

"Would you get a load of those jerks?" Dad said about the Powells and Joey.

The ref blew his whistle, and Poor Rich turned around.

"Whaddya mean 'traveling?'" Poor Rich said. "D'ya need to borrow my glasses?" This was one of the few spots on Earth Dad's yelling was acceptable.

"I'M OPEN, COACH! PASS THE BALL!" T. Pow said.

The Powells had tried out for the team but were told they weren't disciplined enough for league play. Joey hadn't even tried. I figured organized sports weren't his thing.

I heard the Hammond Crew laughing and turned just as Joey spat in an open purse beside a woman wearing a pearl necklace and gold earrings. She didn't seem to notice, just kept watching the game.

Steven had been told the same thing as the Powells, and he came with us to the game and sat next to me.

Luke was having a great game—the best out of both teams—but it wasn't enough. He terrorized the other point guard, putting on a full-court press and stripping the guard every few times he tried to dribble up the court. Luke got rebounds, blocked shots, and led the team in scoring. But he couldn't do it alone, and the rest of the team—consisting of Shane Walsh, Jacob Mancuso, and a few other pricks like them—kept dribbling off their feet and passing the ball out of bounds and getting outworked for rebounds and getting burned on D. They hit some good shots, and Shane had decent handle, but they didn't seem to care about winning. They were all playing for themselves, not for the team. Each wanted to look good for their parents or the girls in the stands and generally played Abercrombie & Fitch basketball while Luke was out there doing all the work. I wanted to lace up and help Luke. With me, the Powells, and my bro out there with him, we woulda fucked those clowns up badly. The other team was nothing special, but they played as a unit, which was more than I could say of the Kirkland Lions. Coach Flemming clearly had no idea how to lead a team and got outcoached badly.

Shane hit a three, and his dad, sitting a row in front of us, cheered. Dude was as big a prick as his son. He had this slimy, I'm-a-Buffalo-lawyer-so-get-outta-my-way air to him.

When Shane got back on D and got burned for the millionth time, my dad yelled, "C'mon, play some defense," and Shane's dad turned and gave my dad a nasty lawyer-look, and Poor Rich shut right up. He didn't say much the rest of the game. He just sat there sweating like a nervous little kid.

The Kirkland Lions lost by twenty to a team they should have destroyed. Dan didn't get a minute of playing time and spent the whole game staring at the hardwood. Beside Luke, Dan was the best player on the team, but Coach either didn't notice or didn't care. I always thought that adults were supposed to know best. Pilots never crashed planes. Police officers never told lies. Judges were always just. And coaches knew how to get the best out of their players. But this clown clearly didn't know what he was doing. Maybe none of the others did either. Maybe it wouldn't matter how well I played in tryouts—maybe Coach would cut my ass too, just like the Powells, who were forces of nature on D. Holy shit! What if this clown was the reason we didn't win a state championship my junior year? As if I didn't already have enough on my mind, seeing this shitshow sent me into a tailspin. I was beginning to see maybe what Dan was looking at whenever he stared at the floor.

That night, I sat on my bed and watched the snow falling on North Buffalo. Big white flakes making everything look clean and whole. I turned around and Dan was lying in bed in a pool of shadow. Jeremy had moved into the bedroom in the basement, so now it was Dan and me again—just like old times. But everything was different between us. Dad had taken apart the bunk beds, so we each had our own separate big-boy bed. I'd put scapulars and rosaries that I'd asked Father Mike to bless on all four corner posts of our beds in the hopes that this would keep the darkness away. But it didn't. Even though it was just us in that room now, we didn't talk anymore. Maybe a few words here and there, but other than that, silence. Dan had stopped playing music entirely, not just at night, and I almost wished he'd pop his Bush or Chili Peppers CDs back in the player, even before bed. I tried telling him that night that Coach Flemming was an idiot, but he just went to sleep.

On weekends it was hard to get him up to deliver papers, even though he always used to be the one who'd wake me. Soon he told me he didn't want the job anymore, and that I could take the whole route. I tried doing the whole thing for a few weeks, but it was too much, so I told Bob that I'd have to quit too. I was able to make enough money shoveling driveways and cutting lawns, but I realized it wasn't really about the money. All this work was about doing something to keep busy. To keep myself distracted so the darkness wouldn't take over. And also to do something good for the neighborhood. It made me happy to shovel driveways and cut lawns and give people the news and serve Mass. If I lost all of that, maybe I'd fall entirely into darkness. It also made me feel special to do all of this with my big brother, even though we'd always divided up the responsibilities and did separate routes and helped different neighbors. But it was all falling apart. Falling apart before I'd even left St. Anthony's. Kirkland High must have been the worst place on Earth. It was killing my brother and it would kill me too.

Maybe dreaming of a state championship was all bullshit. Maybe dreaming *at all* was bullshit. You're gonna be just like Poor Rich someday. You're gonna yell and scream and terrorize everyone at home and then let the whole world push you around when you step outside. You're gonna lose all your friends and brothers and sisters. All your chances to fall in love. You're gonna lose God. He's already slipping through your hands. If you lose Him, Mom will never talk to you again. The nuns will hate you. Sister Rose won't protect you from up in Heaven. Sister Adele will take back her journal and tell you you're writing for the Devil now, not God. Everything is wrong. Just watch the snow fall. Just enjoy the silence. This is your life, James. Screaming and silence. Light and dark. Don't lose the light. Don't let go.

But if I don't turn around and watch Dan in the shadows, maybe he'll just disappear. If I'm not watching, who will?

Chapter 15

Sister Carol called us into the halls, where we dimmed the lights and sang songs while lighting the Advent candles. She called for a moment of silent reflection, and I gazed at Julia standing across from me, her face lit by firelight. She didn't even look at me anymore. There were no more smiles and glances like that night at Emily's party. She didn't look into my eyes anymore like she had that day she came to my house to play basketball. Something about her was different. It was bigger than this school. She was moving on. She'd been light-years ahead of us for so long; maybe now she was finally realizing it. Realizing that guys like me and Tim Lamonz would never satisfy her. She needed something bigger. More exciting. Older. Most sophisticated. And she deserved all of that. I didn't want to stop her. I just wished I could have been all those things. Wished I could have been what she needed. Wished I could have understood what caused her pain and helped her heal. I think she was falling away from God as well, and seeing this happen to her made me realize how serious this change was in me too.

Julia, I know you don't care about me anymore. Julia, I know we've had our differences. I know you probably think I'm a loser, and you have so many more options. But, Julia, please know, even after all of this—after all the pain you've caused me—I still love you. I don't hate you. I could never hate you. Please, I know someday you'll be married to another guy. I know you'll make him happier than any man has ever been. But, please, look at me now. Look at me while this fire is still lit. Look at me before it goes out and the hall goes dark again. Please, just look at me. Please, just give me one moment to feel happy. To feel that hope is still possible. You're the only one here who can save me.

Sister Carol led us in singing "Silent Night." Usually, Miss Amalia would lead us in song, but the school had had to end all Music classes. I heard Monsignor saying to Father Mike before Mass one day that the school was "going under." I didn't know what that meant exactly, but secretaries and teachers were starting to disappear. The nuns were all getting older, and the school couldn't afford to pay new teachers to replace them. They had ended the after-school program, and I heard rumors that they were going to have to sell the convent. It seemed the whole world was coming to an end. Just like the Smashing Pumpkins' song, everything was *right now*. "Today." *Tonight.* There was no past or future. All we had was now. Our only hope was this moment. All we had was this firelight, hopping around and doing its best to stay alive in a cold, damp, dark room. I needed a miracle. A Christmas miracle, but even that was impossible. As much as I wanted to believe—*needed* to believe—I'd waited up on Christmas Eve the year before, then snuck downstairs to see Mom putting presents under the tree while Dad snored on the couch. I didn't make a noise—just slowly walked back upstairs, dragging my left hand on the rail. I was the only one left of my friends who'd believed in Santa, and I couldn't live that lie anymore. I wanted to wait up to do the same with God, but that would never happen. I was ready now to face it. Ready to realize that the whole world my parents and grandma and aunts and uncles and teachers and priests and nuns had built was all a lie. The only thing real was that fire. The only thing I could touch was Julia's hand. And they'd both be gone soon.

It was already dark when I left school that afternoon. Mom and Dad had to drive Dan to a game in Springville, so I walked home. It had snowed hard that day, and I was surprised the game hadn't been canceled. After watching that first game, I didn't want to see any others. I trudged through the snow, and even though I was sad to see that the blue box in front of my house was gone, I was relieved I wouldn't have to go back out to deliver papers. The rest of the family was at Dan's game, so I had the house to myself. I drank eggnog and blasted my favorite Christmas tunes—Nat King Cole's version of "The Christmas Song" being my number one—but I couldn't feel it. I grabbed the boxes of Christmas decorations from the basement and started taping cards and tinsel and holly to the walls, molding, doorframes, ceiling. I covered almost every inch of the living room, then moved on to the dining room. When that was done, I did the kitchen and back room.

When my family came back, I was sobbing on the couch and covered in holly. Dad started bitching about how I'd ruined his new paint job, but Mom said it looked nice. Neither thought to call a doctor. Instead, they went on and on about Dan's pass. "You just dove, and with one hand tossed it behind your back, and that Luke just put it right in. You know, he's really good. You guys should play together sometime. Bring him by the house . . ." Apparently, Dan got some playing time and helped the team pull off a tight win. From what my parents were saying, Luke was the next coming of Michael Jordan. "That guy just does *everything*. He's like a man playing with boys. Who knew he was this good?" Me. Dan. About every motherfucker at Hammond. Even kids out in the suburbs. Anyone with their eyes open. Dan and I could have told them that years ago if they'd ever even thought to talk with us about something other than TV or what we wanted for dinner. Either way, I was glad to hear Dan finally getting some well-earned credit. Maybe Coach Flemming would realize how good Dan was and start him.

We went to Aunt Sadie's for Christmas Eve again that year. Uncle Johnny wasn't there. Mom said it was because he'd gotten into an argument with Aunt Sadie over money. I didn't know who owed what to whom, but everyone was a little tense. Regardless, they all got shitfaced and we sang songs and watched football and all that. While sitting in the living room with my uncles, I started feeling a tightness in my chest, and suddenly I felt as if the room was shaking. I stood up but got dizzy and fell to the floor. My uncles started laughing and saying things like, "Looks like the little man can't handle his alcohol," and "Hey, give him another shot." But I hadn't had anything to drink. Feeling this way was nothing new for me, but I'd never fainted before. I went upstairs to get away from everyone, but Aunt Sadie started yelling that no one was allowed upstairs, so I went to the closet and hid behind the coats while everyone around me celebrated. I checked my watch: ten thirty.

Holy shit! It's an hour and a half past your bedtime. Remember when you'd panic if you weren't in bed by nine? You need to get home now. NOW! Go find Mommy! Go cry and tell her you need to get to bed. Go listen to your uncles laugh at you and say, "He wants to be sure Santa doesn't skip his house," when they hear you beg Mommy to take you home. Don't even bother asking Poor Rich. He won't listen. Mom's your only shot. But what will you tell her? Tell her you're sick! Tell her your stomach hurts.

I waited until I felt good enough to "feel sick," then shot out of the closet and searched for Mom. She was laughing with her sisters in the kitchen. It'd been so long since I'd seen her smile. I felt guilty bothering her, but I was pouring sweat and needed to act fast. "Mom, I'm sick."

"What's the matter, hon?" Aunt Sadie said.

"My stomach hurts," I said.

"You probably ate too much. Go sit with your uncles in the living room. They're having a great time in there," she said.

"I—uh . . ." I said.

"Go on," she said.

I went back to the closet. My shirt was drenched with sweat, and I couldn't stop shaking, but I calmed down a little when I came up with a new plan. I left the closet and stuffed as much ham, turkey, chocolate, potatoes, and cherry pie down my gullet as possible, then stuck my fingers down my throat, just like Gerry used to do after lunch sometimes to make us laugh, and puked all over the kitchen. Aunt Sadie screamed at me, and my uncles laughed and said, "What a lightweight!" and "Rich, you gotta teach your boy how to handle booze." Poor Rich just grumbled some shit and went back to the downstairs bedroom where he'd been watching TV alone.

Mom drove me home, and I lay in bed, fully aware of how the Evil Thoughts would always have a hold on me. It'd been a while since I'd panicked at a party like that, and I knew this was how my entire life would play out. They gave me only so much peace before taking it all away again. I knew Mom was tired of it as well. She didn't even offer to stay up with me this time. When I was little, she'd sleep on the floor beside me and rub my back and tell me everything would be okay. But now I was on my own. And I deserved it too. She was having fun, and I'd ruined it. I made Dad yell. I made Mom sad. I made my brothers and sisters cry. I should just hold my breath until I die. I saw it in a movie. A guy puts a pillow over another guy's head and he dies. I should put a pillow over my head. I really should.

So I did. And I pressed down hard on it, but after about a minute, I took a deep breath and realized the pillow wasn't doing shit. I could have breathed at any time. I'll need to find something else to do the trick. What about Grandpa's gun? We're going to Grandma's tomorrow! Maybe I could sneak away and shoot myself in the head. But where do you aim it? In a different movie, I saw a guy shoot himself in the chin. But how do I shoot it? I'm sure Poor Rich could show me. He goes on and on about how he could have been a sniper in the service but wanted to work in the kitchen instead. Maybe he could tell me where to aim. Hell, he'd probably pull the trigger—make him smile for once.

I was stuck in a spiral of thought and knew I wouldn't be sleeping anytime soon. But who gives a shit anyway? Santa ain't real. Stay up all night. The presents will be there regardless. Do whatever you want. The presents will be there. There might not be any kids there to open them, but the presents will damned sure be there.

We went to Grandma's the next day. I was feeling a little better and had no intention of finding Grandpa's gun. Even if I wanted to find it, we were out of there so fast, I wouldn't have had time to look. Uncle Tommy told a story about how once, when they were in high school, my dad tried to hit my Uncle Wayne with his car. And not at slow speeds either. Uncle Wayne had pissed him off, so Dad had chased him through a field, trying to run him down, but Uncle Wayne hopped a fence before it was too late. A few of my dad's cousins started giving Dad shit about it, so he told us to get in the car, and we went home. I thought about the day I threw a baseball bat at Dan. Did I throw it or did Dad? Or Grandpa? Or Uncle Tommy?

Was Dan Uncle Wayne? Would he get killed if he went to war? Would I protect him?

No, Dan hadn't hopped a fence like Uncle Wayne. After I'd thrown that bat, Dan had turned around and put me straight on my ass. Even though I was bigger and a lot angrier than Dan, when it came to wrestling or fighting, Dan just quietly and quickly put me down. Always. If we went to war, Dan would be the one protecting *me*, and we'd both come out alive. Not like Dad. Dad couldn't protect a hamburger at Paul McCartney's house. Dan was gonna be okay. Mom too. I didn't need to find Grandpa's gun.

When we got home, I grabbed the shovel and headed for Hammond. Champions didn't take holidays off. Michael Jordan would be dribbling his way to the turkey on Thanksgiving, dodging drunk aunts and uncles. I cleared half the court and started running suicides, but I kept slipping on the ice, so I took jumpers instead. First up close, then farther and farther back until I was draining threes from well beyond range. My skin was split and bleeding between my fingers. It stung to touch the ball, but pain meant progress. Nothing good came without it. Something really good must have been coming for me.

Chapter 16

Spring in Buffalo meant new life. Though the world was always a swampy, brown mess, the leaves began to grow back, and the days got warmer and longer. We were all filled with the hope that something newer and better was coming.

After school one day, I was at the coffee shop when Julia walked in with a Kirkland senior. She looked at him the way she used to look at me and touched his arm and laughed at his jokes, and after, they got in his car and drove away. As much as I was a believer, I also knew when to give up. And when I stopped looking at Julia, I noticed that a lot of other girls were looking at me. And some of them were pretty cute too. Tony used to go on and on about how Betsy Washington was the cutest girl in our grade, and I never noticed until she started talking to me one day at lunch. She invited me to the taco place beside the coffee shop that afternoon, and I said yes.

I told her I'd meet her there after school because I had to speak with Father Mike about my schedule for serving Mass that week. When I left the church, I saw her sitting at a table by the window, facing the street. She was really pretty. I started crossing the street, remembering that was where Sarah had given us that stupid name, the Freaky Deaks. Remembering how, when I heard that name, it made my brain attack. When I looked at Betsy, she was smiling. I stopped walking. Why is she smiling? Is she smiling because the taco is good, or because I'm coming to meet her? Why would she smile for me? Julia had dumped beer on my head. Didn't Betsy know that? I'm sure she heard from everyone else. They were all talking about it. Didn't Betsy know my dad throws wrenches and pipes and other shit at me and goes crazy screaming about every god-damned thing in the book, always saying it's all my fault? Doesn't she know I had to hide in a closet on Christmas Eve because Santa-fucking-Claus was no longer real? I should march right in there, take that gumball machine near her, and smash it on the floor. I should take her taco and slap it against the window and start screaming like a madman. Fuck it. Fuck her. Just leave. Don't even go in there.

My muscles tightened like a motherfucker and my head got dizzy. The thought of sitting there and eating made me panic. It made me think of the garden, now all covered in weeds. I didn't have the energy to plant anything new. I knew Julia had every right to date who she wanted, and I was okay with it, even though it made me sad, but the thought of sitting there with Betsy made me crazy, thinking about how Julia was probably getting fingered by drunk old assholes right then. Assholes who only saw her as a pair of tits and an ass they could rub their dicks all over before tossing her out and finding the next pair. The girl I'd loved for years. Betsy, why do you think you can have who you want? Why did I have to try for a year to get Julia to visit, and you call me over with your finger and I come running? How dare you smile! Don't you know where you are? Haven't you taken a look around you? We'll see if you're still smiling in an hour.

I walked back toward the church and watched her through the window. After twenty minutes, the smile was gone. After forty-five, so was she. I walked home into the war zone and prepared for battle. The old man had punched a hole in the wall because the batteries in the remote had died, and he didn't want to have to get up to get more, and Mom just kept saying, "You act so silly," rather than packing her things, taking the kids, and leaving. No one gets to smile in Buffalo. I don't care how fucking pretty you are.

Miss Amalia opened a Mediterranean restaurant on the corner of my street, and I could see it from my front yard. For as far back as I could remember, every other business that had opened in that building had failed, but I knew Miss Amalia would make hers last. There was just something about her. Something special. I knew she would put everything she had into that restaurant, and it made me feel a little safer knowing a part of St. Anthony's was so close to me.

At first, I went over there just to say hi. She wasn't scary like most teachers, so I wasn't afraid to see her. But after tasting the turkey sub and fries, I was hooked and would go over all the time. Sometimes, you could hear my old man screaming even with the restaurant's doors closed, and Miss Amalia would let me stay as long as I wanted. She had a guitar in the back corner, and she told me I could play it, but I just couldn't. She told me things like, "Trust the art inside of you," but it sounded an awful lot like the "listen to your heart" crap Sister Adele and Mom were always trying to heap on me, so I mostly just tuned it out. You don't play guitar in Buffalo. You shovel snow. You work two jobs and never see your kids. You get really drunk and drive into a snow pile. Uncle Tommy said playing music was for long-haired faggots, even though he loved Kris Kristofferson and Waylon Jennings and would play "Long Haired Country Boy" on his CD player at home. I had short hair and grew up in the city and couldn't take any more of them laughing at me, so the guitar would just have to sit there in the corner.

The place was decorated with urns and candles and fake olive branches and paintings of Italy and Greece. Sitting there made me think about how big the world was—so much bigger than Buffalo, and New York even. Made me think of all the places I could go someday. But the thought of traveling made me feel guilty. There were so many problems here in Buffalo that I needed to solve. Who was I to think I could leave? It was too selfish. So, like with the guitar, I'd look but knew I could never touch. I was gonna die in that house and be buried in the yard beside Mr. Rogers's garage. Still, it was nice getting away for a while. And it was also nice watching Miss Amalia bend over to grab napkins off the floor or to put more water bottles in the fridge. Seeing her gave me a feeling a little like the one Julia gave me. I wished I was a little older. Miss Amalia wasn't like the girls I went to school with. If Miss Amalia were to smile while thinking about me, I'd have probably believed her. She had a way of making me feel special and making me believe there was more out there for me.

I thought about asking her if I could work there, but after quitting the paper route, I wanted more free time to practice at Hammond. I also started going with Silas to lift weights at the YMCA by his house. He'd found a workout program called Air Alert that promised to increase our vertical jumps, and we completed the whole thing. I actually added a few inches and was able to grab rim but not dunk. Silas could dunk a soccer ball but couldn't buff a basketball. We were gonna get it, though. That was our goal. To dunk by the end of high school.

We also did some powerlifting. We were both good on the bench, and I maxed out around one sixty. Silas got up to one ninety. One of the few good traits I'd gotten from Dad's side was strength. Yeah, it came with blinding rage, but my dad and uncles and grandpa were big motherfuckers. I didn't get their Hells Angels/bouncer size—thankfully—but I got some of their strength, and it was great. I loved working out. Sometimes I'd go for hours after school. I'd start by running on the treadmill for an hour, then do upper body for two hours, and legs for an hour. The harder I worked out, the less the thoughts attacked me. When I ran, I felt good. When I lifted weights, I lifted the worry along with them. Even so, something never felt quite right about lifting. My muscles were always tight, and I'd feel tension and burning in places that I shouldn't have. When benching, I'd feel an intense strain in my left hip, almost near my butt, and also on the left side of my neck and on the right side of my back. My left side was getting much bigger than my right, and I noticed that this was the side I always turned on while shooting jumpers, almost as if it was a hinge on a door. When I lay down, it seemed all of my weight was on my left side. In fact, my right side didn't even touch the ground, and you could slide a copy of *The Catcher in the Rye* under my right shoulder, and I'd never touch it.

I tried not to think about all this—all the weird aches and pains, and the dizziness I'd sometimes feel when lifting—and just kept going. I saw the girls at school looking at me sometimes and heard what they'd say about my arms and stomach, and that was enough to deal with the pain.

But most of all, I lifted because I wanted to be strong enough to take on any team in the state junior year. Some of those guys in high school looked like grown men, and I couldn't let them push me around. I knew one day there'd be some crucial play—maybe a fight for a rebound or loose ball—and all the work I'd put in over all these years would help me come away with it and put in a game-winning layup or jumper. Champions were made in those split seconds, and I never wanted to be one of those guys who looked back, cursing himself for not giving it his all.

Silas was a great lifting partner because he was as dedicated as I was. We pushed each other and made sure we'd lift even if we were tired or sick. We got pretty big that spring and summer and seeing that something I was doing had actual results—that I wasn't just throwing endless, desperate, unanswered prayers into a dark void—made me want to do it even more.

I think, also, in some way, I was preparing myself for Kirkland High that fall. I wasn't gonna let that place shut me up like it did to Dan. If it pushed me, I would push back. If it spat in my face, I was gonna knock its bitch-ass out.

The summer before I started at Kirkland High was probably the height of Hammond Park. There were a lot of new faces on that court, but the regulars were still there. Kids were always moving back from the Bronx or DC or wherever, and they'd challenge us, calling Buffalo a shit city and saying "Do you know where I'm from?" and some of them put up a good game, but we'd take 'em all down. Luke was still the king, but there were a lot of great players, one being a dude everyone called Ox. Ox was the biggest motherfucker who ever stepped on that court. Probably six foot eight and pushing three hundred and forty pounds. Ox tossed D. Pow around like a doll, but he had a soft touch, and he was automatic with a pretty hook shot that no one could stop. The only way to slow him down was to Hack-a-Shaq his ass each time he shot. One time I tried to block one of his layups, and even though I got my hand on the ball, he was so strong, he finished as if I wasn't even there. I twisted my wrist pretty badly and had to sit the next few weeks out. We didn't have health insurance, so Dad gave me an ACE Bandage, and I kept it wrapped until the pain went away and I could lift and hoop again. Ox was much older, so there was no chance of getting him to play with us at Kirkland High. Still, we imagined how great it would be to have him on our team. We came up with a ranking system and determined that Luke, Ox, Silas, me, and a dude named Alfonso but who we called Tiny, were First Team Hammond Offensive players, and Luke, Dan, Silas, Ox, and D. Pow were First Team Hammond Defensive players. I made second team on D, and Dan made second team on offense. We held an all-star game near the end of the summer, which started as a joke, but actually turned into something serious, and Luke dominated. By now he was able to dunk, and he started buffin' on everybody, even Ox. Dude had serious ups, and those combined with his long-ass arms made him able to do the sickest dunks. No one else was even close.

After playing together for so long, we knew how to maximize each other's talents. On D, Dan and I would guard our men tight on the wings so the other point guard wouldn't be able to pass, allowing Luke to put the pressure on and strip the ball. If Dan or I was covering a man with weak handle, sometimes we'd let 'em cross us, then back-tip the ball right into Silas or T. Pow's hands, and by then we'd already be on the other side of the court for a long pass and an easy layup. On offense, the Powells set great picks, and Dan and I would run from wing to wing, Reggie Miller-style, running our men straight into the Powells' elbows and shoulders. Luke would back up to give us space, then hit us with passes, and we'd turn and shoot in stride, knocking down jumpers from all over—I preferred the corner and Dan the wing. When we got hot, no one could stop us—the rim just kept getting bigger and bigger until I felt as if I could even drop-kick the ball in. If the defenders started double-teaming us, we'd kick it back up to Luke, and he'd drive and hit T. Pow or Silas with pretty passes as they cut backdoor.

Silas was quick and strong and always found a way to score. He was probably the most creative guy on the team when he had the ball in his hands. He could pass, hit mid-range jumpers, and outwork anyone in the post, using Hakeem the Dream-style ball fakes and footwork. The Powells got rebounds and steals and had great vision in the paint, even when it was clogged. Luke wasn't a big scorer, but he could put up big numbers if needed. Mostly he made it so that the rest of us could score. Dan, Silas, and I usually put up the biggest numbers, while Luke worked the ball around and found who was hot that game. He could jump out of the gym and out-rebound guys a head taller, and his passing was surgical—probably among the best in the city. But what he did best was play defense. When he'd slap the blacktop and spread his arms, you knew you were in trouble. D was all about heart, instinct, and conditioning, and dude was Dennis Rodman. He'd run up and down the court all day, then go lift and hit the treadmill after. He smoked hella weed and drank almost every night, but it never slowed him down. Quite simply, he wanted it more than anyone. On offense, he could hit mid- and long-range jumpers and put in layups over just about anyone. He'd drive the lane, and if he didn't have a shot, he'd kick it out to me or Dan on the wing or in the corner, and we'd sink twenty-footers. If we missed, he or Silas or D. Pow would get the offensive board and put in a tough layup or hook shot. We were good. We were fucking good. So often, kids don't realize they were a part of something special until years later, when that thing has long passed them by, but we knew it. In that moment, that summer, we knew we were badass, and we were coming for everything you had. We didn't always play on the same team, but when we did, that was the best squad in the city, and we'd stay on the court all day.

That summer was my favorite time to be a Hammond All-Star. I'd get up at six some mornings and hit the Y to run and lift until lunch, then I'd head to Hammond and hoop until dinner. Even if I was starving, I never wanted to leave. The second you walked away, you always missed the biggest fight of the summer or the best game of the year or your crush was there and now was the time to take off your shirt and school all the others fuckers on that court, but you were at home eating Sahlen's hot dogs and drinking Aunt Rosie's loganberry, and she had already walked off with another player before you got back. Usually we'd stay for Afterhours until late in the night, and then I'd get up and do it all again the next day, never slowing down. Never taking a break. Hammond was happening *right now*, and I needed to be there for every minute of it.

People knew me. When picking teams, I was always one of the top picks. I was usually a high scorer and made some plays over the years that people still talked about. Dan too. They knew who he was. They cheered for him and screamed, "Shoot it, Harvey!" They knew he had the best jumper out there and it was like poetry watching that ball go right through the hoop time and time again. In those moments, I truly believed fuckers when they'd say someday they'd see me and Dan playing in the NBA. There was still a chance. There was always a chance. I was always coming home with scraped knees and elbows, black eyes, split lips, chipped teeth, pulled muscles, and sunburned skin. But the pain felt good. I loved sitting on the couch at night and feeling the deep aches and pains all over my body. Loved knowing I was getting the best out of my body. The best out of my mind and instincts. The pain meant I was alive and using every ounce of my ability to become a champion someday.

During the last week of the summer, we were dicking around between games at Hammond when Luke came sprinting through the park. He shouted, "SCATTER, HE'S GOT A KNIFE!" as he ran past the court and continued on down the street. Just then, Gus rounded the corner, swinging a nine-inch kitchen knife. As he ran toward the court, everyone scattered. Most took off running, but a few climbed trees, and one kid even pulled himself up and sat on the rim. I hid in the gazebo, but Gus saw me and came straight for me.

"LUKE TOOK MY JERSEY!" He stabbed the air with the knife.

I held out my hand. "Friend, Gus, friend!"

He kept coming. "LUKE TOOK MY JERSEY!"

"I-I'll help you get it back. Just put the knife down." I started backing away slowly, but the sides of the gazebo were pretty high, and if I tried to hop them, Gus would have a clear shot at my back. Gus lunged at me, trying to stab my chest, but I shifted out of the way, pushed him in the back, and ran like hell out of there. Two cop cars tore around the corner, and Gus ran to the bushes and threw the knife into them, but the cops grabbed him and put him in the back of their car, then asked me where he threw the knife. I showed them the general area, but they couldn't find it. I felt so stupid for having hidden. Why hadn't I run? It was almost as if I knew I wasn't allowed to. Almost as if a lifetime of abuse had taught me it was best to just take the knife inside of me, then bleed out and die. It made me feel as though Gus *should* find me.

I watched Gus pound on the back window and point at me as the cops drove him away, and I didn't even realize I'd dropped to my knees in the middle of the street until a driver honked at me. Silas helped me to my feet.

"C'mon, man, let's hoop."

Chapter 17

Dan, Steven, and I locked our bikes on the rack outside of Kirkland High and walked toward the gorgeous three-story brick building. The grounds were twice the size of St. Anthony's, but instead of blacktop, Kirkland was surrounded by grass. Even before school, kids were playing guitar, tossing a football or Frisbee, sitting under trees and talking. A young male teacher stood on a chair under the flagpole, reciting poetry as we passed. This was the first time in my life I'd walked into school without Sister Carol or one of the other nuns there to greet me. I liked the poetry thing, though.

Third period, I had math. Over the summer, I'd scored high enough on an entry test that they skipped me to second-year math, and I sat in the far front corner by the windows. The classroom was packed—maybe ten more kids than in the typical St. Anthony's class—and it was much crazier. At St. Anthony's, if you even took your eyes off Sister Verona, she'd make you write a five-hundred-word essay about how all disrespectful children go to Hell, but here, kids talked to one another freely, swearing and throwing shit and telling off the teachers. Something about that terrified me, but also intrigued me. I felt less shame about being the "bad kid," and it didn't seem that God was standing over us watching every horrible thing I did. And it was nice to be able to go to math class and actually learn about math, and go to science class and really learn about science, and not have every class turn into a fire-and-brimstone lecture on the irrefutable evil of boobs, which were hanging out of gorgeous girls' shirts everywhere.

Fate had brought the Hammond Crew together—in that math class, at least. Joey sat in the back corner behind Dan. On that first day, Joey slapped the kid beside him and said, "Give me a fucking pencil." The kid didn't have one, so Joey leaned forward and asked Dan, "Yo, Harvey, can I get a pencil?" Dan nodded and gave him one. Steven had failed the year before, so he was in that class too, but he sat in the other front corner, eagerly taking notes. When the teacher turned around to write something on the board, Joey pulled off his shoe and threw it at the back of Steven's head. Steven didn't even turn around. He just gave this look as if he wanted to set the world on fire but the only match he had wouldn't light, and after taking a deep breath, he continued with his notes. The teacher must have seen it happen, though, because he shook his head and muttered, "Another year of this shit."

They didn't have scheduled bathroom breaks here, so you just had to go between classes. After math, I went to the men's room on the second floor, but I couldn't relax enough to pee because two guys were arguing in one of the stalls. One of them made a loud sniffing noise, and then they walked out. I should have known better than to look at them, because the one guy pushed me into the urinal.

"The fuck're you lookin' at, shithead?" he said.

"N-nothing," I said. I didn't feel any wetness on my shirt, but I knew I'd be checking for piss stains the moment they left, which they did soon enough.

Leaving the bathroom, I almost walked right into Shane Walsh. He was with Jacob Mancuso and a few other pricks I recognized from the JV team, and they surrounded me. Shane had grown a few inches since I'd last seen him and was now taller than I was, but he was still a scrawny prick who only acted tough when flanked by friends.

"Fuck you, Potato McWhiskey," I said.

"Look, I know starting at a new school can be tough, so we'll take good care of you. You still ride your shitty girl's bike home, right?" Shane said.

I probably gave him the same look as Steven gave after getting rocked by Joey's shoe. Shane motioned as if to hit me, but he didn't, and they took off just as Luke Harrison walked by in the other direction. I didn't want him to see me like that, but it seemed as if he did anyway. Even with all the chaos in those halls, Luke saw everything—every angle, every open player, every dead end and inch-wide opening.

At lunch, one of the guys from my Honors World History class invited me to sit with him, but I told him I already had a spot with the Hammond Crew. I invited him to sit with us, but he took one look at that chaos and declined. Silas, Dan, Steven, and I sat with a few other guys at one table, and Joey, the Powells, Luke, and some others sat at another table pushed against ours. T. Pow burned his dick when he stuck it in his mashed potatoes, and the other guys couldn't stop laughing. "Yo, dawg, I think I got third-degree burns an' shit. This ain't funny." But they kept laughing and slapping him in the dick.

"This shit's about to get serious, man," Silas said.

"Yeah, but it isn't varsity," I said.

"We could be the number one JV team in the city," Silas said. "That's nothin' to look down on."

"You think we'll do all right with those other pricks like Shane and them on the team?" I asked.

"We'll be straight," Silas said. "Shane and Mancuso can play, and that new kid Travis Tailor's got game."

"It'd be better with just us," I said.

"Yeah, we'd dominate," Steven said.

"You're too old for JV, Stevie," Silas said. "You gonna try out for varsity this year?"

"Does Jerry Garcia shred the guitar?" Steven said.

"You're a wild dude, Stevie," Silas said.

Tony Da Luca walked by. I said hi, but he just kept walking as if he didn't even know me. We hadn't spoken much in the last few months, and he'd already made a lot of new friends at Kirkland. Ray had moved to Florida, and we hadn't spoken since June. Julia was going to Lakeside Academy, a private school downtown, and all the guys called the girls there the Lakeside Skanks. I hated that name, because Julia wasn't a skank. Yes, she drank and smoked cigarettes and dated older guys, but she was still a good person. She wasn't a skank or a slut, like the guys said. She was my beautiful Julia. I hadn't spoken with her either, and other than the few times she'd come by Hammond that summer to see Joey, whom she'd been dating, I hadn't seen her. It was so weird to be in school without her. We'd been together since kindergarten. At St. Anthony's, they broke up classes into As and Bs when we went to Music and Art and other classes, and for some miraculous reason, every year, I had always been with her. I didn't like that she was at another school. It made my stomach hurt to think I wouldn't see her over the next four years and, after that, would probably never see her again.

Emily and Sarah went to Kirkland, but they did the same thing as Tony when I tried to say hi. We'd all been together for years, and it was as if everything had vanished over that summer. Kirkland High made us all forget who we used to be. Emily wore so much makeup I hardly recognized her, and Sarah dyed her hair black and wore Bad Religion and Black Flag shirts, though she'd never once mentioned liking punk before. In fact, as far as I knew, her favorite singer was Mariah Carey, and she'd had Lisa Frank stickers all over her middle school locker. Seeing them dressed up like that made me realize that maybe I needed an identity too. All my life I'd been wearing uniforms and buzzing my hair and had no idea which group I actually belonged to. The majority of my clothes came from my older cousins, and I mostly wore shorts and T-shirts in the summer and jeans and sweatshirts in the winter, sometimes with Bills or Sabres or Mickey Mouse designs on them. But no one here was wearing anything with Mickey on it. Most of them wore cargo khakis and polo shirts and tight long-sleeved shirts with words like AMERICAN EAGLE and AÉROPOSTALE written on them.

Joey dumped some milk down T. Pow's pants, then slapped him in the face while the other guys laughed. It was good to see that some things never changed.

Dan, Steven, and I rode our bikes home that afternoon. We passed St. Anthony's on the way. Mom had probably already picked up Jeremy and the girls before work that afternoon. I was hoping I'd see Sister Adele or Sister Carol walking through the parking lot, but they weren't there. Maybe it was better they didn't see me now. Over the summer, I'd read a book about the Crusades for my world history course, and after reading about the sale of indulgences, I knew I'd never be able to see God the same. I told Mom about it one Sunday morning when I refused to go to church, and I'd never seen her so angry in my life. She'd screamed every terrible thing at me, calling me an animal, saying I'd burn in Hell, saying God was watching, but she didn't realize she was only making it worse. Hearing someone I loved and respected calling me such terrible things, further driving a wedge between me and the Lord, made me realize how dogmatic and straight-up loony religion was. I lost God that morning. In a big way, I also lost my mother. Poor Rich didn't give a shit. He threw a temper tantrum because his Eggo waffle had burned in the toaster, and he refused to go to church too. Mom didn't talk to me the rest of the day. She was so mean. She talked to Dad plenty, though. But I was worse. "A cancer in this house." The reason everyone was so upset all the time. The reason Baby Jesus cried.

But it didn't matter if I lost my family or friends or God; it was impossible to un-know what I knew.

I felt such shame riding by St. Anthony's—as if I was naked in church. But I couldn't stop riding by. Even if it changed like Emily and Tony and Sarah, it would always be a part of me. How could you spend so much time with someone, and then forget all about them? How could you have so many experiences somewhere, and yet pretend like they weren't a part of you? I missed St. Anthony's and all my friends, but riding by there, I realized it was best not to go back. Best to keep riding forward. It was done, gone. And if I stayed holding onto it, I'd be gone too. Even more gone than I already was. Hell was a certainty for me now. Like the Pink Floyd song, all I had was what was in my hands—what I could touch. And turning my back on God and my friends and St. Anthony's meant I could touch something new. And the music—Floyd, Pearl Jam, Bob Marley—all felt like a map to a better place. Away from the suffering and sacrifice and toward a place of acceptance and peace. I didn't know what I was doing—just following my heart, like Sister Adele had told me. But how could something she told me take me away from her?

Please, Sister Adele, don't be mad at me. Don't hate me. I'm still the same Jimmy. I'll still help you after school, lock the windows, put the books away, clean the closet. But I can't listen to your crap about God anymore. It's not for me. Please accept me as I am. I can't keep living that way. It was killing me. I can't keep thinking the Evil Thoughts. I need to leave them behind with you. Please, guard them. Don't let them invade some other kid's head. They're so powerful, they could kill a weaker person. I was lucky to be strong. To be able to outrun and out-jump them long enough to get by. I was born with a powerful body, one of the few gifts from my father's side. I could hold so much pressure inside of me without bursting at the seams. But another kid would blow the moment those thoughts entered their brain. They'd fuck up Jeremy, I know it. Please, I know you're strong too. Keep the thoughts in a jar and lock them away in the convent. I'm feeling better now. I'm ready to move on. I think I could actually like Kirkland High. The teachers are really smart, even though they don't seem to know shit about God. Please don't be mad at me for being happy to be in a school without Him. You didn't waste your time with me. I still want to be good. I still want to help people. I'll just have to do it in a different way than I once thought.

By the time we got home, I realized Dan hadn't said anything to me on that ride back. Nor had we talked at lunch. It was as if he was there but wasn't. Almost as if he had this invisible barrier around him no one could enter. And I didn't even think to try.

He spoke to Steven, though, and Silas too. Steven had spent a lot of time at our house that summer. He and Dan were becoming good friends. They talked the way Dan and I used to, and it made me realize how much I missed him. We hadn't been friends since he'd left St. Anthony's, and it didn't seem we'd ever be friends again. He probably still blamed me for all the problems in our house. Blamed me for wanting more than Mom and Dad could give. For wanting to go to the places in the pictures on the walls of Miss Amalia's restaurant. For getting most of the attention on the basketball court and in math class and from girls. I knew he liked Melanie Diaz, so when she asked me out, I told her no. She had such big tits too. I would have loved to have felt her up like everyone said Joey had. But it didn't matter what I did or didn't do—Dan still hated me. And I was starting to hate him for it. For always hanging his head and not fighting back. For letting Dad and some of the other guys at school push him around. You gotta push back, Dan. You used to fight back. You used to walk up to the Gates of Hell with me cowering in your shadow. What happened to you? Like Dad says, be a fucking man! What Would John Wayne Do?

I cut Mrs. Prendergast's lawn, swept the driveway, cleaned her gutters, and took out her trash. Afterward, I got some hummus and pita at Miss Amalia's place, where I'd spent a ton of time that summer, and then I went to my bedroom to do homework. At St. Anthony's, I'd never had homework, unless I got in trouble and had to write twenty-five Our Fathers and twenty-five Hail Marys. I could BS my way through most assignments and finish them in school. But Kirkland was different. The work was hard, and I had about three hours of homework that night. I was in all honors classes except for math, and I could already tell I wasn't the smartest kid in my grade. Some kids knew so much about the Arab–Israeli conflict or the economy of China, while I knew how to talk Sister Adele out of giving us a Religion test.

Even with all the homework, I made time to work out after school. Silas and I would go to the Kirkland weight room, which was much better than the shitty YMCA gym, and spend hours there. The machines at the Y were ancient and there were always super-old guys walking around naked with their balls swinging around, sagging down to their knees. But the Kirkland gym was great and had a Supercat leg machine and a Ground Based Jammer, which were my favorite machines. One of the gym teachers, Mr. Mitchell, would spend hours in the weight room after school, teaching all of us how to work out properly, and he took a special interest in me and Silas after we told him we were training to win a state championship junior year. He just said, "Well, that's fuckin' great. I wish the other guys in here had half the heart you two have. We're gonna get you that god-damned trophy." He gave us personalized exercises, and we saw results faster than ever before. Silas got huge, but no matter how big I got, when I looked in the mirror, I always felt so small. The girls would give us looks and sometimes invite us to hang out, but this would always go right over my head. After, Silas would say shit like, "Dude, can't you see she wants to slob your knob?" The thing was, I probably did see, but there was still so much of God inside of me that I couldn't shake out, no matter how many Masses I'd missed or how many times I screamed, "God-damn it!" just like Dad did, and I knew He was against fornication in any form, so I pretended not to see. But maybe it wasn't really God inside of me, but the Evil Thoughts disguised as God. Even though I had stopped believing, I still prayed each night, only instead of talking to God, I was talking to *something*, begging it to save me the way I'd begged God when I was a kid. Maybe it was the Evil. Maybe it was still with me. Maybe I'd flip out in science class and start laughing like a maniac and talking to myself, and all the kids here would do much worse to me than Ray, Tony, and Julia ever did. Gotta stop thinking about it. Just work out. Play basketball. Do your homework. Cut the lawn. Moving makes you feel better. Keep moving forward, Jimmy. It's the only way. Even if the end of the road is, and always will be, Hell.

Chapter 18

My calves and thighs burned. Coach Flemming blew the whistle, and we took off again. One minute to run seventeen widths of the court, which might sound easy, but try it sometime. This was our fifth seventeen in a row. Only me, Luke, and Dan had finished the first on time, so we all had to run another. But no one finished that one in under a minute, us included, so we all had to keep going, and after that, we were all too shot to finish on time.

"We're not going to stop until at least five of you finish in under a minute," Coach said from the sideline. "And the next time, you'll be shuffling, not running."

He was trying to weed out the weak and fickle. The first two days of the five-day JV tryouts had been entirely running. No one had even touched a ball. He put garbage cans on the sidelines so kids could puke, and a few did.

Dan almost finished on time, but no one else was even close, so we had to line up again and this time shuffle instead of run. "We're gonna keep doing this until five of you finish on time." But he couldn't keep up much more of this, because if we couldn't do it sprinting, there was no way any of us would finish in under a minute shuffling.

Again Dan led the pack, and when the last person crossed the line, Coach said, "Okay, get some water."

I put my hands on my head and took huge breaths. Two days a week, Silas and I had been running suicides on the football field after lifting, but even so, my whole body felt as if it was on fire. About fifty kids had shown up the day before, but that number was now down to thirty, and two more took off during that water break. The Powells were there, as was Silas, and so were Shane and his jerkoff buddies, who mostly finished in the middle or last during those drills. Shane was a pretty athletic kid and could have probably finished at least one seventeen on time, but he clearly didn't give a shit, and it showed.

When we went back in, Coach had us run suicides until it was time to go home.

The next day, twenty-five kids showed up. Coach had us do zigzag drills, where one person dribbles in a zigzag down the court while another defends. Dan guarded Shane and kept stripping him all the way down the court as Shane bitched, "C'mon, Lombardi, you're taking this shit way too seriously."

Afterward, we did a shooting drill, where one person in the paint passes to another person on the wing, then runs up to play defense as the player shoots the ball. I sank all of my shots and stripped a kid while I was playing defense.

We did a five-on-five scrimmage after the shooting drill, and Dan, Luke, and I played on a team against Shane, Silas, and the Powells. D. Pow dominated the paint, and Shane hit a few threes, but we killed 'em. I got hot and couldn't miss, and Coach kept cheering each time I sank another three. At

Hammond, Dan would have shot up a storm, but here he always passed the ball, even when he was open. He dished it to me a few times when he had open threes, and I sank 'em instead. I wasn't sure why he wouldn't shoot here, but it had been the same thing last year when he'd gotten into JV games. He'd pass before shooting almost every time. Maybe it was because he felt comfortable at Hammond. It was our place to shine. But here in the *real* world, there were rules and expectations. Hammond was ours, but everywhere else was *theirs*.

At the end of the week, Coach posted a list on the gym door, and we all ran down after school to check it out. As I rounded the corner, D. Pow threw a garbage can across the room and T. Pow karate-kicked a vending machine. "Yo, this whole fuckin' school's a joke! I got mad skills!" How Coach could cut those two was beyond me. Yeah, they needed discipline, but how the fuck were they gonna get it if no adults in their lives had ever shown them what it was? They outworked so many of the Abercrombie bitches who had made the team that it was ridiculous. Luke, Silas, Dan, and I all made it, but we weren't whole without the Powells. Mancuso played center like a statue. He was the kind of cat who'd stop playing just so he could flex for some girls in the crowd. The type of guy who'd miss a game because he had a hair appointment—and definitely not with Gino the Barber.

When we got home, Dad was waiting for us by the door. "Congratulations, boys!" He handed us each a box of Nikes. Not cheap ones, either.

"How'd you know we made it?" I asked.

"How could you not?" Dad said. "You guys are terrific. You just do it like . . ." He started hopping around like a lunatic, throwing his arms all over the place and almost falling over. I had no idea where our athletic talent came from. With a sledgehammer in his hands, dude was like Beethoven, but he could barely function in the world outside of the construction site.

Mom walked over in her diner gear. "We're so proud of you." She gave us each a hug.

"You better bring home that championship now," Dad said.

"My old sneakers are still good," Dan said.

"Yeah, this is too much," I said. "You never buy anything for yourselves."

"You boys earned them," Mom said.

Steven came over that night and sat with the old man, and together they watched old John Wayne war movies. Sometime in that last year or so, those two had become best buddies. I didn't know quite how it all worked out, but Dad certainly yelled a lot less now, and never when Steven was around. Steven was thrilled to help Dad hang drywall or put new windows in the kitchen, and the two would joke around and laugh as they worked. It was incredible. Maybe Dad just wanted someone to *want* to work with him? I almost wished Steven would move in. He took a lot of the heat off of me. When the old man screamed, everyone always blamed me. Now, with Steven there to calm the old man down, I could finally get some peace too. I was so sick of them all calling me a jerk and an asshole and selfish. Them calling me an asshole made me want to *be* an asshole. No matter what good thing I did, I was always the asshole, and I think this hurt me more than I had realized.

Steven tried out for the varsity team that year but heard

the same thing he had the two previous years.

"You might as well give up!" Dad said to the TV.

"Yeah, nobody bests the Duke," Steven said.

"I tell ya, I never shoulda left the service," Dad said. "It was the best time of my life. I got to see the world, work with my hands, booze it up with all sorts of wild animals. I've been telling this guy for years he should join the Marines. He's got the brains for it. The military'd do wonders for you boys. Straighten ya right up and give you purpose."

"I don't need anybody else's purpose," I said.

"Don't be ungrateful, Horace," Steven said. "What the hell else you got goin' for you?"

I pointed to my new sneakers, which I was wearing to break in. "A lot."

"Hey, whaddya say we get back to work, Steven?" Dad said.

"Let's go," Steven said. They got up and went to the basement.

I went up to my room, and when I flipped on the light, I saw Dan sitting on his bed and staring at the floor again. He had his sneakers out of the box and sitting on his lap.

"Whoa, you feelin' all right?" I asked.

"Headache," he said.

I backed out of the room and headed to Hammond. By the time I got there, the sun had already set, so I played one game and went to the gazebo with Silas for Afterhours. It'd been a warm October, but the nights were getting cold again.

"He said he's trying out again next year?" Silas said about Steven.

"Yeah, he was just telling my dad about it. Those two are best friends now."

"I'm not surprised," Silas said. "Damn, that kid doesn't give up, does he?"

"Nope."

"Good for him. This year, we're gonna be I-double-L. We got Luke pushin' point, you and Dan at two guard, me in the paint—"

"I don't know. Some of those guys weren't lookin' so hot. And Shane shoots the ball every time he touches it. He's like a black hole."

"Naw, they're all right. It's not gonna be easy, but we'll win the championship."

"We should run some drills this weekend to be ready for practice next week," I said.

"I, uh, I'm gonna be at my cuz's this weekend."

"Your cuz on the East Side?"

"The one and only Grape Street."

"Damn, all right. Either way, we'll be fine. I just wanna trim Shane's bitch-ass so bad that Coach won't play him. Dan didn't get shit for playing time last year, so I need to destroy Shane."

"Take it easy, Ho-dingies, everything's gonna work out fine. Just watch."

"Doesn't feel fine."

"Yo, relax, man. Damn I'm just trying to stay positive here, all right?"

"Yeah, I'm cool."

When I got home, Dan was still on the bed holding his sneakers, while Steven and Dad laughed together in the living room.

I called Shane a piece of shit during practice because he shot a contested fadeaway three-pointer from the baseline when Dan was wide open on the wing. When we walked back to the locker room, I knew he'd have something to say to me, but he just kept going, not even looking at me. It was weird. In fact, he hadn't fucked with me since that day outside of the bathroom. I turned around and watched him walk away as I pulled a sock over my foot.

"I know about you and him," Silas said as he grabbed his backpack from the locker next to me.

"What are you talking about?" I said.

"I know what he's been doing to you," Silas said.

"I don't know what you're talk—"

"It's cool, man. Let's just say that word got out, and that fool won't be botherin' you again. You got a lot more friends than you realize." Silas looked at Luke in the back corner. "Shane gives you any more shit, you just let me know."

"O-okay." Similar to when I had watched the cops drive Gus away, I felt a relief hearing those words that made me feel as if maybe life was possible.

"All right, gather around." Coach came in holding a clipboard, and stood in front the chalkboard, and everyone sat in a U facing him. "Okay, we got our first game at Rucker High in a few weeks. I haven't decided yet who'll be starting, but I'll pick from those who've been working hardest in practice."

I nudged Dan sitting beside me, and he gave me a look as if to say, *You saw D. Pow destroy that garbage can when he didn't make the team, right, idiot?*

"Make sure you get a good night's sleep and come ready to practice tomorrow. Let's bring it in."

We brought our hands in the middle and did "Team"

on three. I was having a pretty good day until he mentioned that "good night's sleep" shit. How the fuck do you get a good night's sleep? Doesn't that moron know that the harder you try to sleep, the longer the Devil keeps you awake? Doesn't that fucker know to not say all that shit, otherwise he'll curse me and the rest of the team to a sleep-deprived, panicked, winless season?

Fuck, even in the locker room, surrounded by teammates, I wasn't safe. Even while planning for battle, my thoughts could jump me at any time. Beat my ass down. Steal the new sneakers Mom and Dad bought me. Maybe Sister Adele had taken the thoughts out of the jar. Maybe she'd never put them in. Maybe when she found out I'd turned against God, she got all the nuns together to say a super prayer to make the thoughts even worse. Maybe they were all in church right now, praying for the Devil to take my soul.

Chapter 19

We huddled around Coach in the Rucker High visitors' locker room, and he gave some shitty, pornstache-style pump-up speech about trying our hardest and all that shit, then he announced starters. "Shane at point; James at two guard; Luke, small forward; Travis Tailor, power forward; and Jacob Mancuso, center." I gave Dan a look as if to say, *It should be you, not Shane, pushing the ball*, but he'd already been through a year of that and I don't think he cared anymore. Now he was going to watch his younger brother start for a coach who'd benched him most of the last year. Was I supposed to apologize?

"All right, bring it in." We did "Team" on three, then walked out to the court. The starting fives from both teams stood around the half-court circle. I looked into the stands, and my family was there with Steven, cheering. The ref tossed the ball, and the other center tipped it back to their point guard. Almost instantly, Luke stole the ball from the point guard and took it in for a layup. The other power forward passed it in to the point guard, and Luke stayed on him all the way up the court. After he crossed half court, the point guard passed it to Shane's man on the wing, and he missed a fifteen-footer. Mancuso got the rebound and passed it to Shane. Shane pushed the ball up court, but even though I was wide open for a three on the wing, he tried to dribble between two players and got stripped around the top of the key. The other point guard dribbled up court where he and the other small forward had a two-on-one fast break against Travis. Luke and I sprinted back on D, but the small forward put in a layup before Luke could block it. I passed the ball in to Luke even though Shane was calling for it, and Luke pushed it. We set up on offense, and Luke dished a nice bounce pass to Mancuso in the paint, but he did a weak drop step and got stripped by the other center. The center passed to the point guard, and he took it the length of the court. He went in for a layup, but Luke swatted it out of bounds.

Joey and the Powells went wild in the stands. "Fuck him up, Lukie!"

The other power forward passed the ball in to the point guard and he passed it to the small forward, whom Shane was guarding. The small forward crossed the shit out of Shane, and Shane stopped playing D, so I ran to contest the forward's fifteen-footer, but I was too late. The shot went right in as Shane yelled at the ref about a wet spot on the floor or some other bullshit. I wanted to punch him square in the face. We needed Dan, Silas, and the Powells out here. The other team was dogshit, but we were making them look good. We'd killed teams way better than these clowns at Hammond. Put Steven in the game, and he'd come down with every rebound. He'd hit pretty ten-footers from any angle. T. Pow would drive the lane, pulling all defenders on him, then kick it out to Dan, who'd hit threes all day.

But Shane, Mancuso, and Travis played only for themselves, forcing passes and shots they hoped would make them look good to all the girls in the stands.

At the half, Coach Dumbfuck addressed us in the locker room.

"Okay, we're only down ten, so we're not out of it yet . . ."

It took me the entire first half to figure it out. Shane's parents had paid for a new scoreboard the year before. Mancuso's aunt was Kirkland's athletic director. Travis Tailor's mom worked for the superintendent. That was why Dan had ridden the bench all of last year. This was why neither he nor Silas had yet gotten into that game. Why the Powells and Steven were in the stands watching. I suddenly realized that sometimes pilots flew planes into mountains. That police officers broke the law. Butchers sold spoiled meat. Nurses did drugs. Surgeons made the wrong incisions and their patients paid the ultimate price. Coach Flemming was like all these people, selling us spoiled meat and telling us how great it was. Christ, there was no order in God's world or man's. Where could I go where everything worked as it should? Where could I go and feel okay?

When we went back out to start the second half, Mom and Dad started cheering, "Go Danny! Go Jimmy!" We started with the ball, and Luke drove it up court, ignoring Shane, who was bitching to push point. I set a pick for Luke, and he dribbled to the wing, then drove into the paint. He gave the center a fake, then spun left and put in a fancy layup. My parents and the Hammond Crew in the stands went wild.

The other point guard dribbled up court. Shane's man picked Luke at the top of the key, but Shane didn't call it, and Luke ran straight into it. Shane tried picking up the point guard but got burned badly. The point guard dumped a pass to the center, who got Mancuso to jump after he gave him a fake, then he hit a hook shot. Mancuso hacked him on the way down, and the ref called a foul. That was his third, so Coach put Silas in. Mancuso bitched all the way off the court and continued bitching as he took the seat right next to Coach, begging to go back in. The center missed the free throw, and Silas grabbed the rebound. He passed it ahead to me, and I passed it to Luke who was sprinting to the hoop. He caught it, and in one fluid motion, spun around a defender and went up for a tomahawk jam on the other power forward but finished it with a finger roll instead. Our crowd went nuts.

When the power forward passed it in to the point guard, Silas swiped the ball and put it in for a quick layup. The other coach called time, and we went to the bench.

"C'mon, Coach, put me back in." Mancuso was practically in tears.

"Fine, go back in for Silas," Coach said.

"That's straight bullshit," Silas said to himself as he sat near Dan. Score was thirty-six to thirty, them. Luke put in a few more great layups, attacking the rim, and I hit a few long-range jumpers, but it was useless. Shane shot whenever he had the ball within three-point range, and Travis dribbled off his foot once and got hit square in the face with a pass another time. When the final buzzer sounded, we lost by twenty-four. So much for a championship.

Silas eventually worked his way into the starting lineup, which helped us tremendously, but that didn't solve our problem. Shane continued to shoot anytime he had the ball, and the other two idiots looked like lost kids searching for their parents at the mall. Luke dominated teams, but never seemed to reach his potential. He just couldn't do it alone. I had some big games, but it was impossible to set up on offense when each time you passed the ball to someone, they took a quick shot rather than waiting for the right play to come for the team. We had all the necessary elements on that team to win a championship, but under the leadership of a shithead like Flemming, who would ever know? We finished the season with fourteen wins and seven losses. Some would consider that a successful year, but even if we went twenty-one and zero, it would have still been a failure to me.

After that year, Hammond was never the same. The guys were spending more time getting high and fucking around, and less time trimmin' fools on the court. All the training and lifting and shoveling the court in winter seemed to have been for nothing. I had a champion living inside of me, but he was buried under a Buffalo blizzard, and there was no way I'd ever be able to dig him out. Not with adults keeping charge like Flemming or Shane's dad or the countless other shitheads out there who kept Buffalo a Rust Belt loser town. A place where you drank beer and complained about everyone else "ruining this city" while doing absolutely nothing to improve it. Who see something good—pure—and then find a way to profit from it, destroying everything good about it in the process.

After that year, basketball was never the same for me. I hadn't abandoned it as I'd abandoned God, but in my heart I felt that coming. My only hope was that things would improve on the varsity team with Coach Sterling. He was a great coach, and maybe he'd get the most out of his players. But even he had cut Steven. Steven, who'd outworked everyone in tryouts. Who'd finished first on each suicide, each seventeen. Steven, who'd worn torn jean shorts and Payless sneakers to tryouts, and lived in a small shitty house with his absentee dad. Steven, who'd had no one looking out for him in the world. Nobody nudging Coach and saying, "C'mon, there's a new, solid gold shot clock in it for you." I wanted to have hope but knew already that hope was for other people. Was for Shane and Travis Tailor and Julia and Doug Warsaw. Hope isn't for street trash like you, Jimmy. You made a deal with the Devil years ago, anyway. How'd you think this story was gonna end? Not happily. It ends in tragedy. It ends in death. Don't fool yourself for a second thinking it can happen otherwise.

Chapter 20

"Go Jimmy!" I could hear Mom shouting as I pushed it up court. The Kirkland gym was packed—far more packed than at any of our JV games. But varsity was the real show. Though we'd been playing together at Kirkland for three years, the team had never been able to get it together. Despite our inability to unite, we had enough individual talent on that team to win most games. But without a unified front, there was only so much we could do.

The Powells were in the stands again. They'd tried out again, and again smashed garbage cans outside the gym when Coach posted the list of his twelve picks. Our only hope, Coach Sterling, had retired at the end of the previous season, and Flemming took over varsity, so we were stuck with another two years of that clown. Though I was in eleventh grade, I started at two guard, and we had pretty much the same starting five as we'd had at the end of my freshman year, except Shane and Luke had switched positions, with Shane playing small forward and Luke pushing point. Even after years of playing on the team, something always felt off about my game. When I played at Hammond, I played my best—even with the biggest crowd watching. In fact, the bigger the crowd, the better I played. I fed off their energy. I felt us all working as one. But playing on the school team, it almost felt as if those crowds were against me. I could hear every shitty parent out there screaming for me to pass it to their shitty kid. I could hear every drunk dad telling me to "SHOOT IT!" or "DRIVE TO THE HOOP!" I felt as if I could hear everything every person was saying, and it overwhelmed me. There were several times when I fucked up, almost on purpose—tossed the ball out of bounds or took a stupid shot—and I didn't even know why. I wasn't calling the shots. Something upstairs was. It was short-circuiting. Sacrificing itself for the greater good. I wished we could have played those games at Hammond. I wished all the parents fucked off back to their selfish, ignorant worlds where at most you only ever heard them calling you for dinner or bitching about their sore backs or knees.

"Go, Jimmy, go!"

But still, it was nice hearing Dad yell *for* me and not *at* me. My parents never missed a game. Mom worked out her schedule so she'd see every minute I played and every minute Dan watched from the sidelines, and she and Dad and the rest of the family would follow us all over snowy-ass Western New York, driving that station wagon to Fredonia and Springville and Newfane and Medina. When we'd get home, no matter if we'd won or lost, it was always, "Oh man, and that shot you hit from the corner, Jimmy. Wow, what a move!" and, "Dan, when you stole that ball, the other guy didn't even know what to do, and you just drove it down there and put it in and everybody was going crazy!" Sometimes, if we won, we'd get pizza and wings. Gino the Barber came to a bunch of games, and when I'd go in for my monthly buzz cut, he wouldn't shut up about, "No, I'm serious. I know a guy who knows a guy who works for the Knicks, and—I'm tellin' you—when he finds out about you, they're gonna be beatin' down your door. Hey, feel free to pop in back and fix yourself a drink—on the house, of course."

Luke kept getting better and better, and after four years of playing with shitheads like Shane and Mancuso, he'd learned how to play for himself. At Hammond, Luke was part of a unified group that worked together to dismantle teams. But at Kirkland, it was every man for himself. I'd had to learn the same. I'd take shots I'd never take at Hammond. Silas was Silas no matter the situation. He was always solid and could play with just about anybody. I don't know how he did it, but at almost every game, he knew half the other team, and half the people in the stands. We started calling him Phone Book, and then just Phone, because he knew just about everyone's number. He was never pissed at anyone, even when people fucked with him. He always had a quick comeback and a smile, and he'd win over even the biggest of pricks in an instant. It was an incredible talent—maybe even more so than his talent for basketball. One thing I noticed about him was that, whoever he talked to, he made them the center of the world. He'd build the person up, hitting them with compliments and highlighting their strengths. It wasn't that he was lying to them or humoring them. It was as if he could see the best in everyone and knew how to bring it out. Other kids, like Shane and all them, were always putting everyone down. But Silas built people up, and I rarely heard anyone talking shit about him.

I wished I had that talent. No matter how I tried, I

had such anger and disgust inside of me, and it was almost like a barrier cutting me off from the world. But despite the millions of good reasons Silas had to feel just as shitty as I did, he was always great to people. After thinking about it, and about all the people who had come to Hammond over the years, I realized Silas was the reason why Hammond had happened at all. He was the guy who'd brought kids out from the Fruit Belt and Niagara Falls and Amherst. He'd go sneaker shopping, start talking with one of the salesmen, and the next week, the salesman and five of his friends would be hooping at Hammond. That kid was a force of nature, and I was truly starting to believe that someday he really would run off to LA and become a star. He'd been talking about getting into acting and music for the last year. He had the best chance of any of us to make it. To get out of here. To turn shit to sugar.

Silas dropped thirty that night, and Luke had a triple double. I hit six threes and had twelve assists, but it wasn't enough, and we lost a close game to a great team from Lovejoy. Shane fouled out in the third quarter, and Dan got some playing time. Dan dished a few great passes and had four steals in only about seven minutes of playing time. When Shane fouled out, he took off his jersey and kept it off as he sat at the end of the bench and pouted like a bitch. Coach tried getting him to put it back on, but there were some freshmen girls in the crowd he was trying to impress, so Coach had no luck. Our team was dysfunctional, but so was everything else in our lives, and we learned how to make the best of it. At least I got to play.

Nobody said much in the locker room until Silas, covering his crotch with his hands, walked over to Brad

Davies. "Paprika or nutmeg?" Silas moved his hands, revealing his balls, which were hanging out of the zipper in his cargo pants.

"Oh, that's fuckin' sick." Brad threw a penny loafer at Silas's nuts, but Silas blocked it and kept grinning.

"Yo, we just got our asses handed to us. Can't you at least show it?" I said.

"Maybe this is how I mope, Ho-dangles," Silas said. "Besides, you're doin' enough of that for all of us."

"I thought you cared about winning," I said.

"Who said I didn't? Man, we're gonna take it to those foolianis next week. I'm gonna beast it out like J. Peg. He showed me this sick-ass move—"

"There he goes with that J. Peg shit again," Mancuso said from the corner.

"Yo, did I tell you guys?" Travis said. "Maybe I forgot. Anyway, my older brother's good friends with a guy who used to play ball with J. Peg, and they were over at my house the other day, and when I asked J. Peg if he knew who Silas Macker was, he said he had no fuckin' clue."

"Well, that's 'cause he knows me as 'Bones,'" Silas said.

"No, he doesn't," Travis said. "Please stop telling people you know J. Peg. It's fucking annoying."

"You callin' me a liar, motherfucker?" Silas said. He was able to keep cool in most situations—unless someone called him a liar.

"Whoa, take it easy, man, it was just a joke," Mancuso said.

Silas pushed Mancuso into a locker so hard it left a dent.

"Hey, what the hell's going on over here?" Coach Flemming said.

"Nothin', Coach," Silas said. "Just helping him tie his tie."

"Is that right, Mancuso?" Coach said.

"Yeah, that's right."

"All right, get cleaned up, fellas. We're gonna huddle it up in five. And cut the shit, will ya?" Coach went back to his office.

Silas was still shaking with rage. I put my hand on his shoulder, but he pushed it off and walked away.

We sat in a U around Coach and the chalkboard. "Today's loss puts us in last seed for the playoffs, which means we play Archibald—and Eugene Pegos—in the first round, and they've been number one since Eugene's older brother Jerome was a freshman years ago. That's the bad news. The good news is that, this season, we've already beaten every other team that we could face after Archibald. We get past them, and we should be okay. The game's gonna be next Saturday at Fillmore State, so we're gonna need to work on conditioning all week. And to address what happened today in the locker room: if I see anyone else attacking another player on this team, they'll be suspended for a game. Am I clear?"

We all nodded and said yes.

"No practice tomorrow," Coach said. "I want to give you an entire weekend to recover. We'll pick up again on Monday. Let's bring it in."

We did "Team" on three. Dan took off with Steven, who had his own truck now, and I walked to the parking lot behind Silas. Over the last year, something had happened between us. We no longer lifted together, and he had stopped coming by the house. Hammond was almost nonexistent at this point, so the only time I saw Silas was at practice or games or in the halls. I'd been spending most of my time with some of the guys from my AP and honors classes, mainly Ryan Hedman and Billy Wolenowitz. Ryan was waiting for me in his car. I started heading over, but then told him to hold up a minute, and ran over to Silas at the bus stop.

"Listen, man, I don't need anyone pilin' on any more shit," he said.

"I didn't bring a shovel," I said. "You all right?" It was starting to snow—big white flakes set against the dark Buffalo night—adding a clean layer to the dirty slush soaking through my boots.

"I'm fine."

"You don't look fine."

Silas backed against the glass bus stop wall. "Remember a few years back at Afterhours when you asked me why I hit that kid in the St. Anthony's parking lot?"

"Terry Stanford, right?"

"Yeah, that punk. When I first moved out here, I told people I was from some suburb in DC. Didn't want cats knowin' I grew up in the hood. Well, Terry was over my house one day and heard my pops talkin' about our place in the Fruit Belt. The next day, ol' Terry started tellin' everyone in school I was a liar. So I knocked his ass out. You don't know what it's like bein' one of the only brothas out here, man. All my friends back home are either junkies or pushin' rocks. Here or there, I got no place to go."

"Yeah you do. Fillmore State next Saturday. You think Archibald deserves all those championships? Don't get soft on me now. We've been working for this practically all our lives. We're gonna shut down E. Peg and start a new dynasty in Buffalo."

Silas smiled. "Hell yeah. They don't even know what's comin."

"Where you headed now?"

"Just home. You?"

"Some of the guys are getting together for a Stanley Kubrick movie marathon."

"That sounds cool."

"You wanna come?"

"Naw, I'm good, man. Do your thing."

We bumped fists, and I went back to Ryan's car. I felt a heavy, throbbing guilt over the fact that I was glad Silas had said no. The other guys weren't really friends with him, and I knew it'd be awkward having him there, even though he got along with everyone. I sat shotgun and watched Silas standing all alone at that snowy bus stop as we drove away. It reminded me of all those times I'd seen Sister Carol or Sister Adele walking across the St. Anthony's parking lot to the convent after graduation. Reminded me of all the effort they'd put into teaching me about God, and how now I didn't even believe in Him anymore. Reminded me of all the hours Silas and I had played together. Laughed together. Lifted together. And now I was leaving him behind in the cold, all alone. It made me feel like a phony riding in Ryan's car. Made me know full well I'd be leaving *him* at a snowy bus stop or parking lot one of these days too. Made me realize friendship and faith were all bullshit. All we had was tonight. All we had was the snow melting in our cracked, bleeding hands.

Ryan drove us to Billy's mansion in Central Park. Place was like the McCallister house in *Home Alone*. His dad was a surgeon and his mom was a psychiatrist, but they never made me feel awkward for being there. I always felt as if I should wipe my feet on the mat harder than the other guys and try not to touch anything, but Billy always told me to make myself at home. The first time he told me that, I said, "Then you'd better ask your dad to start screaming and smashing shit," and he gave a nervous laugh.

We went to the basement, where Manish Praj and Eitan Goldberg were already on the couch watching *The Shining*. I was glad they'd started with that one and that it was almost over because I couldn't handle scary films, especially ones as psychological as *The Shining*. They always reminded me of the Evil settled way down in the deepest depths of my being that could start creeping its way to the surface at any moment, especially while watching films like this. When it did rise inside of me, I could feel it twisting up my spine, rushing like a raging river. I put in my earplugs, which I always carried with me, and played ping-pong against the wall until the film was over, then sat down when they put in *Paths of Glory*.

The plan was to stay up all night, but I was exhausted from the game, so I left after *Full Metal Jacket*. Ryan offered to drive me, but the walk was only about a mile and a half, so I went on foot. Besides, I loved walking through the park at night. The houses and snow and streetlights and stars so bright above. The city was all mine. No screaming or smashing or threats. No prayers or lectures or judgments. I could walk at my own pace and stop and look at a tree covered in snow or a pile of trash in the street and just think about it and how it related to something so seemingly different, like faith or honesty or friendship. I could see a gum wrapper in a snow pile and think about the time Silas swiped that toothpick holder beside the gumball machine at Denny's and how it had never stopped dispensing toothpicks even after all these years, and how I thought our friendship would be the same—just going and going—but now the toothpicks weren't coming, and this gum wrapper made me think of all the ways change could be good or bad. It made me think of God and Satan and Michael Jordan and Stanley Kubrick and Pink Floyd, and it made me think that maybe I could someday write songs or movies and use the insanity in my head for something good. Maybe I didn't need to be a priest to save the world. Maybe I could just be James.

But I could only get so far with these thoughts before they'd start fucking with me. Once I realized what I was thinking—once I'd made some breakthrough or had connected seemingly disparate things—it was almost as if my brain would start seizing up, and I'd lose my train of thought. I couldn't come at anything head-on—I had to come from the sides. Sneak up on it. Pretend I wasn't thinking in order to think. I couldn't go for a walk with the intention of thinking. I had to just do it—and at an off moment, just as I'd done leaving Billy's house.

The other guys could go at anything head-on. Billy was a fucking genius. The other guys were also smart as hell—way smarter than I was—but Billy was at a different level. He knew everything about current politics and economic policies and could talk for hours about NAFTA or why some piece of legislation Bill Clinton signed was crap, and he had clear, articulate reasons to support his positions, not just, "They're all a bunch of crooks!" He could talk without screaming or smashing shit, and I could listen to what he was saying rather than fear the repercussions of not blindly following his dogma. I'd always assumed liberals must have been the worst people on the planet, but Billy said he was a liberal, and he wasn't bad. I had no idea what was going on with politics. No idea what liberals or conservatives were. I didn't even want to know. Talking about that stuff always made everyone so angry I'd have to leave the room. Besides, liberal or conservative, I was still getting my ass beat either way. Either way, we were still eating fried bologna and potato chips for dinner and watching TV on our thirteen-inch RCA. Who cares who was in the White House? Who cares who was running our city? Our family? Our mind? Sometimes the other guys would make me feel like an idiot because I didn't know what they were talking about. They'd call me a conservative loon, but I was just telling them the things Dad told me. Things I'd heard that angry guy on the radio say whenever Dad drove us anywhere.

But Billy was nice. He'd listen to what I was saying, then explain to me why he thought that thing was wrong. And I always agreed with him. Anytime I'd ever heard anyone talk about things like abortion or affirmative action, they'd always get real angry and scream about how terrible Black women were and how everyone was "trying to steal my money!" and suck off the teat of the government. But when Billy and Ryan and the others spoke about it, they made affirmative action sound like a reasonable and positive thing for society. And I agreed with them. It was almost as if I'd always agreed with them—as if the answers were already living deep down inside of me—but I didn't even know it, because I was always told that gay people were the Devil and Puerto Ricans were gonna rape our daughters and the Russians were coming to take over America and make us all eat borscht or whatever the hell and all that shit. That God was going to wipe out the Earth because teenage Mexican immigrants were having abortions using rusty coat hangers, and then immediately stealing some good, God-fearing White person's job.

Hanging out with these guys both inspired and terrified me. It was almost as if the more time I spent with them, the further away I moved from my family and religion and former friends. I knew that when they spoke about the Arab–Israeli conflict and about how religion was the opiate of the masses, I'd never be able to think otherwise again. It scared me to think that maybe I was just listening to more Sister Verona-style lecturing, only from a different viewpoint. But Sister Verona never had good reasons as to why she thought what she did. God was all things and always right and blah, blah, blah.

I couldn't talk about these things with Mom or Dad, either. Mom didn't seem to care about much other than raising kids, putting out her siblings' fires, and coming to our basketball games, and Dad might punch me in the face and start screaming about Uncle Wayne's dead body if I brought any of this up. I don't even think Silas would have understood what these guys were talking about, and the more I hung out with them, the further away from him I felt too. Hammond felt less and less important. The world felt less insane and chaotic. More and more I wanted to get to those places from the pictures on Miss Amalia's restaurant walls. I thought about Mexico and Spain and all the places calling my heart. I was glad that I'd chosen to take AP Spanish rather than have another free period, even though Uncle Tommy told me that in America, people should only be speaking English. Every time Señora Perez played a film by Almodóvar or read a poem by Neruda, I wanted to rush right off to Spain or Chile or Argentina and learn how to tango and play flamenco guitar and make paella. In Spanish class, I'd always get this feeling that maybe I'd been born in the wrong city, the wrong country, the wrong time period. I could be so happy in Madrid. I needed to see the Andes. I needed to live in Mexico.

Billy and Ryan and them were so far ahead of me, I'd never catch up. I couldn't think abstractly. Just like when thinking about things like gum wrappers and friendship, once I realized I was thinking about justice or philosophy or logic, it would all fall apart. Plus, after a lifetime of being told by Mom and the nuns that God was the reason planes stayed in the air and people recovered from heart surgery and geese flew south for winter, and after a lifetime of hearing Dad screaming, "White is white!" one day, then, "White is black!" the next, I had no ability to think critically. To think for myself. In my world, the loudest person always won the argument. I knew I'd been left behind. It made me want to shut down, but another part of me was ready for the challenge of learning how to think for the first time. It reminded me of when the Evil Thoughts first came on, and I was rushed with the feeling that I now knew everything— every truth of the universe belonged to, and overwhelmed, me. I felt that, by realizing how little I knew, I was capable of learning anything. I was only seventeen. There was still time for me. I refused to live my life like the others—always afraid of what was around the corner. Terrified of the Blacks or Mexicans or gays invading the neighborhood. It always confused me that I didn't hate any of these people, and now

I felt as if I was more on their side than on that of my own family.

Everything was changing, as it always had. The city alternated between the greenest of greens, the grayest of grays, the brightest of whites, and the darkest of blacks. I had all those colors inside of me and wanted to be on a natural cycle, just like the city. To change and allow the old leaves to die and the new leaves to grow. To allow the snow to reflect the moon and brighten the darkest night. To allow the sky to be dark enough to show the brightest of stars. This was my Buffalo. My beautiful city full of doctors and crackheads and professors and lunatics and armchair revolutionaries and drunk dads and hero athletes and guys who wake up at 4 a.m. to plow snow and teachers who grade papers until the twilight hours on weekends and politicians who skim so much off the top they had to bring in a control board to run the city. The city of gorgeous architecture, heart disease, and Wide Right dreams.

When I got home, I ate a bowl of cereal, then went down to the basement to throw my sweat-soaked uniform in the wash. But when I turned on the light, Dan was sitting there, wide awake in the dark and staring into the void. He had this look on his face like that guy in *Full Metal Jacket* before he kills the drill instructor, and it terrified me. He looked at me with those eyes that screamed for rest but couldn't find it anywhere around him. Like all the others, I didn't say anything to him. I just put my clothes in the wash, turned off the light, and went upstairs to sleep.

Chapter 21

With *It's a Wonderful Life* on TV and Bing Crosby's *Merry Christmas* in the CD player, we decorated the tree. Afterward, Mom called us over to light the pink Advent candle, but I went to the basement to call Rachel Abrams instead. I'd been calling her nearly every day for the last few months, and even though we'd talk for nearly an hour each time, I had no idea where we stood. Rachel was in my AP Bio class, and she was one of the smartest people in the school. I could listen her talk about the Krebs cycle or Golgi apparatus all day. We'd talk a lot in class, and her friends all said she liked me, but I wasn't sure what was up between us. I'd also heard rumors that Brian Kramer had felt her up in his Honda after the Sadie Hawkins dance last month, even though she told me she wished she'd asked me to go with her instead. Either way, I couldn't stop calling her, even if I'd wanted to. It didn't feel right. Old stuff from way back. I wasn't in control here, the Thoughts were. Like a junkie goes to a needle, I went to that phone each afternoon. Maybe I would have stopped if she never answered, but she always did—even during Hanukkah. Was she just humoring me? I got the feeling that Billy was humoring me sometimes when he tutored me after class. Maybe they felt sorry for me.

Either way, Rachel picked up that afternoon.

"Hey, Jimmy, I knew it was you just by the way the phone rang," she said.

"Oh, uh, cool. So, what are you up to?"

"Oh, you know. Homework and all that."

"What's going on tonight?"

"Uh, I'm heading to Amanda's for kind of a girls'-night-in thing."

"Nice. You gonna watch a movie or something?"

And so on . . .

My goal was to keep the conversation going so there was never an awkward pause. I was a speeding train, and the second I slowed down, it'd take me forever to get started again, so I couldn't stop. No finesse. No articulateness. Just a train chugging down the track, barreling through grace, charm, and wit.

But I was a seventeen-year-old speaking on a rotary phone in a cold, moldy Buffalo basement. She could hardly expect Cary Grant. Still, she always answered and would keep the conversation moving along. But she'd never meet up with me. She'd say, "Yeah, sure," whenever I asked her to go to Denny's after school, but then she was always busy with soccer practice or student council or whatever. Deep down, I knew she wasn't interested. But I couldn't stop calling. It felt terrible to pick up that phone each day. Terrible to hear her mom shouting for her to answer my call. Dude, she's got homework. She's applying to fucking Swarthmore. She's gonna be a senator someday. Leave her alone. Stop asking her how her cat is doing. She probably told you it was sick just to keep the conversation going and avoid having to hear your crass, minimum-wage mouth breathing into the phone.

But it's good to hope. You need hope. Maybe she *does* like you, but you're not putting on the right moves. Brian Kramer probably just slid his hand right up her shirt—no talk about sick cats or invitations to fucking Denny's. You gotta grow a pair. Chicks want you to be in charge, not fumbling through a phone call. Come, climb the lattice—sneak into my room. Crawl on all fours to my bed and eat my pussy until I cum like Niagara Falls, then stick your fat hard dick in my ass all night. High school girls don't want to talk about AP Bio. They wanna get plowed like Main Street in January.

It all drove me mad. Always waiting when I should be doing, and doing when I should be waiting. I wanna feel those tits too. I wanna rub my hard dick between 'em. I wanna be like Brian Kramer and all the other guys who don't give a fuck and bang girls all over the city: in their cars, in the Denny's bathroom, on blankets under the blue water tower. But you're a fuckin' chump, man. Talking about cats and how's Grandma and did you study for the mitosis test? You're a hopeless fucking loser. You'll never get laid. You're co-captain of the varsity basketball team, and you can't even get your dick wet. Briana Allen said a lot of girls like you, you just need to learn how to talk to them. But I don't know how to talk to them. I don't know how to talk to anyone. Not even Dan or God anymore.

I could hear Mom upstairs singing "Silent Night." They must have already lit the candle. I'd rather light Rachel's menorah. Just hang up the phone. Leave her alone. It's so embarrassing. She never calls you—you know that, right? You know that means something. Debbie Carson does, though. Downtown Debbie. Debbie with the five-hundred-pound father and mom with a mustache and lazy eye. All last summer, Debbie would come over and show you her tits. She's got a great body. All the girls in school call her a whore, but fuck it. None of them are giving you the time of day. And Debbie's not even a whore. She sucked one dick and now everyone makes fun of her forever. Debbie's in your league, Jimmy. You're not gonna marry a senator. You and Debbie can have ten kids and you can get a job at Radio Shack and sell weed on the side and eat Taco Bell every night and jerk off to Brooke Burke on TV until your dick stops working at the ripe old age of twenty-nine.

Rachel said she needed to get ready for Amanda's, so I let her go. I knew I'd be asking her all about it tomorrow. So what'd you girls do? Oh yeah? How cool. I wished the phone service would cut out so I couldn't call her. I was ruining whatever shitty reputation I already had, which was the only thing most high school kids like me ever had. I'm done. I'm not calling her again tomorrow.

But that's what you said yesterday, you weak fucking fool.

At least Julia came over that one time. Julia, where are you? Julia, my love. I don't care about Rachel. You're the girl for me. I'll do whatever it takes to marry you someday. I'll be a champion. You'll see. I'll hold that trophy up, and they'll take my picture and put on the front page of *The Buffalo Times*, and you'll see it and finally realize how much you love me. How you need me. You'll leave your millionaire French model boyfriend and eat potato chips and ice cream in bed with me. We'll squeeze the zits on each other's backs. You'll yell at me for leaving the toilet seat up, then we'll laugh about it when you're no longer mad that you fell in.

"Jimmy, come help us with the Christmas lights," Mom said as I walked through the kitchen.

"Fuck that Mickey Mouse shit, Ma," I said.

"What did I tell you about that language?"

"That you fucking love it."

"Well, maybe somebody's not gonna get any presents this year."

"Ooh, you mean Santa won't bring me a six-pack of tube socks and some tighty-whities from Kmart? I'll cry myself to sleep all Christmas night."

"You're making Carolynn upset."

"Carolynn." I dropped to a knee and looked her dead in the eye. "Santa doesn't exist."

"Yes, he does."

"No, he fuckin' doesn't, and it's best you learn that right now."

She started crying and ran to her room.

"You're such a jerk sometimes, James," Mom said.

"Fuck you, I'm leaving." I grabbed the keys to the station wagon and headed to Billy's to play *GoldenEye* and listen to some of the Zeppelin records Ryan had loaned him.

On Monday, Mom let me drive to school, because St. Anthony's was closed over a power failure or something, and she didn't need to drive the kids in. Dad was talking about moving them over to Kirkland Elementary and Middle because "the tuition is too god-damned high now. They think we're sittin' on gold bars or something over here?" It felt terrible hearing that. For some reason, having the kids at St. Anthony's made me feel as if a part of me was still there. I'd hear them talking about Sister Verona and Sister

Carol and the lunch lady and all them, and for a moment I'd forget I was in the big city that was Kirkland High, and get transported back to a small safe place. Forget I no longer talked to Tony, Ray, Julia, or anyone else from St. Anthony's. Forget I hadn't set foot in the coffee shop in years. Forget that they'd found Gerry's body that summer, in his bedroom with a needle sticking out of his arm. Made me forget how I didn't really think about him anymore. The kid who was once my best friend. Made me forget how numb I was becoming to life. Made me realize how easily I could become like Dan, staring into the dark all the time. Made me not care so much about basketball or Hammond.

Dan rode to school with Steven. Steven had gotten a waiting job at Denny's after graduating from Kirkland, but he still always gave Dan a ride each morning on his way in for the morning shift. Steven kept talking about how he wanted to join the service, and my dad loved it. Dad told Steven he'd take him to a recruiter himself. Since then, Steven had been running all over North Buffalo, miles and miles, stopping every so often to do pushups and sit-ups on people's lawns. He was getting jacked as hell. He'd lift free weights at his house and would spend hours doing dips and pull-ups and everything. He had to have been pushing two fifty now, all muscle, and was almost as big as Dad.

I parked the station wagon as far back in the lot as possible and made extra sure no one was looking when I got out. I'd heard tons of kids talking about how cool the wagon was, because "imagine how great it would be to blaze and fuck in there," but that back seat only came down when Dad needed to get lumber or pipes back from the Home Depot. I never told them it was mine and just nodded along whenever they'd discuss it. It was usually the rich kids who went on vacation to Tuscany and the south of France who'd talk about how "kitsch" that wagon was. How they wished they had one too. I would have loved to have seen any of those pussies pushing that thing uphill in the snow, then see if they still thought it was cool. God, I don't even know why Dad still had it. Instead of buying a new car, he just kept pumping more and more money into repairs. It was as if he just couldn't let go.

Fourth period, I had AP US History with Mr. Samson. I sat next to Billy and Ryan in the front corner, and followed along for about half of Samson's explanation about the *Marbury v. Madison* case, but once I lost him, I never caught up. We had study hall next period in the library, and Billy explained it to me. Afterward, I made up a song about how Mrs. Wilbers, the gray-haired librarian, gave the janitor head in the men's room every morning before school, and when I repeated a part about how "she strained his mop," which almost sounded like a mantra, Billy joined in. Soon other kids joined, too, and we chanted louder and louder until Mrs. Wilbers came out screaming, "I can hear every filthy word! You should all be ashamed of yourselves!" Some kid told her to break a mop handle up her ass, and she stormed off into the reference section.

At lunch, Ryan, Billy, Manish, and a few other guys took turns telling jokes. The best was Eitan's joke about a voodoo dick that wouldn't stop fucking a woman's pussy.

Across the cafeteria, I saw Silas sitting under a table where the Powells and Luke were eating, and he kept saying, "Ms. Winters, you gotta come quick. They're puttin' it in my ass." Ms. Winters, one of the lunch monitors, kept searching the cafeteria, trying to find who was saying all that crap. "Hurry, Ms. Winters, I can't take it no more. Bring the cavalry." The other guys were laughing their asses off, and when Ms. Winters finally saw Silas, she smiled, blushed, and walked away.

Dan didn't sit with those guys anymore, either. He hung out with the cross-country kids, who were big-time potheads. People usually thought football players were the biggest partiers, but at Kirkland, no one out-partied the cross-country guys. They did all kinds of weird shit, including sticking ball pump needles in their dick holes and eating mushrooms then going for naked runs during winter. The craziest was a guy named Cisco, who once swam across the Niagara River about a mile south of the falls. He played bass in a band with a guy named Ian Morricone, and they were always coming by the house to hang out with Dan. Ian would try to get Cisco and Dan to move out to LA with him and start a band, but they thought he was nuts. They'd sit in the backyard, even in winter, and I was pretty certain they would get high—I didn't know for sure, though, because I always did my best to avoid them. Something about those guys scared me. I didn't know how much Dan was getting into any of that shit himself, but I heard rumors that he was into pills and weed. He never told me about any of it, but he never told me about anything, so what'd it matter?

Maybe all that shit was helping him cope with the darkness in his head. Or maybe it was making it worse. Either way, I couldn't keep worrying about him. I had boulders and dynamite in my own head. Everyone was on their own, anyway, so who gives a fuck? He'd gotten into SUNY Brockport and would be moving away soon, and then he'd be the state university system's problem, not mine or Mom's or Dad's. Soon the school would be the one to have to worry about him sitting in the common areas or bathrooms in the dark and staring at the walls.

But that was all bullshit. Dan was, and would always be, my problem. I'd never stop worrying about that kid—not now, not ever. The thought of him moving away made me sad in a way I'd never been. Sadder than when I'd heard Julia had dropped out of Lakeside Academy and moved to Brooklyn and was supposedly dating some huge indie rocker. Sadder than when I'd heard Ray was arrested for selling crystal meth in Jacksonville. Sadder than when I'd heard they were probably going to have to shut down St. Anthony's because the diocese was going under. It had always been me and Dan since the day I was born. We were together in Virginia Beach before Mom made us move back to Buffalo when Aunt Sadie kept telling her she couldn't watch Uncle Jake by herself anymore. Together when Mom was still happy. When she'd take us to the beach and to Chuck E. Cheese and we'd get ice cream and laugh together. When she'd color with us and sing to us and have water balloon fights with us in the backyard. Together when Dad would tell us jokes and scare the monsters out of our closet and never scream. Sure, we wouldn't see Dad most of the time when he was off on his ship, but we knew he was happy out there in a way he'd never since been. He'd come home and give us sailor hats and presents and we'd get pizza and dance around when the *Magnum, P.I.* theme song would start. We were together before Mom made Dad have all the other kids, who fucking ruined everything, and Dad started turning into a psycho, and Mom looked as if she'd never smile again. We were always together, building forts out of couch cushions and making spaceships out of cinderblocks and believing that someday we'd live on clouds with the Care Bears. We were always a team. Even now, when we didn't talk, we were still part of the school team. What would happen when we were no longer playing together? What would happen in twenty years, if we even survived that long? Would we be bald old men who never spoke? Would he have a kid I'd never meet?

Dan, no matter what happens, you can't give up. You have no idea how much I love you. I've never told you, and I know how gay it is to say it, but I love you so much more than anyone else. They can all burn in Hell. It was always just you and me. Why aren't we friends anymore? Seeing you like this is killing me. You can't give up, Dan. You're a starter somewhere. Somewhere in this world, you're a star. In a world of games, you gotta find your team. That's the only thing keeping me going. Someday, I'll find the team where the best parts of me are able to shine through. Maybe that won't happen in Kirkland. Maybe it won't happen in Buffalo. But I'm gonna keep trying. You gotta try too. Promise me you'll be okay at Brockport. Promise me it won't just get worse.

"Ms. Winters, they stuck a whole three-liter bottle of Sprite inside. Ms. Winters, you gotta come quick. Bring a mop . . . and some Jujyfruits."

At practice that afternoon, we ran a Shell Drill to work on defense, but when Shane passed the ball to Dan, Dan must not have been paying attention because it sailed right past his face and out of bounds.

"All right, let's get some water," Coach said.

We left the gym and went to the water fountain, and

Shane bounced a ball off the back of Dan's head. "Anything going on in there?"

I grabbed Shane by the neck with such power, I felt as though I'd lifted him ten feet in the air, and then I pinned him against the trophy case. I clamped down on his throat with a grizzly's strength and felt that I could tear his esophagus right from his neck. I didn't say anything to him but spoke to him with my eyes. Stared right at him. Right through him.

Shane, do you understand that I will fucking end you? Do you understand that for all these years, I was just letting you win because I was terrified to think of what I'd do to you if I fought back? Do you know my grandfather used to bend horseshoes with the same hands now gripping your throat? That these are the same hands that killed Nazis and shoveled thousands of tons of salt from the asshole of New York? Do you know these hands are strong enough to crush every bone in your body? That I'll turn your whole being to dust? Your life to ash? Shane, if you touch him again, I will grab Dad's sledgehammer and go to your house at 4 a.m. I will break into your room. I will wake you from your perfect little sleep, and I will kill you. I promise you, I will kill you.

"Fuck him up, Horace," Luke said. I could see his smile reflecting in the glass.

I said nothing, but I could tell by the fear in Shane's eyes that he understood. I knew he couldn't breathe.

"Yo, Horace, ease up, man," Silas said. When he touched my shoulder, almost instinctively I released Shane. Shane took a huge gasp of air and said, "My dad will destroy you!"

"I'll destroy you first," I said, looking straight into his eyes. He shut right up.

"My office, now!" Coach said.

Coach sat behind his desk and told Shane to speak first. "I didn't even do anything, he just went crazy. He's a complete psychopath and should be in jail." He was crying—actually fucking crying.

"This true?" Coach said.

I didn't say shit.

"All right, Shane, I've heard what I need from you. Go get dressed," Coach said.

Shane walked toward the door, then turned around as if he wanted to say something to me, but I gave him this I-fucking-dare-you look, and he just kept going.

"So, what's going on?" Coach got up and closed the door.

"Coach, you gotta play my brother in this next game. He's been bustin' his ass for you for four years but has absolutely nothing to show for it." I didn't even realize I was crying until I felt the tears drip from my chin.

"I know your brother works hard, which is why I've always kept him on the squad, but he just doesn't have what it takes to make it out there."

"That's bullshit! He *does* have what it takes. You just don't see it. Nobody ever fucking sees it!"

"You know I have grounds to suspend you from this next game, right?"

"Fine. Do it. Put me in prison for all I care. Just watch Dan. Watch him closely. You'll see he does everything right. He knows exactly how to set a pick to make it most effective. He knows how to box out guys twice his size. He knows exactly when to pass, when to shoot. He hits every shot he takes, but he's not going to shoot for you unless he feels safe. Unless he feels like he's not taking the shot away from someone else. He'll give everything he has for you and more. All Shane does it bring us down. Can't you see that after all these years? Nobody ever watches! Nobody ever sees shit! We got something that's so beautiful, and you're fucking ruining it!"

"I'm going to have to think about all this, James. You can go, but stay away from Shane."

I wiped away my tears before I opened the door.

All week in practice, I saw Coach actually watching Dan. Watching every scrimmage and seeing how every team Dan was on won. Watching Dan get rebounds over Mancuso. Watching Dan stripping Shane in drills. Watching how Dan made me and Luke play better. I don't know what was going on in Coach's head, but he seemed to have actually listened to me.

A part of me was terrified by what I had done to Shane, because, in a way, it felt good to hurt him like that. I mean, I didn't like it after, but in that moment, something inside of me had wanted to hurt him badly. Maybe not kill him. But put him in the hospital. Make him have to eat through a tube for a few weeks. I didn't want to allow that kind of violence into my world. It was hard enough keeping the Evil away without any outside influence, and I didn't want to put myself in a place where I'd start fighting regularly. I feared that if I started punching, I'd never stop. I'd punch through a human life. I'd punch through my own.

Shane's dad called Poor Rich, and I could hear a lot of screaming on the other line, but Dad just said, "G-go fuck yourself!" and hung up. Sometimes it was nice having parents who didn't give a shit.

Chapter 22

That Friday night was our winter dance. I asked Rachel to go with me, but she said she was already going with Greg Ramirez, so I went with Downtown Debbie. Though I'd been driving for about a year, I still didn't have a realistic concept of how long it would take to drive anywhere, and I figured I could pick up Debbie, Ryan, and Ryan's date downtown in about twenty minutes. The school had a rule that if you weren't at the dance by nine, they wouldn't let you in, but our practice ran late that night, so I assumed they'd give us some leniency. Even so, I figured I could get us there on time. I got Debbie first, then Ryan, but by eight fifty, we still hadn't picked up his date. We got stuck at a long-ass red light that seemed as if it would never turn, and I started steaming. Debbie put her hand on my shoulder and told me to relax, and I started punching the shit out of the window and screaming, "FUCK!" I didn't even realize I'd exploded until I saw the horror on her face. What, Debbie? Don't you know that when a guy loses his mind you're supposed to pretend nothing's wrong, just like my mom does? That you're supposed to just turn off your brain and pretend everything is okay?

But seeing the horror on Debbie's face made me realize that maybe Mom and Dad were wrong. That maybe my family was far more fucked up than all the other fucked-up families in our neighborhood. That maybe it really wasn't okay to scream like a maniac at girls. I already knew it wasn't okay to hit girls. I'd only seen the old man put his hands on Mom twice: once, when I was about eight, he grabbed her shoulders and started shaking her, but let go when Dan climbed up the steps and jumped on his back and I started punching him in the kidney, which was the spot Uncle Tommy told me to aim for if I really wanted to hurt someone. The other time happened a few years later: Dad lost his mind and pushed Mom, and I grabbed the tennis racket from the closet and started hitting him in his bad knee with the hard edge of the racket so he'd come after me instead. And he did. That was a bad night. Those were the only two times that I knew of, though. But screaming at women was always okay in my house. It happened literally every day, often for hours. It happened in Grandma's house in Bumblefuck, too, and it'd probably happened in Great-Grandpa's house in Sicily as well.

Maybe this shit wasn't right? I needed to end the Lombardi curse. I apologized to Debbie and told myself I had to be more aware of my temper in the future. It's not okay to yell at girls, James. No matter what you've seen, you gotta be better.

I picked up Ryan's date, and we got to the gym by nine thirty. The vice principal wouldn't let us in, even though I told him about practice running late, but Mr. Mitchell, the gym teacher, overheard, and he gave me this look as if to say, *Meet me over there*. We walked to the side of the gym, and he opened the door and let us in. I thanked him, and he just smiled and nodded as if to say, *Anything for an athlete*.

Debbie, Ryan, Ryan's date, and I started dancing with a group of people, but I couldn't stop searching for Rachel. When I saw her, she was dancing with Greg Ramirez, grinding her ass all over him. Debbie kept doing the same shit to me, but I wasn't into it. When Greg went to the bathroom, I thought about asking Rachel to dance, but after having watched her move, I'd just . . . lost interest. She could dance all right, but she was all shoulders and head bobs—not like Julia, who would have danced up and down that gym, doing shit nobody else could. When Greg came back, I figured maybe it was better I was with Debbie in the corner, where I belonged.

Eventually, the DJ played "Piano Man," as he always did near the end of dances, and all the cool kids did the usual, locking arms in a circle and drunkenly swaying as they sang every word of the song. As much as I hated them, I wished they'd let me in that circle as well. When I first started at Kirkland High, a few of the cool girls had told me they liked me, in more words or less, but because of all that shit with Julia I'd turned them down, and they'd turned their backs on me. After Julia, I was just waiting for girls to pour beer on my head the moment they found out who I really was, and I couldn't go through that again. Other girls would say, "you have no idea how many girls like you but you just need to learn how to talk to them." But I didn't care. I'd find one girl I really liked and obsess over her, calling her all the time—like I did with Rachel—and all the while ignoring everyone else. The thing is, I don't even think I wanted Rachel, or any of the other girls, for that matter. Maybe I just obsessed over one I couldn't have so I didn't have to think about all the others I *could* have. Maybe it was better not to invite any girls into my twisted world. Better to keep everyone away. I mean, what would we even talk about? How my dad punched holes in our walls? How I used to obsess over hurting kids when I was younger? How they were moving to New York City after high school, and I was sticking around Buffalo to cut people's lawns and shovel snow? If they even brought up New York, I'd probably start ranting about how we needed to stay here and save Helen and her cat and the lady who always walks up and down Hertel Ave. pushing her dog in a shopping cart, and all the crackheads sleeping at Hammond Park and how we needed to find a way to bring the factories back and make the city proud and hopeful again. How could you just walk away? After all the wars we'd fought together here? Don't you know New York is an illusion? They're just selling you a new Heaven with all the same hellish features. It's all Hell, every last inch, don't let them fool you, too. It's Hell in LA and London and Paris too. Don't you see we're doomed, no matter where we go? We need to stick together in Buffalo and prepare for the long grueling winter of adulthood.

Any teenage girl hearing some guy talking like this would be right to keep on walking—and quickly. I didn't understand these people, and they didn't understand me. I didn't know why they all wore the same turtlenecks and shell necklaces and backwards visors and pants that could be unzipped to form shorts. That night, I was wearing the sweater I'd bought at Abercrombie with the gift card Uncle Salvatore gave me for my birthday. I felt so awkward going into that store, and I'd ended up picking something with the smallest logo on it, but no one seemed to care that I was wearing it. They didn't let me in their circle.

They were always saying and doing shit I didn't understand. They'd go on and on about who was going out with whom and who had the best style and threw the best parties, but nobody was ever *saying* anything, and it all changed week to week anyway, so how could anyone keep up? It made me feel crazy, and I never knew what to say to them. "Oh, yeah, Frank's totally wrong for her," "Yeah, he's such a fucking fag," "Yeah, uh, of course Rob Thomas is a much better songwriter than Dylan." Every conversation felt like a compromise. Every time I spoke with them, I felt as though I was giving away pieces of myself that I'd never get back. They'd make plans to talk to each other on this computer website called AIM, where they all wrote messages to one another, but why wouldn't they just meet up and talk in person?

Regardless, every time they got into that big circle, arms locked together, forever united against the world, I'd wish I was a part of them. Ryan wasn't a part of them. Neither was Billy, even though he was probably the smartest kid in the whole school. What did I have to do to fit in? For homecoming a few months back, we'd each filled out a long questionnaire that got sent to an outside company that calculated how romantically compatible we were with one another. I was literally the least compatible guy in the entire school. Ryan and them never let me hear an end to it.

When Billy Joel gave that line about the guy knowing he could be a movie star, I realized I was that guy. I knew that when I was forty—if I even lived that long—I'd be the guy at the bar talking about how he should have moved to LA when he was younger, but he had to stay in Buffalo to take care of everyone. Who had to sacrifice everything to save everyone, just like Mom had. But Mom tried so hard to save everyone that she never actually saved anyone. Don't even try to help, James. Fuck 'em all. You're not even compatible with them anyways. Let them suffer. Let 'em squirm. Run away now while you still can. Head to LA while you're still young. You gotta try. You can't let Buffalo bury you in snow-covered shit.

After the dance, everyone went to a house party at a mansion in Central Park, and I went off to a dark corner with Downtown Debbie and had my first kiss. I'd always imagined what it would be like. I used to dream about it. Prayed to God to let it happen—with Julia, of course. But it was messy and awkward and all I kept thinking about was Julia dumping beer on my head. If I couldn't be hers, I couldn't be anyone's.

When I got home, the old man was asleep on the recliner and snoring like a chainsaw. As I passed by him to walk upstairs, I could have sworn I saw tears streaming from his eyes.

God, maybe hope never really does go away.

Chapter 23

I sat in the back of the cheese bus by the window. The glass was covered in frost, distorting the lights of the Kirkland High parking lot. Even with the heat on, there were always pockets of cold in Buffalo. My chest and upper back were sweating even as my legs felt the chill. Coach stood beside the driver and kept checking his watch. He'd told me that because of what I'd done to Shane, I wouldn't be playing in tonight's game. At first, I'd felt completely helpless—that this motherfucker was taking away from me the one thing I'd been fighting for since I was a kid—but then I realized that I was giving Dan a shot at playing. Coach really seemed to have been watching him in practice, and, with my position as shooting guard now open, Dan might get some serious playing time. I felt helpless but hopeful. Dan was just as good as I was, and he was even a little better on D, so we still had a chance at winning.

Silas ran up the stairs and onto the bus. "Sorry, fellas, I was takin' a wicked pre-game dump."

"All right, we're all here," Coach said to the driver, who closed the door and took off. Silas walked down the aisle toward the back.

"You wipe?" Luke said.

"You wanna check?" Silas stuck his ass in Luke's face, then took the seat next to him.

In the Fillmore State locker room, we got ready for the game. I usually dressed quickly, then spent my time stretching. Even after all these years, my muscles were still so tight, they always felt like bone. Normally, when I finished stretching, I would dribble all over the locker room—and I mean *all* over. I'd dribble off the lockers, the walls, the floor, and benches, all while crossing fuckers as they got dressed or tried to pass on their way to the bathroom. I loved feeling the blood pumping to my hands. I'd wipe the bottom of my sneakers with my palms to get my hands sticky so I had better control with the ball. Some of the other guys, like Shane and Mancuso, would spend their time fixing their hair and tucking their jerseys in just right. But I was preparing for war. Like Mike Tyson, I was preparing to go out and eat people's children. I wanted to crush them. To break them down. To make it clear to everyone in the gym that we were the dominant team. That we were in control. That despite how it may have seemed, I was actually Genghis Khan, and they were all about to die.

But that night I sat quietly and watched Dan get ready. Dan, this might be your chance. Prepare for war. Prepare to eat souls. This world will fuck with you as hard as it can. It'll take everything you have. You gotta fight back, man.

Coach called us to huddle around him. "Gentlemen, I don't think it needs to be said how important this game is tonight. Archibald is the best team in Buffalo, but we've got a chance if we stick to our game plan and push ourselves. Now, you all know James won't be playing tonight, so we're gonna need the backcourt to step it up. Brian, you're going to be starting for James at two guard. Lukie, you got Eugene Pegos. Don't let him drive—force him to shoot from the outside. As for the rest of you, box your men out, call out the picks, and make smart plays. Let's bring it in."

We did "Team" on three then walked to the gym. The moment we left the locker room, I could hear people cheering and it got louder as we neared the court. I stood at the back of the line, wearing a shirt and tie and khakis, but when we got to the double doors leading to the court I walked ahead. Archibald was already doing a layup drill, and a few of the guys got up high enough to dunk but then just rolled the ball in.

"We're gonna get killed," Shane said.

I wanted to break his little bitch legs so he could never play sports again.

Shane, you stupid fuck, don't you realize that, with the right team, you can beat anyone? That if you play together, you always have hope? But we don't play together, because of shitheads like you.

I stepped aside, and Shane led the team for a lap around the court. The Kirkland crowd went nuts, and the DJ played "Bombs Over Baghdad," which, along with "Welcome to the Jungle," was the song we always listened to in the locker room before games. Hearing André 3000 starting on that first verse made every fiber in my body want to race out into the gym. The bigger the opponent, the bigger the opportunity. Giants fall every day. But it wasn't going to be me hacking at their shins with an ax that night.

I walked with Coach to the bench. "Go Jimmy!" Right away I saw Poor Rich sitting with the rest of my family. They were cheering louder than everyone else.

After warming up, the starters from both teams met at half-court. Even though I sat next to Dan at the end of the bench, our parents kept screaming, "Go Jimmy! Go Danny!" No matter our playing time, no matter where that game was—Antarctica, the Sahara, the moon—they would have been there cheering. Seeing them made me smile.

The ref tossed the ball, and the other center jumped a foot higher than Mancuso, tipping the ball back to Eugene Pegos. Luke got on him immediately and put on the pressure as the rest of the players got into position. The Archibald shooting guard picked Luke as E. Peg crossed the half, and E. Peg drove to the hoop, then stopped on a dime and sank a ten-footer over Silas.

"Brian, call the screens!" Coach said.

Silas passed the ball in to Luke. Luke passed ahead to Brian, who drove toward the baseline and took a wild shot that missed the rim. The Archibald small forward grabbed the rebound and passed it to E. Peg, who dribbled up court slowly, allowing his team to set up on offense. Luke stayed right with him but again got back-picked around the top of the key. E. Peg drove the lane, then kicked it out to the small forward, who sank a three in Shane's face.

"Call the god-damned screens!" Coach said.

"Go Lions!" My parents still had hope.

Joey, the Powells, and a few other Hammond All-Stars were in the crowd too, but they could sense the beatdown we were about to get, so they kept silent. Silas made an errant inbounds pass, and E. Peg stole it and dunked on Mancuso. The other crowd went nuts. This was the biggest crowd I'd ever seen at one of our games, and they were all going to watch us get picked apart slowly, while Dan and I sat here with our cocks in our hands. I wanted to get out there so badly.

At the half, we sat in a U around the chalkboard in the locker room, waiting for Coach.

"Yo, fellas, these cats ain't all that sweet," Silas said. "We're beating ourselves."

"You guys really gotta call those picks," Mancuso said.

"They're killing us with those," Silas said.

"Relax, big boy, I know what I'm doing," Shane said.

"Looks like it," Silas said.

"Look, guys," I said, "we've got so much talent sitting here, but it's pointless unless we use it. I . . ." I felt tears coming, but I held them back. "I might never get a chance to play with you guys ever again."

Luke looked at me, then Dan, then Silas. He said nothing, but I could see he had something on his mind—like a switch had been turned on.

"Yeah, tell Randy that'll be fine . . ." Coach said to someone in the hall as he walked into the locker room. "And watch that number forty-two. He's been campin' his ass out in the paint all night." Coach stopped in front of us. "I'm sorry for that, guys. Okay, the reality is that we're down fifteen. With the way we've been playing, it could be far worse. Shane and Brian, you've gotta call those picks and step in to play D. They're targeting Luke. Andy, I want you in for Shane at the start of this half . . ." Andy nodded, and Shane looked ready to call his lawyer. "Gentlemen, we've got one half of basketball left. This game isn't over yet, but if you don't do something about it soon, this may by the last organized game some of you will ever play. All right, we've gotta get back in there. Bring it in."

We did "Team" on three and then went back out to the gym.

The Archibald power forward passed the ball in to E. Peg., and he dribbled up the court with Luke staying on him the whole way. E. Peg tried to cross Luke at mid-court, but Luke stripped him and took it in for an uncontested layup.

"There it is!" D. Pow yelled from the stands.

The power forward again passed the ball in to E. Peg, and Luke, who pretended as though he was running back up court, turned around and stole the pass. Luke shook E. Peg and put in a wild reverse layup over the power forward.

"Go Lukie!" Mom yelled.

The power forward passed the ball in to E. Peg. Luke stayed on him so tightly that E. Peg made a bad pass up court to the small forward, and Silas stole it. Silas took it to the hoop, drawing the two defenders, then he dished it to Luke, who put it in for an easy layup.

E. Peg pushed it up court again. Andy's man picked Luke around the top of the key, but Andy didn't call it nor did he step up to cover E. Peg, who shot a ten-footer. Luke, however, came out of nowhere and spiked the ball to the ground like a volleyball. It took a high bounce, and Silas caught it and dished it to Luke, who pushed it up court. The Archibald power forward caught up to Luke, so he passed it to Silas, and Silas put in an uncontested layup.

Our crowd went nuts. Even Dan started clapping along. I felt useless as fuck on that bench, not being able to help in any way other than offering water and support, but it gave me a taste of what Dan had gone through those last few years. It was shitty to feel so powerless. To want to lead your team but to be held back on the sidelines. To have a head full of steam and nowhere to release it. It's one thing to be on the court playing with a dysfunctional team; it's another to be on the sidelines watching it all fall apart. On the sidelines, you have nothing but time to think about how the whole game of life is just passing you by. On the court, you're too busy to think. You're just reacting. Letting instincts take over. Maybe this is how he feels trying to lead my brothers and sisters and me. Maybe this is how Mom feels being the oldest in her family. Knowing that no matter what they do, Uncle Jake will still reach for that bottle. That no matter what they say, I'm still going to run around screaming and smashing things while trying to outdo Dad. But, Mom, Dan, if you could just get in the game you'll see that you're both so much better than you ever realized. That the chaos is so much bigger than just our family. Just our city. It's not your fault. Let it go. Shoot the god-damned ball! We *need* you!

Luke stole it from E. Peg again and crossed the shit out of the Archibald power forward, then put it in for an easy layup. He could have dunked it. He got up high enough for a tomahawk jam, but he just ended it with a smooth finger roll. This was real Buffalo ball—no flash. Here, you ate what you were given. Here, you wore the same Bills hoodie for twelve years until it fell apart in the dryer. Here, you got your hair butchered at Gino's, laughed at some racist jokes, drank some whiskey, and left. Buffalo could buff it. Fuck buffin' it. Two points were two points. This was Buffalo ball, and Luke was the King. And the King doesn't have to do shit to please you other than keep the kingdom from getting looted by rival clans. Luke wasn't playing for applause. He wasn't playing to make highlight reels or get his dick sucked after the game. Luke was playing to win. He was playing for revenge. Luke was playing to hurt you and everyone you loved. And what better way to do that than to put in a layup when you can dunk it? To show that you don't even have to try in order to win? That winning is such a fundamental part of who you are that the other team stands no chance? Shit like that gets under the other team's skin. Gets deep down in their psyche. It lets them know exactly who's in charge. And it's exactly what you'd expect from a King.

Basketball had been my life since Dad had put up that hoop over our garage when I was twelve. I'd watched hundreds of NBA and college games, from Laettner's last-second game winner to Reggie Miller dropping eight in the final sixteen seconds versus the Knicks, and I'd played against some serious athletes who'd owned courts and seemed almost unstoppable. But I'd never seen anybody take over a game the way Luke Harrison did that afternoon. He was relentless, grabbing boards and loose balls like a man possessed. He blocked shots of players almost a head taller, stripped the ball from anyone nearby, and terrorized the other team's offense. When we had the ball, no one could stop him. He drove the lane, splitting defenders and putting up shots that had no business ever going in. And he did all of this against the best team in Buffalo with the best player in the city guarding him. For a moment in our lives, Luke Harrison carried us all on his shoulders. He finished the game with forty-one points, thirteen steals, seventeen rebounds, eleven assists, and seven blocked shots—a quadruple double, the majority of which came in the second half. Archibald was stunned, beaten by nearly a single player.

When the buzzer sounded and we won by seven, our fans rushed the court. The Hammond Crew lifted Luke on their shoulders and paraded him around the gym, shouting how they owned Buffalo and would soon own the Empire State. I'd always known Luke was capable of this and felt he could have pulled off such a performance during any of our games, but he'd waited until the stakes were at their highest before showing us what he was truly made of. I can't imagine what it would have been like if it had been all of us, the whole Hammond Crew, out there playing together at the height of our potential. We could have beaten anyone. But maybe we didn't need a whole team now. Luke had learned how to win all by himself, which was a beautiful and terrifying thing. A power far too great for most people. But Luke wasn't most people.

When the Hammond guys brought Luke back over to us, he looked down at Dan and me and said, "They'll never break us *all* up." I'd never heard Luke say anything like that. Dude was always cool. Always stone-faced. Never a drop of emotion. Just killer instinct. But maybe we mattered as much to him as he did to us.

There was really no reason now we couldn't win out, then head east to play the best from NYC. For years, everyone had been going on and on about how E. Peg was the best in the city and maybe the state, and that he'd end up in the NBA someday. But Luke had made him his bitch. I'd always believed we could win a championship, but now I thought we really would. I saw myself with that trophy in my hands. I saw myself holding it up as people paraded me around the city on their shoulders. As Mom and Dad smiled and hugged each other, as Julia blew me kisses and told me she had always loved me, as Ray and Tony toasted me with non-alcoholic champagne, as Sister Rose and Sister Adele screamed out, "It's okay, Jimmy! We know you don't believe anymore, but we still believe in you!" As everyone patted Dan on the back and told him how great he was despite how bad he felt about himself, as the city of Buffalo erupted in celebration—with hope that the depression was finally over, that the rust would wash away, and we'd finally become the world-class city that was supposed to rival New York. That the jobs would come back, and the crime and drugs would go away, and that we'd all be happy again.

Chapter 24

Mr. Bosch was probably the best teacher I ever had. He taught my fifth-period English class, and I understood even the most difficult of concepts he presented to us. He had a way of breaking down complex material into easily digestible nuggets, and I learned a lot about myself along with whatever else he was teaching. There were a few cute girls in that class, and they all loved Mr. Bosch too—probably for similar reasons, but also because he had this bookish-but-hip, classically handsome look that could have easily landed him on primetime TV. Dude was ripped as fuck too, and he put everyone to shame in the weight room. I once saw him bench three-sixty as guys from the football team rooted him on.

"You only have one year left," he said, standing at his podium. He had this young-Brando intensity in his eyes. "Once you graduate, I suggest you put everything that reminds you of high school in a box, and put that box away in the attic for at least ten years. No matter how badly you'd like to look through it, just leave it alone. The time is coming for you to discover who you truly are, and that will be nearly impossible if you hold on tightly to the past. Go forward. Always go forward."

"What if you don't have an attic?" Lenny Daniels said from the back. All the girls turned around and told him to shut up.

Dude, this teaching thing might not be such a bad idea. Look at how they all adore you.

"Attic, basement, whatever, Lenny," Mr. Bosch said.

Great speech, just don't ask—

"Do any of you know what you'd like to be when you leave here?" Mr. Bosch said.

Fuck . . . I hated that question. It had taken a few years, but I'd finally gotten comfortable at Kirkland High—well, comfortable enough. It was different than St. Anthony's and better in a lot of ways. Now I was going to have to find my next path in life. I knew that path would include college, but after that . . .? School was bumper bowling, but soon those bumpers would be gone. What would it be like when you were all alone working some shitty job and coming back to a small dark apartment with poor heating in winter and no AC in summer? What would it be like eating TV dinners every night because the stress of cooking and cleaning would push you to the limit? What would it be like to work for a boss who'd fire your ass the second he sniffed out how crazy you are? I never knew what I wanted to be when I grew up. Billy and Manish and Ryan and Rachel all had their sights set on Harvard, Yale, Brown. And Julia—hell, she was already out living her dreams, dancing in NYC. But thinking of what I wanted to do sent my brain into such a frenzy, I always did my best to avoid it. I couldn't ever think of anything more than what was directly in front of my face. I knew now that I wasn't good enough to make it to the NBA. Maybe I could play college ball, but I wasn't talented enough for the main stage.

The truth was that I did have an answer to that question, but I could never say it out loud, especially not in a place like school. When I was a kid, I never thought I'd make it past eighteen. Never thought I'd make it without Mom there rubbing my back as I wept, trying desperately to fall asleep on the couch. All those long, dark, terrifying nights, all I'd ever wanted to be when I grew up was alive. Who can think of Brown when they can't even imagine breakfast?

Some dipshit in the back of the room was talking about wanting to go into business with his father to sell puppets or some other stupid crap, when I heard people yelling in the hall.

"Get your fuckin' hands off me, narc!"

I knew that voice. The whole class watched as the cops hauled Luke Harrison away in handcuffs. They marched him outside and put him in their car, and then they took off, along with my hopes of ever winning a state championship.

For years, Kirkland High had been flooded with cocaine. School administrators had been doing random locker searches but could never find anything. The problem got so bad that they had the cops bring in a drug-sniffing dog, which led them right to Luke's locker. Apparently, he was a huge dealer in North Buffalo, but no matter how much time we'd spent together, I'd never known it. He had nothing fancy—no gold watches or chains or a nice car. He ate BK, wore dirty old sneakers, and always took the bus everywhere. He was all business all the time. What made him great on the court also made him great slingin' coke. Knowing Luke, it probably had nothing to do with the money. It probably had more to do with him needing to be the best. He probably wanted to run the streets like he ran the court. And I was sure he hadn't been doing it alone. I was sure that shit had been happening at Hammond under my nose for years. The thought of it depressed me in a way I hadn't ever felt. Though it was the spot where many had lost teeth, spilled blood, and broken bones, Hammond had always been a sacred place to me. Had they just been playing there to meet new customers? How important had the game even been to them? Had I been more alone on that court than I'd ever realized?

How could you be so fucking stupid, James? So naïve? Don't you realize the whole world is passing you by, even with your eyes wide open? How do you miss this shit? You're so fucking concerned about God and Santa Claus being real that you miss the real world at your feet. In front of your face.

What about Silas? Was he in on it too? No, he loves basketball more than anything. He'd never do anything to jeopardize our shot at a championship. Nobody worked harder for it than he did.

Don't be naïve, man. Santa is fake. God is fake. Hammond is fake. So are all your friends. So are all your dreams.

That night, I was watching MTV in my room when I saw an interview with the singer Julia was supposedly dating, and he mentioned her—*actually* mentioned her by name. Mentioned her being the inspiration for his latest album. He was so elated talking about *my* Julia. She was out there, living the life. She'd made it happen for herself. She'd taken fate into her own hands. And now she was a star. All the rumors

I'd ever heard about her must have been true. I'd heard Luke and the Powells talk about her sometimes to piss off Joey, and all the shit they'd said probably really had happened. She probably was a cokehead. She probably did fuck every big underground band in New York. She probably did shake her ass in rap videos and let guys rub their hands all over her body.

I'll never be good enough for you, Julia. I can't do what they do. I can't get tattoos or do drugs because Sister Verona said that was bad and I wouldn't get into Heaven. Hell, if I ever let my guard down and got a tattoo, even a small one, I might wake up sweating and screaming some dark winter night with a head full of Evil Thoughts, and the only way to silence them would be to run downstairs, heat a kitchen knife on the stove, and scrape and burn that ink off my skin. I can't play rock music because I'll end up like Kurt Cobain, shooting myself in the head all alone in the garage, and people who commit suicide spend eternity burning in the deepest pits of Hell. Julia, I think I may have the ability to write songs like that dickhead you're dating, but I can't seem to do it. Whenever I start thinking about something, it vanishes. I have such powerful thoughts. They give me ideas, then take them away before I can understand them. It'd be better if I never had any ideas. If I was happy just marrying Downtown Debbie at age nineteen, then getting fat and never thinking again. I think that's the only way I can get by. The moment I try, it all caves in on me. I have such beauty inside of me, Julia. I wish you could see it. If you could, maybe you'd love me like you love him. Maybe you'd realize I'm not just some sack-of-shit street punk who'll be living in his parents' basement until he dies of heart disease at fifty. Who eats tubs of ice cream and drinks gallons of beer and talks nonstop about the high school championship he coulda won, "If that damned coach just knew how to run a team!" Julia, can't you see I'm not allowed to be cool? I can't just run off and follow my dreams. Dad needs my help in the bedroom upstairs, and Mom would die if I left her. Who'll guard the box of Honey Bunches of Oats in the cupboard? If I leave, they'll throw it out. Who'll watch Dan and make sure he doesn't slit his wrists like Uncle Vinny?

And if I do start following my dreams, how will I know they're not really the Evil Thoughts disguised as something good? How do I tell what's real from what's fake? Julia, my brain is so fucked up, it's beyond repair. Even if I did start a band, the moment people started praising me, I'd probably OD on heroin like Gerry. Why doesn't anyone talk about him anymore? How did this happen to all of us? Julia, you're supposed to be here helping us. Taking care of us. But you took your talent and ran far, far away. Do you hate us, Julia? Are you too good for us? Billy thinks he's too good for us. Manish too.

But fuck, you *are*. You know, I was listening to that Tragically Hip song that we loved when we were younger but that we never understood. It came on the radio the other day while I was thinking about you, and I think I finally got it. Something about those cryptic lyrics always felt just like the Thoughts. The ones that I didn't quite understand but always knew were powerful and concealed something real and truthful in the chaos and darkness. The ones that a part of me knew I'd be able to hold in my hand someday and call my own, even though there was no reason why I should ever think I could. Julia, I died when I was nine. When all those

Thoughts rushed me and changed me forever. I'll always be a terrified little kid lying on that bed, praying to God and Santa and Mom and Michael Jordan to save me. To help me sleep. To help me feel okay. But you, Julia, *you* were able to grow. Develop. Realize your dreams. You had such talent and you never doubted it. You believed in it and you became something so much bigger than the small world we grew up in. Julia, *you* were "Ahead by a Century." You always were. It's because of you that I understand this song now—that I understand this thing that was always with me but that I never quite got. You've given me clarity. I love you so much. Take me there with you. Show me how I can catch up. Show me more about how I can understand this darkness and light inside of me. Show me what I can do to be like you. Please don't give up on me. Don't turn your back on me. If I stay here, I'm going to die. I think about doing bad things to myself. I think about cutting myself too. Putting a rope around my neck like Grandpa. Sticking a needle in my arm like Gerry. But I know if I can just get to where you are, those Thoughts will stop, and I'll understand how to make them work for me. If you won't take me with you, at least show me the way. I'm confused. I'm incompatible. I'm furious. I just need some help. I think there's still time to save us all. Just show me how I can do it. Show me how to be beautiful like you. I'm worried that if we lose our next game, I might lose everything. Please, Julia, show me what else is out there for me.

Chapter 25

"As you all know, Luke Harrison was arrested yesterday," Coach said as we stood on the baseline at the Kirkland gym. "Obviously, his career as a Kirkland Lion is over. I know this news hurts, but we're going to have to learn to play without him. We've got Delaware High next, and we're up against Doug Warsaw, who's one of the deadliest shooters in the city. I know it's Friday night, but please make sure you get a good night's sleep and be at the bus no later than five p.m. You got that, Mr. Macker?"

"I got it like Magic got the hiv, Coach," Silas said.

We did "Team" on three and then headed to the locker room.

Silas approached Dan and me while we were changing. "Yo, can one of you scoop me home?"

"I'm walking to Cisco's," Dan said.

"I'll take you," I said. I had the station wagon that night.

We went to the parking lot and got in the wagon, and then I took off onto the snowy streets.

"Shit, my Black ass is gettin' as far away from snow

as possible the second I graduate," Silas said. "Hey, can we make a pit stop first at Pepe's?"

"Sure," I said.

"I've been working on some new tunes," Silas said. "I got the lyrics, just need the music."

"You got any lyrics on you now?"

"Yeah, I'll give you a little somethin'." He freestyled a few bars, which blew me away. I'd never heard him rap before, and it sounded like something you'd hear on the radio.

"How the hell'd you come up with that?" I said.

"You just gotta relax your mind and let the words flow from deep inside. Just hit a thought or emotion and shit starts flowin' like an oil well."

"And you can say anything you want?"

"Hell yeah. There ain't no rules to art. There ain't no rules to life either. Just let it rip, man, and do what feels right."

"I dunno. I don't think I know what feels right."

"Horace, you got the vision. You see the game. You just gotta see yourself. I think you're just one of these cats that takes a little longer to figure it all out."

"I hope so. I feel like there's something inside of me trying to get out, but I have no idea what it is."

"Why you worried about what it is?"

"I don't even know how to explain it."

"It'll come. Trust me."

I did trust him. And that fucking terrified me for a lot of reasons.

We parked at Pepe's Tacos, across the street from St. Anthony's, and the Hammond Crew was all over the parking lot, looking more intense than usual. I knew it had to do with Luke. Silas got out, and D. Pow came over to the station wagon.

"Yo, Horace, you guys gonna pull it off tomorrow?" he said. He was swaying and looked drunk.

"Fuck, I don't know. It's gonna be tough without Luke."

"Fuck Luke. You can still win. You just gotta play for yourself. You're the best player out there now."

That hit me in the gut. It meant a lot hearing him say that. A part of me wanted to do as he said and play for myself. The other guys like Shane and Mancuso had been playing for themselves for so long that I doubted anyone would blame me for doing the same. But I'd been born Catholic. Born in Buffalo. Born to a huge, crazy-ass family who shared everything short of used toilet paper. I knew I had no business ever playing for myself in anything.

And it haunted me to think that, right then, Luke was sitting in a cell because he'd chosen to play for himself. Shane and Mancuso were clowns. Their version of playing for themselves would, at worst, lead to hangovers or bumps on their dicks. But Luke was a champion with a raging heart and countless talents, and those talents had turned on him. Ruined him. Always think of the team first, Jimmy. You start listening to that voice inside of you telling you to go rogue and it's gonna bring you to the cell beside Luke. Just do what you're told and shut up about it.

"I heard there'll be some scouts out there tomorrow," D. Pow said. "Show 'em what you got."

"Yeah, maybe."

D. Pow walked back over to the others and took a swig from a flask his brother handed to him. They were all smoking cigarettes and drinking clear liquid from plastic Coke bottles, and their faces looked so old and tired, with the misery of adulthood already settling in. It seemed they already knew their time was over. These guys had ruled middle and high school. They'd fucked all the girls, sold all the weed, and thrown all the best parties. But now T. Pow was hacking up a lung, and he kept smoking. Now Joey, who'd always been so athletic and muscular, had to sit on a car hood to give his knees a break from carrying around the fifty extra pounds he'd put on that year.

Silas came back to the station wagon. "Yo, Ho-dingies, can you scoop me up to my cuz's?"

"On Grape Street?"

"The one and only."

Though I had an idea of what was going on, I needed to see it with my own eyes. I got on the Kensington Expressway and got off in the Fruit Belt.

"This may seem a little strange, but I got this feeling like I never really existed. You know what I'm saying?" I said.

"Yeah, I feel you."

"I'm just so sick of playing with losers—carrying these fucking losers. They have no heart. They're all beat before they even get in the game, and that's if they even man up and decide to play."

"Yo, lemme tell you something, Horace. My daddy grew up right over there in the East Side of Buffalo. Now that's one of the poorest areas in one of the poorest cities in the country. But he had one dream that he never let go of: he was gonna get his ass outta the ghetto. Wasn't raisin' a family in the hood. I remember walkin' on crack pipes in my front yard when I was little—fiends killin' each other just outside my door for Lord-knows-what. Now, my old man ain't never gonna win no father of the year award. That mothafucka never really helped me with shit. But at least his ass got us out of the ghetto. At least he put food on the table every night and heat in the house every winter. How many niggas can say that about their pops? Not everybody has the heart of a champion, Horace. But that sure as hell don't make 'em losers. You look up in the stands the next time you go talkin' about losers. No matter where we go, you always got someone up there cheering for you, and that means something. Not everybody has that. You need to go easy out there, man."

"I just feel like I'm being buried under an avalanche here, and nobody's even trying to dig me out."

"I get it. Yo, we're gonna make it big someday. A lotta those guys we just saw . . . this is as good as it gets for them. But you and me are goin' somewhere. Yo, it's a left here."

I pulled into a driveway, but it didn't belong to Silas's cousin—unless he'd moved. Silas walked up to the door, and a light-skinned guy who looked Puerto Rican answered. Silas went in and came back out a few minutes later carrying a backpack. He hopped into the car and tossed the bag on the back seat. A cop started tailing me before I pulled back on the Kensington Expressway, and I got seriously spooked, but he turned onto a side street. When I got to Silas's house, I reached back and grabbed the backpack before Silas could. It was unzipped about an inch, and I purposely stuck my finger in the hole and pulled up on it, opening the backpack enough to see a brick of white inside. Silas reached over, closed the backpack, grabbed it, and got out.

"This doesn't change anything, man," he said.

Chapter 26

I woke up the next morning to the old man screaming about money or some other horseshit and couldn't get back to sleep. When I sat up in bed, I was overcome with a feeling of total exhaustion—as if my body was wrapped in a stone blanket and my blood was heavy as molten lead. Though it was morning, it was a gray Buffalo winter morning, and even with the blinds open, the room was still dark. I just sat there, wrapping myself in the darkness and staring at the floor. I couldn't get up. There was nothing more in front of me. Just a wall of misery. Everything good in my life was now gone. Even with a trophy in hand, I'd still be a loser. A loser from a loser town with loser friends. A loser who couldn't even get Rachel Abrams to meet him at a fucking Denny's after school. She and all the others were probably spending the weekend deciding which Ivy League school they'd go to. Weighing their options. Trying to decide which school produced more CEOs, senators, US presidents. Making informed decisions based on class sizes, student-to-teacher ratios, the prestige of professors.

I felt as though I could just die right there—could die, and no one would even notice. They'd probably make an announcement about it at school and everyone might feel sorry for about a second, then they'd go on with their lives as if I was still invisible in the back of the room.

The only thing that got me up and moving was the thought that maybe there was some blow scattered on the back seat of the station wagon. I rushed outside and triple-checked to be sure there was nothing there. I looked down the street and checked parked cars for what could be undercover cops, then went back up to my room.

Silas, you made me a criminal. Bullshit! James, you did this to yourself. You *had* to see. Why can't you just be like all the others and close your eyes and pretend everything is okay? Why can't you just close your eyes and pray, and lie to yourself that God will make it all better? Don't you see that's how people survive here? Don't you see that all the battered wives and drunk dads and miserable kids survive here only because they're able to adapt? To kill it all away? Bury their hope in wooden barrels that they toss over the falls? Don't you know what's coming, man? You can't escape this. This prolonged delusion of adulthood. This blind faith in misery as our only salvation. This is what you inherit here. Don't ever blame Uncle Vinny or Grandpa for what they did. They were the smart ones. They *knew*. The others don't. You can know too, man. Get a knife. Press down and drag it across your wrists. You'll get dizzy, fall asleep. They'll find your body four days later when the smell gets to be so bad someone finally comes upstairs to check.

There are anvils on my hope. Boulders on my inspiration. The good is so tightly wrapped around the bad it has no chance of ever seeing the light. Get a dull knife. Like everything else in life, this can't be easy. You gotta fight for it. Fight for the right for control. Rest.

Eternal Damnation.

Fuck.

The old man was still screaming, now about how he couldn't afford new windows because of the god-damned Democrats or whatever. The phone rang, and every part of me hoped it'd be Rachel, finally calling *me* for once. Wishing me luck with my game that night. I picked up the phone in my room, but it was Grandma. She said she was feeling a little sick and that she was going to the doctor but not to worry because it was nothing serious.

When I hung up, I saw the marble notebook Sister Adele had given me sitting on the dresser. Over the years, I'd written a few things here and there in it, and felt that maybe I had something to write that morning, so I grabbed it. But everything in me seemed so dark, I felt that if I started writing, the Evil would sneak out and everyone would finally see how psychotic I was. They'd storm the house with pitchforks and torches and drag me out into the street and hack pieces off my body until all the Evil was gone and they were "safe" again. We never escaped the Dark Ages. Angry mobs are as possible and powerful as they were then, and don't ever convince yourself otherwise.

I put the journal back on the dresser and went downstairs. Poor Rich was now laughing at the TV. Mom was wiping the dining room table down with a soapy rag.

"Ma, you ever think about going back to school?" I said.

"What? Don't be silly."

"I really think you could—"

"Go get ready. We're heading to afternoon Mass before your game tonight."

"Fuck that. You know I don't believe in that bullshit anymore."

"You need to pray to God so you win tonight."

"We won last game without me *or* God, so I ain't too concerned."

"You never do anything without God."

"Yeah, whatever."

"If he doesn't have to go, then neither do I," Dad said from the living room.

"See what you've done?" she said to me.

The phone rang, reminding me about Grandma. Dad screamed for someone to get it, but after the third ring, he got his big ass up and answered himself.

"Hey," I said, "Grandma called a little while ago and said she was going to the hospital."

"What? How long ago was this?" Mom said.

"I dunno, maybe half an hour?" I said.

"Are you kidding me? And you didn't say anything?" Mom said.

"What does it matter if I say anything? Nobody does shit about anything anyways."

"Sometimes I think you're more animal than human."

"H-how could you say that to me?"

"Do you even have a heart?"

"Do you even know . . . do you even know what goes on in my head? Do you know what saying something like that means to me?"

"Me, me, me. Always *me* with you, isn't it? Why do you always have to be so selfish?"

"Selfish? How can I be selfish when nothing in this whole fucking world is mine?"

"What makes you think you deserve anything? Blessed are the meek—"

"For they're a bunch of fucking retards! I'm tired of being a sacrifice, Ma. I'm not like you. I don't want to die for anyone anymore. I'm tired of giving my life away. I want my own life. I want to be happy."

"You sound just like your father. Always so dramatic about everything."

"Don't you compare me to him! I'll kill myself before I ever become him. I'll kill myself right now."

"You're such a jerk sometimes."

"I will fucking blow my brains out."

"Why can't you be more like Dan? He never complains."

"How can he? He sits all alone in the dark basement, buried under the weight of this house. What are you doing about that, huh?"

"You know the doctor says he has headaches."

"And you know that's bullshit! Why aren't you helping him? Why isn't anybody helping him?"

"God is helping him. Come to church so we can pray—"

I punched the wall so hard, the drywall cracked. Poor Rich hung up the phone and said to me in an unusually calm manner, "Hey, I just painted that. Take it easy."

I picked up a chair from the dining room table and put its legs right through the wall.

"Hey, Jimmy—" Dad said.

I dropped the chair and grabbed him by the throat, pushing him into the living room where he fell to his knees. I wrapped my arm around his neck like a python and squeezed with everything I had. I expected him to erupt. I expected him to get up and throw me through the window. But he just gasped for breath with this helpless fucking look on his face. Like a terrified, bullied kid. It disgusted me. This monster who'd destroyed so many of the sparkling cities of my youth. This animal who I'd thought could push that house over with his bare hands. He begged me—please, I can't breathe. All these years, the strength had been a lie. All these years, he was a bigger bitch than any of us. My veins didn't hold a miner's blood or a Nazi-killer's. I was the son of a coward. I wanted to kill him. But I felt so sorry for him. Sorry for that little kid, whose eyes begged me to let go. Sorry that my arms, like Grandpa's, were crushing this poor kid's will to live. I let go of him, not even realizing that Mom had been screaming at me to stop, hitting me in the knees with the tennis racket from the closet. You know what? Fuck her. She never did any of that shit to Poor Rich while he was beating the shit out of me. She just looked away and let it happen.

Dad gasped for breath and rubbed his neck. I bent over and looked into his dripping wet eyes and said, "You died with God. I don't believe in you anymore. You never get to tell me what to do ever again. You never get to tell me what to do ever again."

I took off for Hammond, which was empty and had been for most of the last year. Some of the kids who once used to go there were now in jail for stealing cars or smoking crack or breaking and entering. The others were too busy getting high or working full-time jobs. A few even had kids now. I was alone on that court. There wasn't much snow on the blacktop, so I didn't bother clearing it. I shot jumpers from a few feet, moving in a U around the rim, then moved out about a foot when I got to the other side of the rim, and shot my way back. I kept doing that until I was taking threes. I drained three in a row, then four, then five. I kept counting and stopped at twenty-three in a row. If I shot one more, maybe I'd miss. You gotta know when to walk away. Gotta know when to stop.

When I got home, the wall was patched up with a fresh sheet of drywall. Mom was at church, and Dad was laughing at the TV again. I didn't realize how late it was until I searched for Dan and he wasn't there. He must have already left for the bus. I got ready, and Mom came home, so I had her drive me to the Kirkland High parking lot. She didn't mention anything about that afternoon. But I guess after a lifetime of eating shit and saying it tasted like strawberries, she'd probably already forgiven and forgotten—or just plain forgotten.

Everybody else was already on the bus. Coach gave me crap for being late, but fuck him. I passed Dan in the front and took an open spot in the middle. There was an open seat next to Silas in the back, but I felt bad enough just being on that bus with him and I wasn't about to get any closer.

In the locker room, we sat in a U around Coach. Silas tried apologizing, but I wasn't like Mom. I couldn't just forget that shit. He said he was just saving up to buy some recording equipment and then to head out west, and that I could come and all that shit, but how much of that was lies as well? I felt as if our entire friendship was bullshit. How many times had our family station wagon transported bricks of cocaine throughout the city? How many times had he told me that all he cared about was winning a state championship?

"Okay, gentlemen, we've reached the second round of the playoffs. If we take this one, then we make the city championship game, and from there we play against the best in the state. Luke's absence is going to hurt, but we've already beaten Delaware High this season, and we can do it again without him. Dan, you're going to be starting for Luke tonight. Make sure you stick to number thirty-four like glue . . ."

Dan gave Coach a look as if to say, me? But once it sank in, Dan's energy seemed to change from benchwarmer to champion in only a few seconds. He, like Mom, could forgive and forget an entire career's worth of being benched, and I knew he'd be coming out strong.

"The only way we're gonna win this game is if we play together."

We did "Team" on three and walked to the court, and when we stepped on the hardwood, Shane said again, "We're gonna get killed." But when the DJ played "Bombs Over Baghdad," I was ready to take on the '96 Bulls. Dan and I led the team in a lap around the gym, which was packed with screaming fans, and we broke into a layup drill. I was so pumped, I dunked the ball. I wasn't even trying to either— just ran up for a layup and the feeling came over me. I'd never gotten up high enough to dunk before, but the energy from the crowd boosted me the extra few inches. Andy pushed me and said, "Dude, you're gonna get us a technical." Apparently it was a technical foul to dunk in warm-ups, but the refs weren't looking, so we were cool.

Mom and Dad were cheering in the stands beside the Hammond Crew. I wished Steven was there, but he'd enlisted in the Army and was already gone.

Billy, Ryan, and Manish were there with Rachel Abrams and a few other people. I heard Billy yelling my name. It was nice to hear him acknowledge that I was better than him at something. It made me feel a little worthier of his friendship.

When Mom and Dad saw Dan line up for the tip, they lost it, screaming his name and leaping up and clapping. That made me smile. I don't know why Coach started Dan that day. Maybe it was because he finally realized how Shane brought us down. Maybe he'd seen how poorly Andy had played the day before and figured why not give Dan a try. Maybe he was tired of hearing me bitch about it.

Mancuso actually won the tip, and Dan grabbed it. He passed it to me, and I waited for our offense to set up. As great as the energy of the crowd was, it overwhelmed me. Right from the start, I felt I could hear every word everyone was saying. *Pass! Shoot! Drive!* I could feel them all judging the way I dribbled and ran and shot the ball with one foot behind the other.

Dan set a pick on Doug Warsaw, who was covering me. Even though he'd hit a growth spurt a few summers back and had grown to be six five, they kept him at point. I think this was the work of his father, a prominent surgeon with considerable influence at Delaware High, who wanted to prepare Doug to play point at somewhere like Michigan or Duke, where he'd be too short to play forward or center. He had me by a few inches, but I'd kicked his ass so many times when we were kids that those inches didn't mean shit. I knew how he played. Knew every one of his ball fakes and crossover moves. When Dan set a pick, I knew Doug would sense it coming, so I faked in the direction of the pick and went the other way. I drove hard to the hoop, but the center got in my face, so I kicked it out to Shane on the wing. He launched a hurried three that hit the side of the backboard and went out of bounds.

"Work it around, Shane," Coach said.

Doug pushed point, and I got right on him after he crossed half court. Shane's man set a pick on me, and Doug used it to sink a pretty three in Shane's face.

Silas passed it in to me, and I pushed it up court with Doug on me the whole way. I hated playing point guard. It was much harder than it looked. There were a million ways to fuck up, and if you did, the other team could get an easy layup out of it. The pressure from the team and all the fans superheated my brain. I remembered hearing all the greats like Magic, Jordan, and Bird talking about benefiting from having experience when playing in the playoffs, and now I knew what they meant. This shit was more mental than physical, and I didn't trust my brain. Once I was aware of this, my brain started attacking me. I passed ahead to Dan before I could do something stupid. Though he had an open shot, Shane started screaming for the ball, so Dan passed it to him. Shane tried to launch another three, but his man was on him, so he bounced a pass to Silas in the paint. Silas did a drop-step but the center picked him up, so he dished me a behind-the-back pass as I ran to the hoop, and I put in a layup. I could hear D. Pow screaming, "Yeah, Horace!"

I picked up Doug at the half again, and again got picked by Shane's man at the top of the key without Shane saying shit. Doug drove and sank a fifteen-footer.

I pushed it up court again and passed to Dan. Shane called for the ball, and Dan passed it. Shane tried to bomb another three, but he was covered, so he drove the lane. He dribbled off his foot, and the ball rolled out of bounds.

The ref called for subs, and Andy came in for Shane. "C'mon, Coach, I'll hit the next one," Shane said on his way to the bench.

I looked up at Mom helping Carolynn blow her nose, and I walked over to Dan. "I don't care if you have three men on you, the next time you touch the ball, shoot it."

Silas heard and said, "Yeah, Harvey, we need you right now."

"C'mon, Coach, put me in for Dan. He sucks," Shane said. He was sitting right by Coach.

I know Dan heard, but it didn't seem to faze him.

When Doug pushed the ball up, I stole it just past half court. Instead of taking it in for a layup, I waited for the offense to set up. I shook Doug and drove to the right, where Andy was on the wing. I drew some defenders, then kicked it out to Andy. I ran and set a pick on Dan's man, and Dan ran to the top of the key. Andy hit him with a pass and in one fluid motion, Dan sank a deep three right in Doug's face. Highlight reel stuff.

Our crowd lost it. I could hear both Powells and Joey screaming shit like, "Harvey! Have my baby!" "Harvey! You rock my world!" Mom and Dad were screaming for him too. Silas and I both gave him high fives, and Dan smiled.

Silas stole a lazy Delaware inbounds pass and kicked it back to Dan, who sank a fifteen-footer.

Doug pushed it up court and passed it to the center, who took a hook shot over Mancuso. The center missed it but got the rebound, and I fouled him trying to block his shot, which he put in. He hit the free throw, and I pushed the ball up court. I passed to Dan on the left wing, and he dumped a bounce pass to Silas as he cut backdoor. Silas did a spin move and put in a reverse layup.

On D, the small forward sank a three with Andy on him.

As I pushed the ball up court, I caught their D sleeping, so I threw a pass to Dan, quarterback-style, and he put in an easy layup.

When Doug pushed it again, he drove past me, but Dan back-tipped the ball right into Silas's hands. Silas passed it to me, and I dribbled up court, taking it right to the hoop. When the power forward stepped to me, I kicked it to Dan in the corner, and he drained a three.

Doug hit a three the next time down the court, and Silas put in a hook over the power forward. We kept going back and forth like that until I drew my second foul, and Coach put Shane in for me, and Delaware started pulling ahead.

But before the half, Silas blocked the shit out of the center, and Dan dove to save the ball from going out of bounds, tipping it back to Silas. Silas passed it back to Dan, and Dan dribbled up court. He stopped at the top of the key, faked a pass to Shane, and drained an NBA three in Doug's face. He finished the half with five threes and twenty-one points.

In the locker room at halftime, Coach told us, "Now that's some excellent teamwork out there! Let's keep that up! And, Dan, you just keep right on shooting." He told Shane he'd be sitting at the start of the second half, and Shane went ballistic, tearing off his sneakers and throwing them across the locker room.

We did "Team" on three and went back out to finish

Delaware off. We put on a full-court press right from the start of the second half and wore them down. We went up by six, but when I drew my third foul Coach pulled me out and put Shane in. I think Coach finally realized what a disease Shane was when we got behind by two with him out there. Coach put me back in, but I drew my fourth foul almost instantly. Coach kept me in, though, because Shane was fucking up the game. Dan and Silas were dominating. Silas owned the paint, and Dan kept getting steals and draining threes. Despite the energy of the crowd fucking with my head, I was able to block out a lot of it. That is, until I heard someone in the crowd say something like, "For Chrissakes!" which I heard as, "For Christ's sake!" For a second, I got lost in thought and pulled my groin trying to keep up with Doug. He drove the lane, getting an extra step on me, and when I shuffled to keep up, I felt that old, dull pain—ancient biblical stuff from when God banished Lucifer to Hell. I jumped to block Doug's shot, and even though it was clean, the ref blew the whistle, ending the game for me. I sat at the end of the bench, and when Shane walked back on the court, I knew we were fucked. He took a few wild shots, made some errant passes, and we lost by one.

Dan and Silas both had monster games. Silas finished with eighteen points, twenty-four boards, and eight steals, and Dan dropped thirty-eight points with ten threes and nine steals. Before fouling out, I had twelve points and ten assists—mostly to Dan. God, if we'd only had Luke instead of Shane, we would have been moving on to the championship. But Luke wasn't there, and never would be again. Because he was eighteen, and because of how much coke he'd had in his locker and New York's mandatory drug-sentencing laws, Luke would get fifteen years.

Delaware went on to win the city championship, but they lost to a team from Utica in the first round at Glens Falls. Doug was only a junior, so he'd be back the next year.

But Hammond was done forever.

Chapter 27

The summer between junior and senior year, I got drunk for the first time. I was with Ryan, Billy, and Manish, and we stole a case of beer from Ryan's dad and a bottle of vodka from my parents' liquor cabinet. Neither of my parents drank, but the house was always well stocked with booze because my aunts and uncles were on a nonstop party that would last until their funerals. No one would notice a bottle missing. Hell, no one in my house would notice a kid missing.

Ryan's parents were out, so we drank in his basement while listening to *Who's Next*. Ryan's dad had a great record collection. Ryan had burned a bunch of the records onto CDs, but the songs sounded worse that way than they did on vinyl. Manish and Ryan were big into computers, and they showed me websites where you could find the lyrics for almost any song. We'd spend hours looking through the words to our favorites. The first I ever looked up was "Crossroads" by Bone Thugs-N-Harmony. I was looking up the lyrics to "Baba O'Riley" that night as I struggled through my first beer. The other guys had gotten drunk before, but I'd needed to keep my body clean and pure so I could win a state championship. Now all that was done. I'd also wanted to keep myself pure so I could get into Heaven. Even though I no longer believed, God still had such a hold on me I thought I'd never get away. But once I got that first beer down, God's voice lost some of its power in my mind. The second brew went down much easier. I got up and sang every word to "Behind Blue Eyes" as if I'd written the song myself. Feeling Pete Townshend's words working through my body loosened up words of my own.

Before the school year ended, Mr. Bosch had put a single piece of paper on each of our desks before class one day, then told us, "Don't think—just write." Some of the other kids seemed confused—Ryan included—but I got it right away. I started writing nonsense at first, but then I wrote an entire song. Mr. Bosch asked me to recite it for the class, but I declined. The exercise was liberating; however, the song began, *Hold my hand, my young son. Wrap your fingers tightly. I'll guide wherever you will go.* Even in song, I couldn't escape the restraint. But after that second beer and then the third, I started to feel a liberation I'd never felt before. When I went to piss, this time I didn't hear the voices of my parents and brothers and sisters and aunts and uncles and teachers and everyone shouting for me to get the fuck outta the bathroom! Hurry up! I need to take a shower! I need the hair dryer! I need you to finish your Religion test! Grandma is watching you! Hide your ding-dong! She'll know if you shake too many times! After a few beers, the piss just flowed. I couldn't have cared less if someone knocked on the door or came in and pissed along with me or even on me. After, I looked at myself in the mirror and smiled. I smiled so widely. I'd finally found an answer! I'd finally found a way out of my head. The beer killed the noise. I went for another and another, and when we walked through the park to Denny's, I hit on every waitress in the place. I didn't even care what they said. Didn't care that they rejected me. I asked them all to marry me. Even when they threatened to call the cops, I didn't give a shit. I stole the toothpick dispenser, and we took off running.

We walked back through the park, and I tossed the toothpick dispenser into the front yard of a mansion near the diamond where I used to play Little League games. I kept telling the guys we should go to Rachel's house, but they said that'd be a bad idea. I wanted to tell her how I felt about her. With a head full of beer, I didn't care what she'd say. I just wanted her to know. I wanted to tell her that I could be her boyfriend, that I'd move with her to Pennsylvania when she went to Swarthmore. Hell, I'd fit right in in Philly. We could move there when she graduated, and I could protect her from all the scumbags who'd try to hurt her and steal her money. We could make a great team. I went on and on like that until I passed out in Ryan's backyard.

When I woke up the next morning, my head was killing me, but it was more than worth it. Better than God or basketball, beer was a true escape. Beer was beautiful. Beer was the answer to all my problems. Everyone always bitched about drunks being deadbeats, but Uncle Tommy had his own house and car. Maybe being a drunk was the way to go.

All summer, I'd steal a bottle of whiskey here and a bottle of wine there, and I'd drink myself to sleep. Ryan got a job at a supermarket on Delaware Ave., and we'd bring to the counter cases of beer, frozen pizzas, bags of chips, condoms, and he'd charge us the price of a newspaper. We'd go in waves—me, Billy, Manish, Eitan—filling the station wagon with hundreds of beers for under three bucks. "Big Pimpin'" became our getaway song, and I'd always rap Jay-Z's verse and Billy did Pimp C's as we drove off to whoever's house and supply the whole fucking place with booze. For months, we brought the party with us wherever we went, all for practically free. We'd dump out a Guinness or Sam Adams for each beer we chugged, offering a sacrifice to the beer gods. Billy and Manish would get a little shook about it sometimes, but Ryan and I didn't give a fuck. We'd even go to convenience stores and walk out with cases of beer. Most employees would just stand there shouting, and by the time they did anything, we'd be gone. All my life, I'd known adults weren't watching, and now it was time to punish them for it. It was time to take everything they had while they weren't looking and leave 'em wondering how they could have lost it all. I realized nobody gave a shit, and if you walked around with your dick hanging out of your pants, most people would just get out of your way. Ryan got a cell phone, so no matter where we went, we always knew where the party would be. We were free to head out into the night and let it take us.

I pretty much stopped playing basketball entirely. No one was going to Hammond except the drunks and crackheads, and the court became lonely again. I hadn't heard much from Silas, and people were saying he'd moved to California. I thought about calling to confirm this, but I just couldn't. A part of me was glad he was gone. But another part was devastated that my best friend could just leave like that without saying goodbye. Yeah, we hadn't hung out much over those last few years, but once you bonded with someone the way Silas and I had, you never really stopped being friends. You might get tired of one another, or angry, or whatever, but no matter what happened, you'd always be connected. And he just upped and left without me. He'd said we'd write songs together and make it big in LA, but that must have been bullshit, just like everything else. Anyway, I was glad to stay in Buffalo.

I'd finally started to understand what the others had been saying when they told me if I just tried, I could get girls. When I was drunk, I didn't give a fuck, and I started getting my dick sucked and eating pussy on the regular. At parties, girls would pull me into closets or garages or the back seats of cars, and slobber all over my dick—sometimes fast and sloppy, other times slow and sensual. The first time was in a bush behind the coffee shop near St. Anthony's. Downtown Debbie unbuckled my pants while we were walking home, and I let her do her thing. Soon all the girls said I was a player and a manwhore, and we liked you better when you were just the shy, awkward guy. Yeah, maybe so, ladies, but none of you ever juiced my nuts the way ol' Debbie did. As much as I ragged on her, she had a killer body, and I ate that box after licking every inch of her skin. I would have fucked her, but God was still up there watching me. Sister Rose was still up there rooting for me to make the kinds of choices that would put me back to work in her eternal garden in the sky. That would allow me to enter her eternal library where any book was at my fingertips.

But, Sister, you don't know how badly I wanna work that snatch. Why does everyone else get to fuck, but I have to go home with sore nuts? I'd rub my hard dick all over wet pussy, but I'd never stick it in. One night, Lisa Webber and

Karen Brunetti pushed me into a room at Brenda Carvey's house, and Lisa sucked my dick while I made out with Karen. Then they switched. I lay on the bed, and Lisa took off her pants and sat on my face, and I made her cum. Karen pulled out a condom, but I told her no. I was embarrassed to tell her the real reason, so I said my dick was sore. None of those public school kids would ever know the complexity of the bond I still had with God. St. Anthony's fucked me up royally—but I don't think I would have changed anything. Besides, some of the other guys were getting herpes and crabs and shit, and it was nice having a clean, rash-free johnson.

I must have been doing something right, though, because girls would call and come by and they'd go in the above-ground pool Poor Rich and I had installed in the backyard that May, and they'd take off their tops and pull my hands underwater and put 'em on their prickly pears and we'd rub together until we'd cum. I loved feeling asses and tits and massaging muffs, and I didn't know why I'd locked my sexuality in prison for so long. Why I'd pissed away my time chasing after future senators and all-star dancers and heart surgeons when all I had to do was take a deep, calming breath and let the legs open for me. I spent the whole summer drunk as fuck and face-first in pussy, as should be standard for any seventeen-year-old.

There was something about being seventeen and doing yard work and cleaning the pool and hauling piles of dirt to low spots in the lawn that made me feel alive. I'd put on my Walkman and play the CDs Ryan burned for me. I'd listen to Sabbath and Zeppelin and Floyd and The Who as I cut the lawn. I'd listen to Supertramp and Queen as I sucked leaves out of the pool. I'd play The Allman Brothers and

Hendrix as I ran all over Buffalo. I never wore a shirt. After so many years of lifting and playing sports, my body was solid. But no matter how many hours I spent at the gym, whenever I looked at myself in the mirror, I always felt small and weak. I would say, I need to work on triceps or curls or pecs or whatever. But I'd seen a picture of myself standing next to Luke in the paper a few months back when they announced the first-team all-city players, and in it, I was just as big as he was. I maxed out at two eighty on bench and almost four hundred with squats, and I realized that maybe all this shit about being weak was in my head. When I cut the front lawn, girls would look at me. Sometimes they'd whistle or come over to talk. When I ran by Miss Amalia's restaurant, I'd see her pretending not to notice. One time, I purposely went over and spoke to her as I was cooling down, and no matter how she tried, she kept watching the sweat drip down my pecs, over my abs, and into my shorts. As the drops ran across my fat Italian sausage, I wanted to take her by the hand, lead her to the kitchen, and eat her pussy until she screamed, then titty-fuck her and release a gallon of cum in her face.

That summer, I felt like a Bob Seger song. "Like a Rock." Even though I got a part-time job laying brick for a hardscaping company, I was done pissing away my time and energy on frivolous bullshit. I was done trying for state championships and trying for Heaven and trying for Harvard and trying to get Dad to stop yelling and to make Mom smile. No, that summer I was out to make some money, get drunk as shit, and cum all over every hot horny chick in the city of Buffalo.

I think we all knew that this summer was our last

chance to fuck around and have fun. The next summer would be spent getting ready to go away to college. So we'd drive west into Canada and go to the beach and race cars on desolate country roads and hit up the titty bars with our chalked IDs and pass out all over Ryan's parents' summer cottage. I loved being drunk. Unlike Uncle Tommy, I was a nice drunk. A happy drunk. All I wanted was to joke around and then jizz on a pair of hot tanned tits and pass out. When I was drunk, I could sleep anywhere—no earplugs necessary. Even after I'd given up on God, I still prayed almost every night—the prayers just weren't anything formal. It was more like an informal conversation with God. But when I was drunk, I just fell right asleep. No chitchat. No begging or despair. I got drunk almost every night, just like Uncle Jake. Smiled every night, just like Uncle Jake.

Maybe soon my hands would start shaking every night, just like Uncle Jake's. Maybe soon I'd lose a kidney, just like Uncle Jake.

Chapter 28

In November 2000, I was one of the SOBs who voted George W. Bush into the White House. Despite everything Billy and Ryan told me about him, when I stepped into that voting booth, I felt the weight of a lifetime of shame pulling that lever down for me. Besides, what more damage could one president do? I mean, left or right, my life was shit. It didn't matter which jerkoff's face I'd see on TV; the same Evil would still be inside my mind.

Dan was already off at Brockport studying communications. After his performance against Delaware High, a scout from Syracuse showed interest, but nothing ever came of it. If it had, Dan probably would have played with Carmelo Anthony on their championship team. He could have made Brockport's team, but I think, like me, Dan wanted a break from basketball.

We hadn't spoken since he'd left that summer. Even before that, we really didn't talk. He was spending a lot of time with the cross-country guys, and they smoked a shitload of weed. I got high with Dan and Ian Morricone one night before Ian headed west to start a band in Venice Beach, and it was one of the defining moments of my life.

After toking, I went to my room and listened to Zeppelin, and I felt the music, purple and black, wrapping around me, warming me, filling all those spots in my soul it had never reached before. Ian came in and played "Redemption Song," which I'd never heard before, and after that first verse, I immediately knew what I wanted to do with my life. I pictured myself sitting cross-legged under a tall tree in some ancient forest and holding out my arms, palms up to the sky. After, I saw myself playing an acoustic guitar in that forest as all the knowledge of the world flowed through me. I became a filter for everything in this world beautiful and hideous and clean and dirty.

After that night, I started growing out my hair and wearing clothes with earth tones and holes. I wore sandals and hemp necklaces and smoked weed whenever I could. When I was high, I could see entire films and symphonies playing in my head—could see paintings and sculptures forming and changing colors and shapes and sizes. My thoughts became something beautiful and powerful and aligned. Weed gave me a purpose in a way God never had. Beer helped me kill everything away, but weed helped me build it back together.

As powerful as it was, though, weed couldn't help me rebuild my relationship with Dan. After all those years of not talking, I'd just sort of stopped trying. He had his life; I had mine. Like with Rachel and Julia and God and Santa, I had to give up. If he didn't want to be my brother, then I couldn't push him. Maybe I could be better to Jeremy instead. I'd always been such a prick to him, but he was becoming a pretty cool kid. He was one of the most popular eighth graders at Kirkland Middle, though he'd only been there a short time, and all the hip stoner kids were always coming by the house. They thought Dad was hilarious and would goad him on and on to tell stories about sump pumps and World War I and how to stop the Russians if they attacked, all while they giggled like idiots. While I could only talk to people when I was drunk, Jeremy was a natural at making friends. He was smart and funny and didn't do anything weird like Dad and I did. I was more like Dad with this shit. I'd find myself drifting in conversation, going on and on about the most minute details about something, not realizing that no one gave a fuck. Or I'd start ranting about how shitty music or mainstream film was these days, and they'd walk away to listen to Our Lady Peace and watch *Coyote Ugly*.

My sisters weren't as sociable as Jeremy, and I knew they were having an even harder time in public school than at St. Anthony's. Diane was a freshman at Kirkland High, and Rebecca was a fifth grader at Kirkland Elementary, and they'd both come home crying sometimes because the other kids were picking on them. Mom and Dad never seemed to give a shit, and I probably would have just made things worse, so no one ever really told them not to worry and that it'd be all right. The truth was, it wouldn't be all right. Life didn't get better until you stopped giving a fuck and started pounding beers and smoking chronic. After hearing what the other kids called them, though, I realized that I'd been bullying my sisters for years, calling them fat and stupid and ugly. A part of me wanted to help them, but after all those years of beating them down, it was almost as if I'd made grooves in my brain that, no matter how hard I tried to be nice, I'd slide right down again into a place where I was mooing like a cow at them or barking like a dog. I was disgusted with how I treated them, but no one was stopping me, and the more I did it, the more I realized how little control I had over anything. But even if I had been the best brother on Earth, this world wanted nothing more than to bring us all to our knees, then put two bullets in the back of the head, and there was nothing I could do to change that. You can't be weak, girls. You gotta be strong. What Would John Wayne Do? You gotta fight back. You're not ugly. You're not fat. Go push one of those fuckers down the stairs and step on his throat. That'll get 'em to shut up. But I know you won't, because you were taught by a monster of a father to always let life push you around. You were taught by a monster of an older brother that your whole role in life is to absorb all the ugliness in the world and call it your own.

I knew I was a terrible brother, but who the fuck was showing me how to care about anyone? Poor Rich was a straight loon and Mom was slipping deeper and deeper into Rosary World now that Carolynn was old enough to take care of herself. I felt comfortable shouting every terrible thing in the world at my brothers and sisters, but it was impossible for me to say something nice. There was no way I could ever say *I love you*. The truth was, I didn't know if I even did. We were roommates. We shared a space. I didn't know any of them better than a stranger off the street. I knew the movies they liked and their favorite singers and restaurants and all, but the rest was a mystery to me. Hell, I didn't even know myself. Only now was I starting to realize maybe there was a new person inside of me dying to get out. But I didn't even know how to care for that person. All I had was the party that night. All I could think about were the next pair of tits to fuck.

I hadn't spoken with Silas in months, either. It was weird. As much time as we'd spent together. As many battles as we'd fought together and got bloodied and bruised, I didn't even know his birthday. I didn't even know his middle name. Shit, I didn't know Ryan's either, or Manish's. What the fuck did any of us know about anyone? The month before, one of the kids who was always at every party and smiling the hardest shot himself in the head. Nobody even knew why. We stopped partying for, like, a night when we found out, then went just as hard the next.

Chapter 29

I didn't even try out for the team senior year. With Silas and Luke and Dan gone, there didn't seem to be a point. I was tired—tired of fighting for something that didn't want me. Tired of fighting adults, trying desperately to get them to see the greatness that was Hammond. Tired of trying to bring greatness to people who did all they could to stay stuck in mediocrity or worse. They could all eat shit. Besides, now I had beer and weed and pussy. Organized basketball was for chumps. My best days on the court were behind me.

After our game against Delaware High that last winter, though, Fillmore State was interested in me. I went to a few practices and played with the team, but my heart was no longer in it. Fillmore was a D1 program, and at that level, you had to eat, sleep, and shit basketball, and I just couldn't do it, so I told them thanks but no thanks before they had a chance to reject me first. Just as Dad had given up a decade of drinking almost instantaneously, after that last practice session, I almost entirely gave up basketball. I stopped playing it, watching it, carrying my ball around the house. It fascinated and terrified me that I could give up something so important to me without a second thought, and it made me wonder what else I could give up so readily. I'd already dropped God on His head. What about Mom? Or Dad? Or Dan? Or Silas? Life seemed to be nothing more than a long, exhausting journey of walking away from everything. Pick something up, use it for a bit, then toss it back on the path and keep going. No rest. No enjoyment. Just constant motion. Just hazy memories.

The latest thing I'd picked up off that path was a girlfriend. Apparently, she'd gone to all our games last season and had written my jersey number, forty-two, all over her notebooks and on papers she taped to the mirror in her bedroom—at least, that's what her friend Becky told me. "C'mon, just give her a chance. She'll be at Samantha's house tonight," Becky said in the hallway one afternoon. I wasn't going to go but changed my mind when I saw a wrinkled note in my locker after school. "I heard you weren't playing on the team again this year. But maybe you'll have time now to take me out for coffee?" I smiled the rest of the day. Her name was Amelie, and she was a grade behind me. We'd had a computer or home economics class or something together the year before, and I was surprised I hadn't realized how cute she was. She had this face that didn't catch my attention at first, but the more I looked at it, the more beautiful it became. She was in all AP and honors classes and was ranked fourth in her grade, but she was the type of smart girl who was fucking clueless about life. She knew everything about vectors and derivatives in AP Calculus, everything about which king married which queen to prevent/start which war in AP Euro, everything about atomic theory and molecular formulas in AP Chem, but she had no idea how a lawn mower worked ("Does it just suck the grass up or something?"), no sense of the most basic directions (she once got lost on her own street), and no fucking clue who Bob Dylan or David Bowie or Led Zeppelin or Humphrey Bogart were ("Marlon Brando? Is he one of the Wayans brothers?"). She thought the Bond movie *GoldenEye* had been created after the video game. Regardless, she had huge tits, a perfect stomach, and the best ass in school, hands down. She was a swimmer and set a few school records. It felt good having someone so smart, talented, and beautiful leaving me notes.

The party that night was a shitshow, though. Samantha must have pissed someone off, because people were fucking up her house. It wasn't as bad as the party I'd gone to years back where people had burned down half of the kitchen, but it was still pretty bad. A few football players were pulling up her living room carpet, dumping mayonnaise all over the padding underneath, and putting the carpet back in place. Some guys in the basement were smashing up her pipes with a hammer, shooting water all over as they cheered. Considering how terribly kids were treated, it surprised me that the teenagers of the world hadn't yet united and burned all of civilization to the ground. I got drunk as fuck and saw Amelie talking with her class president, Alex Davis, so I decided to wreak some havoc myself. Ryan and I slid a pack of cigars onto the burners in Samantha's furnace, then we pissed in her laundry detergent and fabric softener, and Ryan took a dump in a plastic bag and then tossed the log into one of the vents in her dining room. We grabbed her car keys and took the Beemer for a spin, blazin' ninety down residential streets, blowing through stop signs and pushing straight through a red light on Delaware Ave. When we got back, Ryan wanted to pull it into the garage, "So none of these other animals can destroy it. This baby kicks," but he drove straight into the garage door instead. We got out laughing, and Ryan puked in the driver's seat. Some kids ran out of the house as Samantha chased after them, screaming, "GET OUT! GET THE FUCK OUT!" One hurled a beer bottle through her front window, and all the people inside cheered. Samantha sat on the grass, pulled her knees to her chest, and sobbed, rocking back and forth. Someone lit a cherry bomb and tossed it in the bushes behind her, and when it went off, she started screaming hysterically and pulling her hair. The cops showed up, and we all split.

We went to Denny's, and while eating my Moons Over My Hammy with Ryan and a few other scumbags in a corner booth, Amelie and her friends walked in. I walked over the table, hopped down, and sat with them. The waitress gave me some shit about it, but I always tipped well, so she didn't push too hard.

"This is why I'll *never* throw a party," Alex Davis said. Dude was equal parts smart to ugly, and he was a fugly bastard, but for whatever reason, chicks dug him. Had that Diego Rivera swagger.

"When I tried to get some ice from the fridge door, a stick of butter came out," Amelie said.

"I saw someone flushing a bag of oranges down the toilet," I said.

Alex gave me a look as if to say, "Go back to the corner with the other degenerates," and that just pushed my buttons. I dropped under the table and squeezed between him and Amelie.

"What are you doing?" Alex said.

I put my arm around Amelie, and she smiled. "Let's get outta here."

Amelie said okay, then she handed Becky some cash for her Grand Slam and took off with me, hand in hand. She lived a few blocks away, but knew a shortcut through some backyards and a park, and after hopping a few fences and swinging on the swings, we arrived at her house. She said her dad was nuts, so we'd have to be quiet, and then she let us in the back door. Almost immediately, I kissed her. Her dog kept jumping on us but didn't bark, so we were all right. We moved to the couch and spent about an hour just kissing. Then I slid my hand up her shirt and grabbed one of those perfect, firm titties. I reached around the back, and with one hand unsnapped her bra. She took off her shirt, got on top of me, and dry humped the shit out of me. My dick could cut diamond and my balls were aching, but soon she took off my shirt, then my pants, and deep-throated the whole sausage. She licked my balls and taint and swallowed every last bit of gravy. I licked her bean until the sun came up, then split when I heard Daddy coming downstairs. I walked a mile home with the smell of her pussy all over my face as the sun struggled to cut through the gray, late-autumn sky.

I started seeing more and more of Amelie, forgetting about Julia and Rachel and all the other girls I'd had no idea how to talk to. With Amelie, it didn't matter if I stumbled through the conversation; she was just as awkward. She said a lot of dumb shit, and I loved it. Apparently a lot of other guys loved it too, and I found myself wanting to beat a lot of asses at Kirkland High. But it didn't matter because she told them all she was my girl. When one of them wouldn't take no for an answer and started following her around town and showing up at her house, I waited for him after school, grabbed him by the throat, and told him it all ended now. At first he tried to act tough, but when I put the squeeze on his stalker-ass, he said he'd cut it out. I'd hooked up with a bunch of girls over the last few months but I'd never had a girlfriend. Whenever the ladies got too close, Julia's face had started dominating my thoughts, and I'd tell them I wasn't interested or I'd just stop talking to them. Some didn't get the hint and just kept coming. Downtown Debbie was always cool because she knew when to cum and go. But some girls just clung onto you and wouldn't let up.

But when I was with Amelie, I only saw her face in my mind. It was nice having someone there who liked me as much as I liked her. Who called me as often as I called her. Who'd hold my hand in the hallway at school and kiss me at my locker. She seemed proud to be around me, and as much as I was embarrassed and ashamed of myself, being with her made me feel a little worthier of receiving love and affection. We'd eat lunch together and work out together and get drunk on the weekends together. We always went to her house. There was no way I'd ever bring another girl into my world. It had to be hers. And she was cool with it. As long as we stayed downstairs, we'd be all right. Her stairs were really noisy, so her dad would hear us if we went up to her room. But downstairs was great. She had a big house by the park that was always clean and well-decorated. My house was always a disaster, with shit all over the place and half-painted walls and wires hanging from the ceiling and kids running around screaming. But Amelie's house was quiet and peaceful and clean. They had pictures on the fireplace mantle where everyone was smiling. She had an older sister who was in college on a cross-country scholarship, and

Mom was a dentist and Dad a realtor. There was something beautiful about being in their home, lights dimmed, snow falling outside, Amelie holding me and kissing my cheeks and forehead. About being young with everything ahead of me, which both inspired and weighed upon me. About being young and having nothing to do with my time other than get high, get drunk, listen to music, and kiss this gorgeous girl.

Amelie and I would watch movies sometimes, but the only one we ever actually got through was *Gladiator*, and that was because I kept telling her, "No, I wanna watch this." With all the others, soon after pushing play, we'd be running our hands all over one another. She loved my stomach and would lick it and rub her face and tits all over it. She also loved my hands and would cum quickly when I massaged her. I knew just how she liked it: slow circles around her bean, then slide two fingers inside while making the "come here" motion against her G-spot. Her pussy would start rolling like a wave and she'd clench her teeth and pull my hair. Sometimes, we'd lie on the living room floor and sixty-nine, sucking on each other's junk for an hour or more—not even cumming, just enjoying the pleasure of both giving and receiving. Taking our time. What was the hurry? We were teenagers with tight, hard bodies and raging hormones and all we wanted to do was lick each other for hours. I could have spent days rubbing her ass, kissing it. Licking it. Putting my dick between her cheeks, squeezing them together, and fucking them until I'd squirt gallons of cum all over her. After a month, she started begging me to put it inside her. I always said no. That I was waiting for marriage. But that was bullshit. Even married, I wouldn't have been able to do it.

God was watching. Sister Rose was watching. Grandpa was watching. Blessed are the Virgins, for they Shall Inherit Hell! Blue Balls! No, I couldn't do it. I wasn't ever allowed to and was already pushin' it with all this blowjob and titty-fucking business.

Regardless, she pulled me onto her one night, grabbed my ass with one hand and my dick with the other, rubbing it all over her. "C'mon, baby, I *need* you." At first, I held out, but when she started demanding it, the blind-faith-Catholic and son-of-a-tyrant wounded parts inside of me felt obligated to do as she commanded. I got as deep inside as the mushroom tip when I heard someone coming down the stairs. I imagined it was her father holding a gun, and upon catching this street-trash drunk, "Raping *my* daughter on *my* living room floor," he'd shoot my bits right off. I jumped off of her and even after I realized it was just her dog, my dog was done. I drove home, stopping halfway to release the tremendous pressure on my balls, then smoked some weed and fell asleep while listening to *Strange Days*.

Chapter 30

"Here, take these," Cisco said, dumping two round orange pills into my hand.

"What are they?" I said.

"THC pills," he said.

"That all?" I said.

"Christ, man, enough with the questions. Just take 'em. You'll thank me later."

While I was always down to blaze, given the insanity natural to my brain, I was terrified of acid or anything like it. I'd seen a few kids take bad trips, and based on the looks on their faces and the shit they were saying, I felt as though I knew what they were going through. I think my entire childhood had been one bad trip, and I didn't ever want to go back. But I'd heard about these little orange pills before—Ryan and Manish had a hell of a time on them—and I figured why not.

Though Cisco was Dan's friend, we'd been hanging out together here and there on the weekends. He went to Fillmore State, which was the only school I'd applied to, and I think I wanted to be around someone who could help ease my transition from high school to college. I knew deep down below the partying and sixty-nining was a huge magma bed of panic just waiting to erupt the second I graduated, and I was keeping Cisco close for damage control. Plus, he was about the biggest party animal I'd ever met. Once I watched him drink five glasses of beer and a cookie jar filled with four beers in under two minutes. He could open his throat and dump a beer down in seconds.

That night, we headed to a Fillmore party at an abandoned warehouse south of the city where a few college bands were playing. Though we popped the THC pills on the drive down, they didn't kick in for about forty-five minutes. But once they did—fuck! Cisco's cousin worked with cancer patients, and he'd swiped some of these pills, which were designed for people going through chemo. It came in waves. First, I felt a body high, but my mind was completely fine. Then I started getting giddy. Then I got really introspective, which was great timing, because the band currently playing had kind of a Velvet Underground meets Joy Division thing going on. I got lost in the music, grooving along and watching the guitarist rock the room. I could have watched someone play guitar for hours. I loved to see where the sounds came from. How they got higher in pitch as fingers worked down the frets and the reverse as they went up. How picking a single note had cleaner tones than strumming several at once. I wished I knew how to play. In that moment, there didn't seem to be a higher purpose in life than playing guitar and singing songs. The pinnacle of human achievement. All around me were people lost in the music—but they seemed to have found something in it that brought them all together.

Whoever threw that party knew what they were doing.

They had set up laser and strobe lights and put kegs all over, and it only cost ten bucks to get in. Cisco's brother was there. He was a big artist in the underground Buffalo scene and had moved to NYC after dropping out of Kirkland High. But he wasn't a prick. In fact, he was a pretty damned cool guy, and he popped some of the THC pills with us.

I'd never been to a party like this before, and it opened up something in me that had been sleeping since I was a kid. It was almost as if all that creativity I'd shut out—that I'd tried desperately to avoid—was the very stuff fueling this celebration. As if the words coming from that singer's mouth and sounds coming from his guitar were the same music inside of me that as a kid I'd tried to block out by popping earplugs in my soul. Something in me was changing. So much had already changed in the last few years. So much since I'd left St. Anthony's years ago. Would Sister Adele even recognize me now? With my shaggy hair, red eyes, and broad shoulders? Would God recognize me? Would Santa know where to bring my presents?

All was going well until I got a glimpse of this gorgeous girl dancing alone in a dark corner. It seemed as if every part of her body was flowing in unison, creating something so beautiful I didn't feel worthy to watch it. She had a shaved head, and deep dark eyes, and a face that looked as if it could be Egyptian or Turkish. She was wearing this loose, white, long-sleeved T-shirt over a pair of equally loose green military pants and heavy black boots. She had several long beaded necklaces around her neck and a ring in her nose, and she was so stunning it rocked me to the core. She didn't seem to be dancing for anyone but herself, and there was something so calming yet disorienting about it that my peace was now gone.

I wanted nothing more than to go over and dance with her, but that was wrong for several reasons. It wasn't okay to interrupt someone's flow, especially when that flow was so beautiful. And I didn't want to get rejected in a place like this. For once in my life, I felt as if I was in the right spot, with all the people I was supposed to be around, and I didn't need any of them telling me I wasn't good enough.

Also, Amelie.

Fuck! Since the beginning, I hadn't thought about anyone but Amelie, but seeing this girl dancing alone in the corner made Julia's face coming rushing back to my mind. Made me realize that Amelie and I had no chance. That no girl would ever satisfy me unless she moved like this girl in the corner. Moved like Julia. Rocked a room like the girl ripping the bass on stage. Amelie with her scholarship essays and weekend trips with her family to the lake and her can-I-buy-tickets-for-the-subway-at-Subway questions. I knew I'd never be happy unless I was flying down the road at a hundred miles an hour, playing music and smoking herb and finger-fucking every pretty girl along the way. I knew I'd never have a steady house and a steady job and a fireplace mantle on which to put pictures of my smiling family. My family were these mutants around me—who'd broken into an abandoned warehouse in a dead part of the city that would be entirely black if you looked down at it from a plane at night, and had set up a stage and lighting and all that crap, knowing full well that the cops could come at any minute and take it all, but they still set it up anyway, trusting in the night, and they'd set it up the next weekend, and the weekend after that, until we were all drug-shriveled, sex-addled lunatics whose eyes had been burned out by lasers and whose ears had been destroyed by feedback, always searching for the next party, the next pussy, the next pill.

It was invigorating and paralyzing all at once. To know now my future. To know full well that America and God and love and family didn't belong to me. But, fuck, Jimmy! They never have. Don't you get it now? Don't you see that's why you've never belonged? You're a mutant. You're a depraved son of a lunatic and you'll never find peace except in a crowd like this. But it's better to destroy only yourself than it is to create a family and destroy them too. Better to be alone in misery. Go off to a corner by yourself. Tie off. Shoot up like those guys over there. Smoke crack like the guys we passed on the way in.

I entered a new phase with the orange pills, one that made me weepy and hopeless. It was almost as if the band had taken the pills too, because they knew exactly what to play—something slow and driving and dark like Lou Reed playing with John Cale. The band played the sadness of that entire city. They'd raised the dead—all those who once had great dreams that they, like the city, would rise up on high. That they'd find hope and glory and inspiration, but got buried in a shit-blizzard instead. I resolved then that I, like Jim Morrison, would go down in a blaze of glory. That I'd never follow any rules but my own. That I'd loot and indulge and destroy on an endless quest to find something pure in this world. Something better than what had been given to me. Something that I knew existed even though everyone would warn me it didn't. Something that I'd felt while listening to great tunes or reading books by guys like Kerouac and Hunter S. Thompson. Something that maybe, if I found it, could save us all.

"Yo, I told you you'd be thanking me for those pills," Cisco said, grooving along with the music. He was in a band and had played bass at a party like this a few months back with Ian Morricone, Dan's other cross-country friend. Ian had some serious pipes and could scream the paint off a wall. Their band had been getting pretty big until Ian had decided to head out west. He'd asked Cisco to go, too, but Cisco wanted to get his degree and become a geologist. I didn't know why. Music was the best anyone could ever hope for in this shitty world. Fuck the rocks. Fuck the Earth. I want the heavens. I want to rock with the gods.

Ian and Cisco had stayed in close touch, and Cisco said Ian was already making a name for himself in LA.

Los Angeles. I'd never been west of Cleveland. LA was like a dream. Some mythical place, and to know someone who was not only living there but also taking the city by storm made me think anything was possible. Dude smoked me up for the first time. He gave me the gift of music. I needed to get out there.

"Let's hit up ETS for some bean burritos," Cisco said.

I didn't want to leave, but he was driving, so I followed him outside.

On the way to the car, some crackhead drew a knife on us and said, "I-I want everything you got. Gimme your shoes, belts, everything."

Cisco took off his belt, then whipped the absolute shit out of the guy's head so hard that he dropped the knife and fell to his knees. Cisco grabbed him by the throat and said, "You ain't gettin' shit but this dick in your mouth unless you get up and run your bitch-ass outta here." The guy ran away, leaving his knife.

There was something about Cisco that got me right away. Some danger in his eyes and swagger in his step. Nothing seemed to scare him. I'd been ready to walk out of there naked, but Cisco wasn't walking out of anywhere naked. He'd fight until his last breath. The only other person I could say the same for was Luke. They were similar in so many ways. But where Luke rocked the b-ball court, Cisco rocked the back alleys and warehouse parties and Highways to Nowhere. I felt drawn to him.

We decided on Jim's Steakout instead, and I got a chicken finger sub and fries. We sat in the corner and watched all the drunks coming in and out, starting shit, grabbing each other's asses, yelling, stinkin' the place up. The herd. The idiot masses. More and more, they were disgusting me. The more I slipped into the underground world of art and drugs, the less patience I had for all these mouth-breathing shitheads. With their Geico-middle-management-seeking, Ski-doo-weekend-riding dreams.

"Yo, fuck Fillmore. You should apply to Conesus. That's where I'm transferring in the spring," Cisco said.

"That's the best school in the state system. There's no way I'll ever get in," I said.

"What's your GPA?"

"Right now it's three point nine seven, but that'll probably drop after this semester."

"Damn, three point nine seven? What's your class rank?"

"I was thirteenth at the end of last year."

"Dude, you could easily get in. Why don't you apply now?"

"It's too late, I think."

"Fuck Fillmore. See all these d-bags? They're gonna be

the ones sitting in the back of the room sleeping their way through bullshit world history lectures. Why not try for something better?"

"I-I can't."

"Why not?"

"I just can't."

I wasn't exactly sure why, but felt it had something to do with needing to stay in Buffalo and at home. There was still so much here to fix. So many piles of trash and snow on the streets. So many husbands beating their wives and kids. So many kids shooting up for the first time. So many people pissing away their last dime on crack. So many people breaking and entering and raping and murdering. I needed to stay here and fix it all. Make it all better. Sister Rose had been buried in Buffalo. Even though they'd sold the convent and the new owner paved over her garden, those roots would always be under the blacktop, waiting for me to water them. Hammond was here. Most of my memories were here.

Plus, how could I ever survive without my mommy? Without her rubbing my back as I wept all night, trying desperately to sleep? What if the Evil Thoughts came back while I was hours away from her, and I slipped into a panic so blinding I slit my wrists to prevent my hands from hurting someone else? Cisco, there's no leaving for me. There is no getting away. I'm gonna die right here, three hundred and fifty pounds with pasty, sun-starved skin, watching the Bills lose season after season but always saying, "Oh, but we'll get 'em next year!"—that is, if I even live long enough.

We smoked some grass in the car and went back to Cisco's place to watch *Imagine: John Lennon*. When they played "All You Need Is Love" at John Lennon's funeral and everyone was crying, I couldn't hold back the tears. My eyes were pools of sorrow and hope and misery and inspiration and absolute fucking horror. Cisco saw me crying, but he was cool and didn't say shit. I think he got it. He understood the terror of existence better than all those other fuckers— even better than Ryan and Manish and Billy. As smart as those guys were, they just didn't get it the way Cisco and I did. The way Ian did. The way Silas did.

I wondered if he was in LA as well. Where are you, Silas? We haven't spoken in months. I don't like us not being friends. Come back. Let's start that band you were telling me about. Together, we'll top the charts. We'll show all these fools we're still champions. We'll make the kind of music that people will raise up on high, bathing us all in warm, guiding light. Showing us what we could be. What this city could be. Saving us. Saving us all.

The week before Thanksgiving, we got rocked by a huge blizzard that shut down practically the entire city—minus the bars, of course. By the thousands, people abandoned their cars on the highways and roads and trudged home in almost waist-deep snow. In times like these, people understood why they called Buffalo the City of Good Neighbors. The whole city worked together to shovel cars out of snow piles, bring elderly neighbors food, snowblow each other's driveways, give each other firewood. Times like these brought us all together, and rather than complain about it, we celebrated. If a blizzard like that hit most other American cities, people would panic and turn on each other, but Buffalonians were used to it, and we turned that entire week off from work and school into a nonstop party. We'd put on our snow pants and boots and heavy jackets and hats, and walk the streets pounding beers and searching for the next party. Ryan, Billy, Manish, and I hid beers in snowbanks and somehow knew exactly where they were when we came back for them days later. Along the way, we'd help push stuck cars and we'd toss the drivers a beer to calm their nerves. Some people cruised the streets in snowmobiles or on cross-country skis, but we went everywhere on foot. In that week, we probably walked over a hundred miles through the city, pounding beers and smoking bowls and pushing each other into snow banks and screaming into the night. There were things I experienced growing up in Buffalo that I never would have experienced anywhere else. For as many reasons as there were to hate that city, there were so many reasons more to love it. No matter where I went, no matter what I did, I'd always be a Buffalonian, and that made me proud.

Chapter 31

I watched Grandma die about a week after Thanksgiving. She'd moved in with us in just before the blizzard, after taking a nasty fall, and her health kept deteriorating. The night she died, she asked me to bring her some water. When I came back to her room, her eyes were closed and she was taking quick shallow breaths, and then they just . . . stopped. I sat on a chair beside the bed and wiped the sweat off of her forehead with a towel. I didn't need to check her pulse. I knew what had happened. I saw death take her. I was more familiar with death than I was with her. I sat on that chair and stared into the darkness, thinking over and over how alone we all were. Thinking how terrible it felt that some part of me was glad she wouldn't terrorize us—Dad especially—anymore. Thinking about how much of stranger she was to me. How I felt no different about her passing than any of the people I saw on the news, dying in Africa or China or Haiti or wherever else people were suffering. How terrible it felt that I felt nothing for her despite all the people throughout my entire life shouting, *Thou Shalt Love Thy Grandma or Else Thou Shalt Burn in Hell!* But I didn't love her. I tried so hard to love her, but I didn't. Do *you* love the angry old lady you sit next to on the bus? The one reading beside you in the library?

I sat there for about an hour alone, staring at the floor, mind racing to the moon and back. Dad came in to check on things, and the house erupted. Mom woke up and went off on me. She gave me the, "ARE YOU EVEN HUMAN?" deal again, and I just sat there, head so heavy it could snap right off my neck. With her screaming at me and Dad throwing shit around the room, for a moment I believed that maybe I had actually killed her. For a moment, I felt like a murderer. Felt the cops would be coming soon to take me away and finally lock me up where I belonged. And I hated Grandma, and all of them, even more for making me think this. I felt even further away. I already knew I was going to Hell. That was never up for debate. All this atheism and drinking beer and smoking weed and listening to The Doors and sucking tits and dreaming about LA were bullshit. In that moment, I knew how fake it all was. How hopeless. I *was* shame. I was the kid and grandkid and great-grandkid of rageaholics. I was Catholic, no matter what I thought. My destiny was already set. I was never getting away. They had me on a long leash, and they were giving it a strong pull that night to remind me who was, and always would be, in charge.

Dan came home from college, and Mom drove us to Bumblefuck in the station wagon for the funeral. About ten minutes into the trip, Dad turned up the music as loud as it would go, but that didn't stop us from hearing him sobbing, crying out for his mommy. In both life and death, she made him cry like a child. The song was Celine Dion's cover of "All by Myself," and hearing those lyrics, as shitty as they were, made me realize what a long, lonely life was in store for me, and probably for everyone around me. I sat next to Dan, and we didn't even look at each other. I wasn't bitter or avoiding him or anything—I just didn't have shit to say to him.

At the funeral, Uncle Tommy gave some speech about Grandma being the best mom ever and all that crap, which seemed to irritate Dad. Uncle Tommy forced some tears, but I couldn't. I tried to cry, but nothing was coming. Everyone around me was crying. Even Jeremy and the girls. Dan looked sad, but he always looked sad, so that was nothing new. I was about the only one in there with dry eyes. The only animal, as Mom would say. Would I cry at *her* funeral? Or Dan's? Or Jeremy's or Carolynn's or Diane's? Would I smile if Dad got hit by a bus? Oh shit, I didn't even realize I was smiling thinking about Dad getting leveled by a red double-decker until Mom gave me a dirty look. I snuck off to the bathroom and took a long look at myself in the mirror, then hung out in a stall as a wave of panic rocked me. Away from the dog and pony show, the tears finally came, but I didn't know what I was crying about. It felt less as though it had anything to do with Grandma and more about the fact that I was happier to be alone in a bathroom stall than with all the other blubbering phonies. While they prayed to Grandma God, I wished I'd brought a flask with me. I was sure there'd be booze at Grandma's house after the service, but I needed some now.

After the funeral, we went back to Grandma's place, and I went straight for Uncle Wayne's guitar. I opened a window, took out the screen, and tossed the guitar in the snow, then I went outside and put it in the back of the wagon. When I came back in, Dad and Uncle Tommy were arguing about something, and I used the distraction to swipe a bottle of whiskey, which I brought to the garage. Jeremy came out and asked for some, but I told him to fuck off, and he went back into the house. As he walked away, I realized I was the Uncle Tommy of my brothers and sisters. But Dad always called me Wayne. Maybe I was a combination of Uncle Tommy, Uncle Wayne, and Dad. Either way, I was as much a monster as Mom always said I was.

We left soon after, and Dad went on and on about how, "He's gonna take everything. Mom left the house to me, but he's gonna take it, I know he will. He thinks he's the boss. He wouldn't even let me talk at the funeral. He always thinks he's the boss of me." Dad, you silly fool, that's why you gotta open a window, toss what you want through, and sneak off with it. You gotta rob the place blind. You can't leave anything in anyone's hands—especially not your brother's.

When we got home, I started messing around with Uncle Wayne's guitar. Ryan had told me you could find guitar tabs online, so I started looking up how to play songs. Being an ever-ambitious young man, I went straight for "Stairway to Heaven." After fucking the song up for about an hour, I put the guitar in the closet and got ready for the night. I'd gotten used to having the room to myself and didn't like that Dan would be sleeping there again. I told him I'd been hanging out with Cisco, and he told me I should watch out for him and that he's a little off. Well, so am I, homie. So are you.

I picked up Ryan in the wagon, and we headed to a party at one of Amelie's friends' places. This party wasn't a warzone like Samantha's had been. People were chugging and cheering and dancing, but no one was tearing out the walls or pissing all over the place.

It was warmer than usual for a December night, so we sat outside by a firepit, telling stories, and Amelie sat on my lap. All of her guy friends were the most pathetically boring assholes. They all thought they were witty and hilarious, but their jokes were *Friends*-level at best. They all reminded me of that cokehead Chandler and the pussy-ass other guy with the dark hair and the dumbass who was always doing the Fonzie "*Hey*, look at me" thing. The only people who'd ever laugh at their jokes were their friends. The rest of us would get another beer, smoke a cig—whatever we needed to get away. All these douches had frosted tips and wore shell necklaces and turtlenecks and backwards visors and all the other Abercrombie gear. Their shirts had numbers on them for some reason, as if being a d-bag were a sport. The only thing keeping me there was Amelie's perfect ass grinding into my man bits. I wanted to carry her upstairs and rub my cock all over her, but another urge won out.

"Hey, let's toke."

I followed Ryan inside, and we smoked a bowl, but then he ran out and no one else had any green, so we drove to the East Side. I parked in front of a house near where Jefferson and Broadway met, but we couldn't remember which was the right place.

"I think that's the fence there, remember?" Ryan said.

"But why's the gate closed? It's usually open," I said.

"Someone probably shut it on their way out," Ryan said. "I'll hop it and find out."

"Dude, you're gonna get shot."

"Why would they shoot someone who wants to give them money?"

Our usual hookup was dry, so we came out here, which we did from time to time. Our other option was a dude who'd pick us up in his Cadillac at a convenience store on Bailey Ave., then drive us around the neighborhood while we did business. But his shit always tasted like Ajax, and there was something about him that creeped me the fuck out, so I'd brought us here instead.

"Yo, I'll go with you," I said. "Just in case shit goes down."

I shut off the car, and just as Ryan hopped the fence, the cops shined a light on us and told us to come over. One was a White all-Buffalo meathead and the other was a big older Black dude.

"Forget your keys?" the older one said.

"Oh, uh, I think we got the wrong house," Ryan said.

"Yeah, you do," the meathead said.

"We followed you boys here," the older one said. "When we saw two White guys drive into an all-Black neighborhood, we got a little suspicious."

"I, uh, got friends out here," I said.

"Come with me," the meathead said.

He pulled my hands behind my back and put cuffs on me while the older guy did the same to Ryan. As the meathead tightened the cuffs, he said to me, "You're lucky. If you were a Black dude hoppin' a fence on Starin Ave., you'd be bloody and broken by now. We beat the shit out of dudes all the time."

As sick as it was, I think he was trying to impress, not intimidate, me. Even now, while he was putting cuffs on me, I was his White bro. They made us march down the block, while they followed behind in their cruiser, flashing their lights and making enough noise for people to come out of their houses. I wasn't scared, but ashamed. I recognized the neighborhood. Years back, I'd eaten Thanksgiving dinner at Silas's grandma's place a few blocks down. Everybody in my neighborhood was always talking about how terrible Black people were and how dangerous "those neighborhoods" were, but all of Silas's family members had always been nice to me. In fact, I'd liked hanging out with him down here, and that Thanksgiving with Silas and his grandma was one of my favorites. I felt a deep confusion walking down her street in handcuffs. Was I the guy saying please and thank you to her during dinner, or was I the scumbag buying drugs just outside of her window?

After we had walked a few blocks, the cops let us go. We got back into the station wagon, called up the other dude, and got in his Caddy. We bought enough to not have to go back there anytime soon and went back to the party to toke. Even with a head full of weed and what tasted like Raid bug spray, those *Friends* jokes weren't funny. Plus, this one dude was gettin' all close to Amelie, and even though I felt as if I was getting further away from her, I still stepped in. I took her by the hand and led her upstairs and made sure those jackasses could hear her moaning my name even with the window closed. Ryan told me that shithead left once Amelie started really screaming. Now, *that* was funny.

Chapter 32

I was hanging out in my room playing guitar and watching MTV one night when a video came on and Julia was in it. She was the girl the singer had lost and was trying to win back. They had a whole dance routine and everything. Fuck, Julia, the world is watching you now. They all want you. They love you. They'll pay money to throw themselves at your feet. But, Julia, they'll never know what I do. That I've loved you since we were kids. Long before you grew those perfect tits that they all photograph and show off in music videos. Long before you started walking around with celebrities. You'll probably be in movies soon. You'll probably be the next Julia Roberts. America's girl. But they'll never know the way you used to laugh when we recited lines from *Billy Madison* in the back of sixth grade Reading class. They'll never know how you were the first to rush to help Tina Sanders when she thought she was choking during our field trip to the zoo, even though she'd just swallowed some water down the wrong pipe. They'll never know how we laughed when we filled cups with each kind of pop at Gerry's twelfth birthday at the skating rink, and Gerry puked in the corner, and that guy yelled at us and you told him to go to Hell.

Julia, I've loved you long before they all did. Long before your face was on magazine covers. I've loved you since the day you asked if we could pray for Gerry's dead mother. Since the day you told Sister Verona that your rosary must be broken because you couldn't feel Mother Mary inside of you anymore. Since the summer before seventh grade when I was watching MTV and saw the video for Mazzy Star's "Fade Into You," your favorite song, and I felt closer to you than I'd ever felt to anyone before or after.

Julia, none of them will ever love you like I do. They want you for what they see. They care about you as much as the media tells them to. But they'll never know what I know—that we came from the same place, Julia. That we came up fighting the same battles. We sat next to each other in class for so many years. We learned how to read together. Julia, I'll do whatever it takes. I know I may look happier than ever now, but it's all a lie. I'm still falling hard. Everything is outta control. I feel as if I'm slipping down a greased slide, and I'll never be able to pull my way back up. I'll learn how to play this guitar and write you the best song you've ever heard. Is that what you need, Julia? Will that make you finally see me and love me and want to be with me? We don't need millions of dollars and mansions and people in Russia and China and Germany knowing who we are. We can have each other and be happy and start a family and be good to our kids. We can break the cycle of anger and abuse that's been passed on to us for all these generations. We can save ourselves. Save our city.

Oh, Julia, I was doing all right just now. Why did I have to turn on the TV?

I could feel words coming up from deep in my gut. I

played a simple arpeggio with variations of the D chord and sang, "I was fine alone last night, until I saw your face. It took me by surprise, my thoughts just drift away."

I'll never get away. I'll never shake this feeling. There will always be another championship I'll strive to win. There will always be another pot at the end of the rainbow that I'll kill myself to find. Julia, stay away from me. I'm poison. No song will ever save me. No kiss will ever heal the excruciating pain in my heart. No soft touch will ever cure the anger I fear will soon destroy me. Stay where you are. Stay with the phonies. At least they pretend to be happy. I know I'm not happy and I can't hide it, and that makes me dangerous.

I got high with Ryan that night, and we watched Oliver Stone's *The Doors*, pausing every so often to smoke another bowl. By the end of the film, my brain was exhausted in a way it'd never been. It was as if the soul of Val Kilmer's interpretation of Jim Morrison leaped off the screen and settled into my own soul, stirring up this need to create both cinema and song. My mind felt as if it'd actually been blown, and I was concerned that maybe something upstairs had broken. Watching this film reminded me of the feeling I'd gotten at that warehouse party with Cisco, and made me absolutely certain I needed to do whatever it took to unearth the creativity inside of me—and to hell with anyone's rules.

But it seemed that the more I tried to write songs, the more difficult it proved to be. Like that night walking back from Billy's house after the Kubrick marathon, it seemed I had to sneak up on the song from the side—never approaching head-on. If I realized I was creating, that'd be the end of it, so I could never sit down with the intention of writing. It had to come to me all at once, otherwise I'd lose it. I started carrying a small notebook and voice recorder with me, filling both in a few weeks. Most of what came out was crap, but some of it was actually good. I thought about asking Cisco to play with me, but he seemed too occupied with his studies, so I left it alone.

Should I go to LA or NYC? Silas and Ian are in LA, but Julia's in Manhattan.

Stop with all this insanity! You think Dad will let you leave?

Fuck Dad! I'll do whatever I want.

Try getting away and see what it does to you. You'll never be able to outrun the guilt of leaving them here. Of leaving Mom, who always cried so hard whenever she watched them take Dumbo away from his mother. Of leaving her and Jeremy and the girls to get screamed at each day while you're off writing tunes and singing like a faggot. Uncle Wayne tried to get away too, and look what happened to him. There was something written in black marker inside his guitar. It was faded but it said something like, SING YOUR OWN DESTINY. My destiny is on these streets. God already chose me to die here. He killed me when I was nine when he filled my head with all that insanity and darkness. He handed me over to Satan to go crazy in this very house. They're gonna have to airlift your bloated corpse out of here. You're gonna go crazy, and then spend your life strapped to this bed, and they'll keep feeding you and feeding you until you weigh a thousand pounds and are covered in sores and scabies and crusted feces. No one will ever love you. No one will ever talk to you again. Fuck LA. Fuck NYC. You belong to Buffalo. You're only allowed Rust-Belt dreams.

Mom called me to help her and the kids with Christmas decorations. We were getting a late start this year, what with Grandma passing and all. I went heavy on the eggnog and tried to relax. Tried my hardest not to get into a fight with anyone. Dad was still pretty shaken up. He'd already lost his father years ago, so losing a parent was nothing new, but now he was an orphan. The reality was, he never really had parents, it was just that now he could probably no longer ignore that fact. Grandma had never once said a single nice thing to him—not that I'd ever heard. She always laughed at him with Uncle Tommy and teased him and told him, "Oh, lighten up," after she'd made her grown-ass man of a son go off to the garage and cry. I'm sure he'd hated her, and he'd probably hated himself for hating her. He'd grown up in an era when Mommy and Daddy always knew best, and if you questioned them, watch out. He should have been like Uncle Wayne—trying to get out. But even Uncle Wayne got sucked back in.

I heard Uncle Tommy talking about it at Thanksgiving. Apparently, Uncle Wayne was "one of them god-damned hippies," and he wanted to get out of Dodge, but when Dad enlisted in the Navy, Uncle Wayne felt guilty and enlisted too, even though he was morally against the war. Everyone in the family, my dad included, blamed Dad for Uncle Wayne's death. But what could he do? They were at war. Uncle Wayne made his own choices. It wasn't even Dad's fault. Why do these crazy-ass people keep blaming everyone else for all the shit that happens to them? I'm not gonna be like these fuckers. I'm gonna get away and never come back. I won't make the same mistake Uncle Wayne did. When I go to Hollywood, I'll never look back. Buffalo is a death sentence. Buffalo kills everyone, often long before they die.

Uncle Tommy also talked about Uncle Wayne's house, which Uncle Tommy and Dad had promised to help fix up when he and Dad got back from the war and Uncle Tommy got out of jail, and everything made sense. I think when Dad left the Navy, he had to give up on his dream of ever saving his brother, and maybe he spent so much time fixing up our house because it was his last shot at helping Uncle Wayne—at spending time with him. He called me Wayne all the time. Maybe Dad was always screaming because he missed his little brother.

We did the whole deal of putting up the tree and lights and all that while listening to Bing Crosby. It was nice having a girlfriend for once. Nice having someone over the holidays. This was the first time I'd ever had a girlfriend, and even though I'd never invite her over, I felt as though she was with me—until we lit the pink candle. Then, all I could see was Julia again. All I could think about was how quickly I'd kick Amelie to the curb if Julia so much as winked at me. Made me think of how quickly any of us would kick each other to the curb for a better offer anywhere else. For a better father. A better brother. A better son. We were bound together by a common misery. The delusion that this was the best of all possible worlds. The best we could ever hope for, so abandon all hope. The only way to get through the holidays.

On Christmas, we stayed at our house for the first time since we'd moved back to Buffalo. We'd always gone to Grandma's, but that wasn't ever happening again. A part of me was glad about that, and I felt so guilty for it. Mom was right to call me an animal. I had no heart. No soul. I was gonna end up like Val Kilmer in *The Doors*, hanging out of hotel windows and setting bedrooms on fire and pushing everyone around me away. There was no Christmas anymore, just another day to remind me how fucked up it all was now. I'd have given up everything—the weed, the beer, the blowjobs—to be a kid again. To believe again. But that was impossible.

For Christmas, Amelie gave me a hemp necklace that she'd made herself. It was cool that she was trying. I should have done the decent thing and broken up with her, but doing that would only confirm that I was, indeed, heartless. Everyone told me how great she was. How kind. How lucky I was. I couldn't leave her. It would make me evil. Bad. So I was stuck with her. Stuck in Buffalo.

Shane and all the other d-bags were back in town Christmas week, and I saw them at a house party downtown, thrown by a Kirkland High alum who now went to Fillmore State. Dan was there too with some of the cross-country guys, but he was staying far away from Shane. When Shane passed him to get a drink, Dan turned away so quickly, he almost spun right into a wall. Dan, you used to be fearless. What happened to you?

Shane was at Duke, and Mancuso was at Brown. Someday they'd move to NYC, get rich, and buy half of Buffalo. But they could have the mansions. The statues and museums. I had the alleys. The abandoned warehouses downtown. I had the syringes in Allentown trash cans and the crackpipes in Fruit Belt streets.

"I hate those fuckin' pricks," Ryan said.

"You and anyone else with any sense of style," I said.

"We should fuck 'em up," Ryan said.

"I-I need to get back home soon," Billy said.

"After," Ryan said.

"I should go now," Manish said.

Those two were getting to be pussies as well. They used to have more of a sense of danger to 'em but ever since they got their college acceptance letters—Manish to Yale and Billy to Amherst—they'd become scared to leave the house. Ryan had applied to Cornell, UPenn, Brown, and a few others, but he didn't give a shit. It was almost as if the closer he got to college, the more shit he wanted to fuck up, and I was right there with him. I'd only applied to Fillmore State and already had my early decision acceptance letter. Fillmore was Ryan's safety school, but he'd probably get into his top choice, so I knew I'd be going there alone. He was always battling with Billy for the top rank in our class, but Billy was now in the lead and would probably stay there. Ryan had one of the worst cases of senioritis in our class—probably *the* worst—and his GPA was dropping like a rock. He'd had a months-long project to complete for AP Physics, but on the day of his presentation, he hadn't done shit. At the start of class, he asked to go to the bathroom, then went to the cafeteria and stole a handful of spinach and iceberg lettuce. He ripped a poster board off a wall, wrote some shit on it, came back to class, and gave a presentation on how spinach fell faster than lettuce if you dropped it because it had a smoother texture. The teacher gave him an F, but because half of the grade also came from peer review, he ended up getting a C. I had stopped giving a fuck too, but I didn't have Ryan's flair.

Shane was in the corner flirting with a cute Kirkland High sophomore. I wanted to walk over and say something to him. Bitch-slap him in the face. Piss on his shoes. But another part of me was over it. He'd moved on, and it was time for me to do the same. As much of a prick as he was, he would probably always be successful. He was a smart, good-looking guy with much better social skills than I had, and who gave a shit if I broke his nose or knocked out his teeth? He'd ice it down and go back to his pretty-boy life of European vacations and dating models. There was no sense in getting upset about it. He hadn't hit me in years. He didn't look at me once, not even when I passed right by him. What was the point in staying stuck in the past?

Manish and Billy left, and Ryan and I got high and drove to the factories south of the city. Amelie called Ryan's cell phone looking for me, and Ryan drove me to her place. I knew that because I'd gotten the mushroom tip inside, technically I wasn't a virgin anymore, but still I held out when she pulled down her panties, turned around, and braced herself against the wall. Instead, I started crying, and at first I didn't even know why. But then I realized it was because I didn't want to be with her anymore. I mean, I'd already thought about all that before, but that was the first time I really *knew* it. I didn't tell her that, though—at least, not directly. Instead, I told her about my dreams. About how I couldn't be here anymore. About how I wanted to head out west and create movies and music that actually meant something. That could save people's lives. That I felt there was a higher purpose for my life. That maybe God didn't want me to be a priest, but a filmmaker. A singer. An actor. And was that so bad? Did that make me a monster? A selfish prick? Was I killing my family? Was I ungrateful?

The tears fell hard, and as smart a girl as Amelie was, I

knew I was creeping her out. I knew dudes probably didn't talk to her about stuff like this. I knew dudes probably just stuffed her buns with their hot dogs, blew their wads, and went home. Amelie tried to comfort me, but I could see how overwhelmed she was—that she knew it was over too. I could see in her eyes the long, lonely future I would have attempting to follow these dreams. Could see the looks other girls would give me when I told them the same thing. The looks that everyone would give me unless I did indeed become famous, and only then would they all tell me how great I was. What a champion I was. How they'd known all along that I could do it.

Amelie would go to college. She'd become a dentist like her mom. She'd probably marry a guy like Shane, move out to Clarence, get a big mansion and a country club membership, and grow old raising babies and going golfing and taking trips to Florida and buying antiques with her mother-in-law.

But I would be riding in boxcars alone like Bob Dylan. Wandering deep into caves to die like Johnny Cash. Heading out to the desert to find the secrets of the universe like Jim Morrison. I was going to be alone and always a step away from insanity. Girls like Amelie might invite me to their rooms or to eat dinner, but the second they saw that insanity in my eyes, they'd run screaming in the other direction. But I had no other choice. Nothing else made me happy. I knew I just had to *know*. Something had happened when those Evil Thoughts hit me and it changed me forever. No matter how hard I tried, I could never be like the rest of them. Could never be like Sister Adele or Monsignor Joseph or Billy or Uncle Tommy or Mom or Dan. I had the mark of the beast, following the false gods of creativity inside of me. I could never be happy just going to work and then coming home and making dinner and eating ice cream while watching TV and going to Mass on Sunday and to Grandma's house where I smiled and told everyone how much I loved them. But you know what? Neither could any of them. Maybe I wasn't able to fake it like they could. Maybe they had the same feelings, but ignored them. Either way, I knew I couldn't ignore them, and I knew my life was about to get even more lonely as a result. Even more weird. With a guitar in my hands, I felt more power and freedom than ever before. But I also felt an overwhelming need to write my masterpiece, which sent my mind and heart and soul into a new kind of frenzy. I could never feel peace until I'd written my "Across the Universe" or "Like a Rolling Stone" or "Heroes." Until I'd directed my *Apocalypse Now* or *Cool Hand Luke* or *Pat Garrett and Billy the Kid*. Once I started moving in this direction, I would never be able to turn back. I'd have to keep going, deeper and deeper into the heart of my own insanity, going all in, in the hopes that someday I'd turn it into something brilliant. Something that would save the world.

Chapter 33

We got hit with a late-March snowstorm that covered all our muddy lawns in a fresh layer of white. That first winter of the new millennium was long and brutal, and it seemed we'd never escape it. A few weeks back, I'd made the mistake of leaving Uncle Wayne's guitar downstairs. Dad got angry that we'd run out of A.1. Sauce or some other crap, and he grabbed his sledgehammer and smashed the guitar to pieces. I wasn't there, but Jeremy told me about it. I wished I had been there and had my recorder on to capture the sound that hammer made, smashing down on generations of family dreams. What an incredible way to end a song. An album. A lifetime. Dad, I don't think you realize you're more of an artist than all the charlatans parading around San Francisco and NYC. I wasn't even mad about it. Everything good in my life had been getting smashed since I was a kid, so what was the point of getting upset? I should have known better than to leave something important out in the open like that. It was my fault. Anyway, I'd recently picked up a job at Taco Bell and had enough cash now to buy my own guitar. It was probably better that way anyhow.

Ryan got into UPenn and Cornell and decided on UPenn. I wished he'd gone with Cornell, but at least Philly was only a six-hour drive, and it wasn't too far from Yale and Amherst. I could do road trips every few weeks. Cisco had transferred to Conesus at the start of the spring semester, and I went up to visit him one weekend. It was fucking amazing—a small campus set in the beautiful Finger Lakes. I wished I could go there too, but everything I knew was here.

That Sunday, the paperboy delivered later than usual—and he was always late. Probably due to the cold. Dan and I would have gotten it there on time no matter the weather. I usually went straight for the comics and ignored the rest. I knew the world was burning and didn't care to read any more about it.

But when I grabbed the paper that morning, Doug Warsaw's face was on the front page—and I'm not talking about the front page of the sports section. He made the front page of the whole damned paper. Delaware High had pulled off an upset over a great team from Long Island, winning the state championship. Little Dougie, who I used to school all the fucking time at Hammond.

Hammond. I hadn't thought about Hammond in so long, but seeing his smiling face holding up that trophy sent me sprinting down memory lane—and not in a good way. All I could think about was how we'd been screwed out of holding up that trophy ourselves. How the Hammond Crew had been told by the Man that we weren't wanted. That we were too unruly. Too uncivilized. That only pretty-boy blonds with rich parents like Dougie were fit to hold that trophy.

My head started spinning and my stomach ached.

Maybe if I ate something I'd feel better. I reached up into the cupboard for a box of cereal and saw that damned box of Honey Bunches of Oats. I opened it and put a handful in my mouth but it was so stale and disgusting that I spat it out and threw the box in the trash.

I filled my flask with whiskey, grabbed the keys and snow shovel, and headed to Hammond. I shoveled off the court, stopping every so often to pound whiskey and shoot jumpers. I slipped and fell on my back, and stayed down, taking another gulp from the flask. I looked up at the rim with the gray sky beyond it. That rim used to be so red, I could see it with my eyes closed. So red, I could see it in my dreams. But now it was so gray, I almost couldn't tell it from the sky above. Just keep drinking until it all disappears. Close your eyes. Go to sleep. You'll be warm soon. It'll all be over soon.

Two women passed by on the sidewalk, and I could hear them talking.

"God, would you look at that? Another loser who's too cool to listen to his parents."

"These kids need Jesus. They're all so darned ungrateful . . ."

Their voices got smaller and smaller until they disappeared into the gray void.

What happened to you, James? You were gonna be a priest someday. A champion. Someday, you were gonna save us all. But staring up at that infinite point where the heavens of instinct and blind faith finally met, all I could think of was what next I'd have to worship in order to survive.

About the Author

Jonathan LaPoma is an award-winning novelist, screenwriter, songwriter, and poet from Buffalo, NY. In 2005, he received a BA in history and a secondary education credential from the State University of New York at Geneseo, and he traveled extensively throughout the United States and Mexico after graduating. These experiences have become the inspiration for  much of his writing, which often explores themes of alienation and misery as human constructions that can be overcome through self-understanding and the acceptance of suffering.

LaPoma has written five novels, thirteen screenplays, and hundreds of songs and poems. His screenplays have won over 160 awards/honors at various international screenwriting competitions, and his black comedy script *Harm for the Holidays* was optioned by Warren Zide along with Wexlfish Pictures (*American Pie, Final Destination, The Big Hit*) in July 2017.

LaPoma's novels have been recommended by *Kirkus Reviews* and Barnes and Noble (B&N Press Presents list), have hit the #1 Amazon Bestseller lists in the "Satire," "Urban Life," "Metaphysical," "Metaphysical & Visionary," and "Religious & Inspirational"

Kindle categories (USA, Canada, and Australia), and have won awards/honors in the 2018 Eric Hoffer Book Award, the 2016 and 2017 Florida Authors and Publishers Association President's Awards, and the 2015 Stargazer Literary Prizes. He lives in Mexico City.

www.jonlapoma.com

Also by Jonathan LaPoma

Hammond, The Summer of Crud, Understanding the Alacrán, Developing Minds: An American Ghost Story, and *The Soul City Salvation* are books one-five of a loosely-linked series. Each novel can be read independently of the others.

Hammond
A group of troubled but charismatic boys in a tough Buffalo, NY neighborhood play basketball at a local park and dream winning a state high school championship.

The Summer of Crud
The summer after graduating from college, a mentally ill 22-year-old takes a cross-country US road trip with a friend, hoping to find the inspiration to reach his songwriting potential, start a band, and avoid student teaching in the fall.

Understanding the Alacrán
A 22-year-old man moves to Mexico and better understands the addiction and mental illness destroying his life.

Developing Minds: An American Ghost Story
A group of recent college graduates struggle with alienation and addiction as they try to survive a year of teaching at dysfunctional Miami public schools.

The Soul City Salvation
Not yet ready to take on Hollywood, a 26-year-old aspiring actor and writer moves to Soul City, CA and begins therapy for OCD, setting him on a ten-year healing journey that drives him to near madness as he explores the limits of his heart, creativity, and psyche.

A Noble Truth (screenplay)
Two friends set off on a road trip to explore what truths unite people in a modern America dominated by apathy and discord. It is soon clear, however, that truth is the last thing either man seeks.